# Hamlet, Prince of Denmark

*A Novel*

David Hewson

A.J. Hartley

❀ Created with Vellum

*This book first appeared as an audio drama on Audible, narrated by Richard Armitage.*

**What the Critics Say**

“It’s a fresh, contemporary take on Shakespeare’s tragedy, one not afraid to create new characters or cut long soliloquies. We get a noirish Hamlet, who, when asked by Laertes if he's ready to fence, blurts out: ‘I’ve been ready all my life.’” (*Associated Press*)

“English literature teachers worried about getting pupils entranced by Shakespeare should plug them in to this imaginative gloss on Hamlet before starting on the real thing. Hobbit-fanciers will rejoice to find that Richard ‘Thorin Oakenshield’ Armitage is an outstandingly versatile narrator. This is the one of the most powerful listening experiences that I’ve had.” (*The Times* London)

# Something Rotten in the State of Denmark

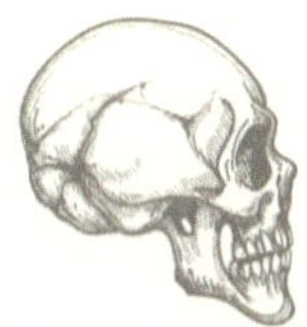

Drunk, full of a righteous fury, the king lay on a couch in the court garden, listening to the laughter in the castle behind. It was November in the year sixteen hundred, a cold still night beneath a clear moon. Gaiety inside. Dancing.

Hamlet, monarch of Denmark, a burly, ill-tempered man of fifty, had left the entertainment clutching his flagon of hard spirit, found space in the courtyard, ordered servants to bring braziers to keep him warm then drank, drank hard, spitting curses into the darkness as he listened to the hubbub inside.

This new century had brought with it a changed world, one he was coming to hate. He was an old Dane, blood going back to the pagan days of the Vikings. Made by a world where a man ruled by strength and cunning alone, left his enemies in pieces on the battlefield, seized by force any neighbouring lands he coveted.

Now the air was rank with fresh ideas from the soft lands of the south. Art and notions of freedom. The idea that life was no more than perpetual combat seemed unfashionable in the chattering circles of plumed dandies and so-called intellectuals that comprised a modern court. Men whose grandfathers had spent their lives mucking out pig farms now went to school and came back with the languages and skill with words and numbers that stuffed the kingdom with lawyers and secretaries and businessmen who could turn their hands to any manner of dealing which turned a profit. Where once there had been peasants and kings and precious little in between, there was now an army of scholars and merchants clawing their way past the venerable old aristocracy in the name of freedom.

And with that freedom – or the illusion of it – came dangers. Treasons made all the more painful since they began so close to home.

He finished the flask of aquavit, bellowed for another, told the lad who brought it to leave him alone.

Alone.

As if that were possible. Try as he might he couldn't still their voices in his head. Gertrude, his queen, prancing 'round in her finery, a confident hostess making up for her boor of a husband. Claudius, his own brother, a silken-voiced courtier who'd worked at Hamlet's side since he first took the crown.

"My own blood," the king muttered in a slurred and drunken tone. "My own..."

There was a storm coming. A bloody one. Vengeance made real. In the morning it would begin.

He drank and drank. Until finally the voices receded and the lights went out in the neighbouring hall.

Still, one was missing.

"The boy," the king whispered, close to sleep.

His son was back where he longed to be. In Wittenberg, Germany, reading books. The perpetual student.

Filling his head with all those Italian ideas about art and culture, statecraft and freedom. Playing with new-fangled firearms when he should have been learning how to hew an enemy's head from his shoulders with a sweep of his broadsword.

These were no lessons for monarchs. Denmark was doomed unless Hamlet acted with a fierce and merciless strength. Unless by force again he brought it back within his iron fist. And the boy... no use at all. A weak, fey creature, so meek in bearing it was hard to believe Hamlet had sired him, let alone given the sullen brat his name.

"Tomorrow," mumbled the man slumped on the damp cold couch, beneath the sputtering torches. "Tomorrow all changes. And..."

The drink closed his eyes. Exhaustion. Nothing else. Not guilt. He'd known none in the cruel past. Would feel nothing but satisfaction when the coming work was done.

He laughed at that thought. Rolled back his head. And in that moment the strangest thing happened. Something liquid, cold and sticky, slipped into his ear.

A roar rose in his throat and stuck there. His eyes opened but as they did a cold thrill of pain raced through his head as a swift nausea rose in his gut.

Hamlet, King of Denmark, looked around him, realised he couldn't even move. There was a shape, timorous in the shadows. Something in its hand.

*Treason...*

A small word for a vile act that might change the world.

*Trea...*

He tried to say it. Tried to shout, to scream, to cry for help. But nothing came except the foamy bile, pouring through his nostrils, spewing from his throat.

His finger stretched out in front of him. A shape emerged from the gloom.

"You..." the king stuttered in his dying agony. "I will see you in..."

The very word choked, stuck in his craw.

"Hell?" asked a cold, mocking voice in front of him. "Not yet, Hamlet. Not yet..."

Then the night came around the dying man, enfolding him like a black shroud. And with it one final terror.

Almost three months on flurries of snow and slabs of rain fell on the castle's grey stones. Hard icy gusts rolled in from the ocean, drifting onto the walls, bringing spray and the smell of salt into every corner. From the woodland by the shore came the nocturnal dirges of hungry owls and the screeches of foxes in heat.

Marcellus listened. In his year as a soldier on the night watch he'd come to hate these things. Had become a man used to snatching a few hours of sleep during the day then waste the endless night waiting on dawn.

Time spent in boredom and stupid routine, usually. Elsinore was the greatest castle in Denmark. Too tall for siege ladders to reach its ramparts. Too well stocked inside its vast interior, with chicken coops, a pig pen, a vegetable garden for the royals. What went on outside the walls didn't much matter.

It was different for the peasants in the hovels by the harbour. They would be left to the mercy of any hostile foreigners who crossed the narrow Øresund channel looking for loot.

But no one worried about them so much at that moment. The castle had a new king. It was still waking from the uneasy hangover of his coronation and an equally unexpected wedding.

There should have been nothing for a sentinel like him to do. Then, three days before, he saw something and after that Marcellus scarcely slept at all.

It started as a garbled tale from an idiot stable boy, one of the usual night time terrors the guards shared around the fire when they had nothing better to do. Then the watch leader, Barnardo, a man with as much imagination as the stone from which Elsinore was built, said he'd seen an intruder beside the chapel tower: a tall figure in full armour, walking the battlements.

The place was searched from top to bottom. There'd been snow that evening but there were no footprints on the ramparts. If it had been anyone but Barnardo the episode would have been regarded as no more than an uneasy joke, one more castle myth, told by a fool. Yet, even with the sun up the next morning, a doleful sense of unease hung over all the sentries who would watch the following night.

They told no one in authority. Enemy spies didn't scale the walls in plate armour. The King's councillors had enough to think about looking out to the flat, low shoreline beyond Elsinore's walls without worrying about what might already be inside, somehow unseen. Yet fear and trepidation proved infectious. By nightfall an air of muted panic hung over the watch like smoke.

Three hours after midnight and still nothing, though every man was awake and watchful, jumping at the slightest sound, the flutter of a bat, the squeak of a mouse, the howls of distant dogs.

Marcellus had worked his way to the eastern wall and was gazing out into the freezing night wondering how much time had passed since the last bell. It couldn't be long now. Still, the watch had been quiet. By the time the guards had made their second circuit of the walls with nothing to report even Barnardo had been shame-faced, muttering about cloud shadows and the dreams that came from boredom.

Snow fell on a light breeze beneath a moon that was almost full, its silver light reflecting on the narrow stretch of water that separated Denmark from its neighbour. Marcellus was feeling a little easier. Soon dawn would come. The cock would crow from the coop. Elsinore would wake to another day ruled over by Claudius and Gertrude: new king, the same queen they had before.

A strange contracted sequence of events within a mere three months. A monarch's funeral. A royal wedding. A coronation. And something strange stirring on Elsinore's heights.

When this odd interlude was over Marcellus would drag Barnardo down the tavern, make him buy a round of wheaten beer, and enjoy reminding his friend how badly he'd spooked them.

He was laughing to himself at that thought when there was the briefest, softest sound, like metal scraping faintly on stone. A sudden chill breeze froze his blood. Sensing something behind he wheeled around, dropping his shouldered halberd so its spiked tip pointed down the battlements to the round tower.

Someone – or something – was standing in the doorway along the wall, a deeper blackness in the shadows.

"Who's there?" he demanded, staring down the shaft of the halberd, his knuckles white.

"It's me," said a familiar voice. "Barnardo. Put that thing away before you kill someone."

Marcellus shook his head with relief and lowered his weapon as the watch leader joined him.

Barnardo was a farmer's son from Jutland, frank, tough, unshakable mostly. He rested his long snaphaunce gun against the parapet then peered over the walls down to the port. The channel looked still in the moonlight. Perhaps it would freeze soon and make Elsinore briefly open to invasion from its twin town across the water in Sweden, Helsingborg.

"You look frozen," the new man said. "Francisco can take over here. Go home to a warm bed and dream of a warm woman."

"Dreaming's all I do," Marcellus grumbled.

"That's because you're an ugly sod. Speak of the devil," Barnardo said, deadpan. Two men were emerging from the chapel tower, one armed like them, the other with a cloak drawn tightly about him, his breath like mist in the freezing air.

Francisco, another guard. The second a younger, slimmer figure. Horatio. Friend to the king's son.

An educated man, Barnardo thought, not kindly.

"I haven't seen a bloody thing," Francisco muttered as they came close. "You?"

"Now there's a surprise," said Horatio, with a wry grin at Francisco. "No ghouls or apparitions then?"

He was a smart-faced youngster from one of the aristocratic families, slim, clean-shaven, fine, delicate hands, unscarred by hard labour. A student through and through. Marcellus hawked and spat over the battlements.

"Seen a whey-faced toff who don't belong here. Wonder what he thinks he's up to."

Horatio laughed.

"Just seeking answers. Francisco's got it in his head that if this thing appears again someone like me might be able to speak to it."

"Someone like you?" Marcellus echoed, an edge to his voice. "A clever bugger, you mean?"

"Not really. I just..."

"He's here because I invited him," Francisco cut in. "Just a thought. I mean... we didn't know what to do last time, did we?"

Marcellus frowned, but Barnardo slapped them both on the shoulders so hard it hurt.

"No arguing boys. Too cold up here for a fight."

"If it does show up..." Marcellus brandished his halberd, "We'd be a sight better equipped to deal with it than a sodding bookworm."

"I don't doubt that, sir," Horatio said cheerfully. "But it's all a bit moot, isn't it? I mean..."

"Shut it!" yelled Barnardo, pointing back to the round tower. "There!"

All four men span round on their heels, looking along the wall.

Just visible in the silver night a hulking shape stalked towards them. It appeared to be a giant of a man, armoured from head to toe, a vast two-handed sword dragging behind him. The visor of his helmet was up. The bearded face beneath it seemed to glow with a soft, pearly light like moonshine on deep water.

But the eyes had the colour of fire, of burning coals, and they stared with menace directly at the sentries with each step the creature took.

Marcellus was the first to come to his senses, once more levelling his halberd and bellowing at the thing to halt. His hands trembled and the hair on the back of his neck stood on end. The others followed suit, Barnardo snatching up his gun and snapping back the hammer. Even Horatio plucked a dagger from his belt though he shrank against the crenelated parapet as if ready to flee.

The apparition didn't break stride. It was closing on them, hoary locks stirring about its face as if in a stiff breeze no one else could feel, still glaring, still noiseless as the grave from which it must have come.

Francisco cringed as it closed on them, but Barnardo stepped forward, shouting "Stop, in the name of the King!" barring its path with a sweep of his axe.

Still it came on, stepping through the weapon as if it was no more than air, then through Barnardo himself so that he cried out in horror and loosed his weapon. There was a flash of flame and a terrible report. For a moment the battlements were wreathed in acrid bluish smoke. Then the armoured spectre emerged through the bitter cloud, unhurt, unmoved. The others were falling back, shouts of alarm and fragments of prayers on their lips. Francisco stumbled to the cold stones, one arm over his face. Horatio dropped to his knees and in that instant a sound broke out over the castle, the distant crowing of a cockerel.

With the first sound of morning the apparition vanished, quick as mist caught in a sudden storm. The four stood in frightened silence. None keen to speak as if words would make it all real.

Marcellus was the first.

"That face!" Marcellus stammered. "Did you see the face?"

Barnardo could only nod and stare at the path it had followed, from the tower, through them, into nothing.

"It was the old king," he whispered. "Hamlet. And I swear..."

The words were gone again. It was the student who found them first.

"The thing wanted to speak," Horatio said.

He leaned against the wall and eyed them.

"To someone. Not to us."

THE CASTLE of Elsinore sat at the narrowest point of the sound between Denmark and Sweden, a glittering stronghold with one foot in the old world, blockish and practical, one in the new, shiny and ornamented. Both were, in their ways, impressive, but its halls and passages seemed caught in transition, hesitating between its fortress past and its palace future.

In daylight it was the latter that was easiest to see. Courtiers in their finery congregated in the Great Hall, loitering in hope of a royal audience, a banquet or dance in the ballroom with its towering ceiling. Some were visiting dignitaries, a few statesmen and their wives, or lawyers with briefs and maps and contracts. Others seemed strictly decorative, lounging and gaming and singing as if to remind the world that this northernmost of the great European palaces liked to think itself a cultured outpost of Renaissance Europe, a walled version of distant Florence reimagined for the cold bleak wastes of Denmark.

Scores of servants ran through tight passageways with trays of food from the kitchens, while others unloaded wagons of meat and vegetables in the courtyard or hauled wood for the ovens and the fireplaces in the royal apartments. Boar were dressed and roasted on spits, tables and trenchers scrubbed, rushes strewn on the floors, beer brewed and kegged, clothes mended, boots heeled, armour oiled, blades – military and kitchen alike – were honed, and bed linen packed for laundering in the river. Behind discrete doors and carefully hung tapestries, the business of daily life in the castle cranked and sweated regardless of day or season.

Outside, for all its newer gloss, the medieval fortress still loomed large over Elsinore's palatial aspirations. The ramparts had been raised and modernized. A square cannon tower had been added which looked down on the waters of the sound and the strip of land which bound the castle to the town. Enemies, after all, could be lurking anywhere.

Inside the perimeter walls were rune stones far older than the castle itself, boulders roughly carved with pictograms and ancient, linear script, remembering exploits from another more primitive world, that of the Vikings, an era the refurbished and glamorous parts of the castle seemed keen to forget.

Elsinore breathed. It pulsed with life, with births and deaths, with whispered trysts, political indirection, meetings, lies, promises kept and broken. It groaned with food and sex and snoring. And it watched. More than anything else, it looked out to the horizon, and down to those who called it home: a parent, a spy, a judge. The castle saw all.

And now, on this bright, cold, January day, it witnessed a little man running, scampering as if his very life depended on it.

LIKE AN IMP SET FREE, like a demon sprinting through the darkness, the dwarf scurried down the icy stone corridors of Elsinore, bouncing off the damp, dank walls, chattering to himself, laughing at the jokes to come.

So many of them.

So much planning, scheming, hoping.

Yorick, son of Yorick. A small creature, big on ambition. Latest in a long line of Elsinore jesters. A fool before royalty. The one true, honest voice among the craven court followers who hung around the throne like flies sniffing the presence of a corpse.

Four foot and a bit. Gross, jowly bearded face. Fat, bowed legs. Big belly, big nose, big head. Through the Great Hall he darted, past the sovereigns' seats, the paintings, the tapestries, the statue of his father, placed there by Old Hamlet. A joke for a joke.

He paused, looked at the object beneath the sputtering brands in the wall. The jest seemed cruel, unnecessary.

Naked, Old Yorick sat on a huge tortoise. Flabby right arm out in a regal pose, acknowledging his people, left on his fat side, holding in his greedy girth.

Gross arse, strong, gnarled hands. Small prick. An expression of fear on his finely-sculptured face. Even the tortoise that bore his weight was laughing.

Everyone did, the dwarf thought. That was why creatures like him existed. To serve as objects of mirth and derision for normal men. To show them a mirror of humanity then raise their spirits as they witnessed the ugly truth.

He stopped for a moment. Tried to imagine this dead stone face alive. Failed. Walked on, more slowly now. Into the east wing, the royal quarters. Past guards who never acknowledged him. Past the quarters of servants who hadn't raised a squeak in protest back when Old Yorick was put to the sword.

The door to the Queen's apartment was ajar. He slunk into the shadows cast by three torches, edged close to the bedroom. Listened to the rhythmic sighs within.

Moved nearer, shrank to the floor like a cellar rat. Spied on them through the keyhole. Claudius and Gertrude. He over her, bed shirt around his hips, face wreathed in a passionate desperation.

All the noises and motions of love. None of the profit.

The King was near fifty. The Queen two years younger. Two months married after the sudden death of Old Hamlet, her husband, his brother.

The jester stopped on the threshold. Finger to lips. Thinking of a joke fitting the circumstances. Something about sowing seed on stony ground. Empty pleasures pursued too late. The waste of warm and wrinkled skin.

Yet he stayed in the shadows. A fool by fate and calling, not by temperament.

The king cried. The queen followed. Hidden behind the long drape Yorick stifled a laugh.

Moved on. One room only. Hamlet had stayed there since he was a child, a closeness demanded by a too-caring, worried mother.

This door was fully open. The jester considered marching in, bold as brass, leaping onto the dishevelled double bed. Tussling the hair of the tall, skinny figure there. Trying to find humour amongst the misery.

Then he took one look and thought better of it.

Hamlet lay stiff on the sheets, head back on the pillow, fists tight over his ears, eyes on the ceiling, listening to the grunts and snorts and creaks his mother made with the king, his stepfather. It was that man, Claudius, who had raised the prince far more than Old Hamlet had. That heartless old bastard had always been too busy with wars and scheming to notice the fragile, solitary child he'd bred in the equally heartless fortress.

Here, or so the seers said, deep beneath the rock, lay Holger Danske, Denmark's Arthur, the hero of legend, clutching his broadsword Curtana, sleeping the enchanted sleep given him by Morgan Le Fay. Waiting for the moment the realm was threatened, ready to wake and save Denmark from her foes.

Yorick wasn't sure he believed the seers. But Holger Danske's time might be near. There were, he had heard, enemies abroad. The nation was divided, ruled by a diffident monarch and a queen whose only son was a reclusive and seemingly perpetual student. An unlikely successor to the throne in Elsinore. Perhaps it was a good thing that it wasn't blood line alone that counted when it came to the selection of the Danish monarch.

The moans from the royal bedroom abated. Pants and low arrhythmic breathing took their place.

The dwarf slunk from the royal quarters, made his way to the western tower, out to the battlements. He'd heard the rumours of strange happenings there. Ever curious he needed to know.

January out in the fresh air. The Øresund channel that separated Denmark from Sweden was narrow here. Frozen in the worst of winters, the ice so thick that Norway's armies, which occupied the territory opposite, might cross from one side to the other.

The jester climbed to the highest wall of the fortress. Dawn was breaking over the dark water below. Small boats, lights at the stern, Danish and foreign, were out chasing the silver rush of herring that fed the Nordic nations and always would.

His limbs were small, deformed, yet strong. The dwarf leapt onto the castellated wall at a run. Stood on the rough stone, stared down at the land below. The hovels of Elsinore's servants. The jetties of the port. Between them the too-small cemetery for the ordinary folk, a place he visited from time to time, watching as the sextons shifted old bodies to make way for new.

This was Elsinore. Hard rock, barren lineage, a black world in turmoil.

Home. The only one he had.

A noise. A cry from along the wall, in the guardhouse by the northern tower.

A single word caught on the icy night air.

*Ghost.*

Nothing there now in the first light of day.

He looked over the battlements at the little harbour, the narrow stretch of sea. Took a deep breath and spat into the fresh breeze like a child.

Then went back down to the royal quarters. Quiet in the queen's chamber now. The king had returned to his own room and the dressers who would prepare him for the visitors waiting in the hall below. There was talk about meetings to come, about the Prince rousing himself from his constant mourning and take part in the business of the court.

Silent as a church mouse Yorick crept back along the corridor. Hamlet was asleep in a tortured, childish pose, clutching the pillows to him, head buried in fine Rennes linen.

The fool shook him roughly by the collar.

He was a tall, handsome young man. Twenty seven though he often seemed younger. A pale, finely chiselled face, nothing like his father's. Long fair hair. Mournful eyes that were the pale grey-blue of the sea in autumn. They possessed a sorrowful cast and had done so long before his father died.

"Why are you waking me?"

"Because it's time to get up. The fornicating's over. For now at least."

A torrent of curses. The clown stood back, folded his arms, looked shocked.

"That's unbecoming of a man who might one day wear the crown."

"To hell with the throne." He pulled the sheets over his head. "The lords would never choose me. Besides I want to sleep. Forever."

"That'll come soon enough."

"Bugger off."

Yorick dragged the bed clothes off him and wagged a fat finger.

"Don't make me spank you. The King's putting on his robes and telling all and sundry he desires your presence downstairs. There's state business to be done. It's expected. Best be dressed when old Polonius knocks on your door."

A sly eye turned to the small library by the desk near the wall.

"Tell them I'm reading. It's work."

"They won't believe you. This is your duty. Your fate. Here. I'll fetch your boots. And some clothes that aren't black for a change. Comb that long hair before I do, which will hurt, I promise."

"Tell me one thing first." Hamlet sat up, suddenly alert. "And don't play the idiot with me. I know you."

A bow, a flourish of his stunted arms.

"Then recognition is all I crave."

"How did your father die?"

A pause. A moment of serious consideration.

"Much like yours, Hamlet. Mortality stole him."

There was a line between impudence and treason. It was a fool's job to tread it.

"Tell me!"

"But I did. Do you have cloth ears to go with your cloth brain?"

"One day..."

He laughed. Winked. Waited. Saw the anger die in Hamlet's eyes.

"I'm just your hideous little pal. Don't be angry."

"I'm staying in bed."

"Oh, no, you're not... "There's trouble coming." Yorick's hand went to the window. "Young Fortinbras has parked his Norwegian army out there behind Helsingborg. If the sea freezes and he's so inclined we could have his fury on us in days. Then the Sound will run with blood like it did in your father's time. So get your lazy arse down there now."

A flourish. A perfect bow.

"Your highness..."

~

"WE DON'T WANT WAR," Claudius said as they assembled in the Great Hall. "Not now." He looked at Hamlet, with affection and concern. "Young Fortinbras has marched into Sweden with an army. How big that force is, how strong, how disciplined... we aren't yet sure. Nor is it clear if this is just political sabre rattling. Or more... personal. I think he wants revenge. Your father killed his. In fair combat..." A nod at the walls. "Out there. But that was twenty seven years ago..."

"Some wounds heal slowly."

Hamlet had rejected the jester's advice and put on black. Shirt, doublet, trousers, shoes. The clothes made his face seem bloodless in the glorious hall with its gold and scarlet drapes, the ornate furniture, the tapestry map of Denmark and its shifting conquests on the wall. And the strange statue of a fat midget, perched on a tortoise, right hand outstretched like a sad emperor in his glory.

Outside the ordinary folk were close to starving. It had been a cold, meagre winter. Some blamed that on the sudden and unexpected death of the old king, as if a monarch's blood was tied to the health of the nation. But within the castle the supply of luxuries hadn't dried up. Servants moved around the room with beer from Jutland, figs from Italy, French wine and meat.

Claudius didn't reach for them. Nor Gertrude, his queen who sat next to him, never taking her eyes off her son.

"I mourn for your father," the King insisted. "Just as much as you..."

Hamlet laughed.

"How's that possible?"

"He was my brother!"

"And now, two months on, you've wed his queen."

"Three," Gertrude cut in. A fortnight before, the first time he'd made that dig, she'd been shocked, offended. Now she was tiring of the argument. "Would you deny me all happiness, Hamlet? Was I supposed to climb onto a funeral pyre with him as if we were still Vikings?"

She gestured at the guard next to her, dressed in finery, the latest musket from the English armourers leaning on his shoulder, a gunpowder flask on his belt.

"We're a modern court. With ambassadors across Europe, seeking peace and trade and continuity. Not the marauders of old. The crown holds everything together. It may be yours one day if you...."

"Behave?"

A cold smile from the Queen.

"If you continue to study what is fitting for a king. If you show yourself to be a friend to Denmark, a leader, someone who understands the arts of the court, of diplomacy, even war."

"If I become my father, you mean? Or my uncle?"

Colour rose in her cheeks. Gertrude nodded.

"Good men to emulate."

Hamlet looked away.

Polonius, Lord Chamberlain to the court for thirty years, stood listening, one hand in his long white beard, the other fingering a pocket watch shaped like a golden drum.

He eyed Claudius and got the nod to speak.

"Fortinbras believes your father's death gives him the opportunity – and the right – to demand the return of those lands Old Hamlet seized after he beat Old Norway in single combat. Through violence true, but legal violence. He has no right..."

"He has youth and vigour and an army," the King objected. "He'll make his own right. The way they do. Here..."

He summoned the ambassadors picked for the job of dealing with Magnus, the Norwegian king in Oslo. They were two nobles, the youngest, Voltemand, from Copenhagen, the elder, Elias, a local. Claudius looked at them. Two very different men, he thought. Elias he'd known since childhood, a decent, loyal lord. Voltemand came on the recommendation of Polonius and seemed more ambitious. Sly even.

He handed the letter to Elias. It was sealed with the mark of the crown.

"Fortinbras has ambitions above his station. He's crown prince, not monarch. What our spies tell us..." A grateful glance at Polonius. "... is that Magnus himself is sick and impotent, weak in the head. Not long for the world. Perhaps he'll nod and give the boy what he wants. But a little diplomacy and haggling about taxes and duties won't go amiss. Let's drive a stake between Magnus and his nephew, set one against the other..."

Voltemand nodded.

"Wise counsel, sir. Fortinbras is a rash and arrogant man from what I hear."

"And if we hear that in Elsinore it must be kitchen gossip in Norway. Get private messages sent. Let's stir matters for our Norwegian upstart cousin."

The two departed. Claudius caught the eye of his stepson.

"There's the scent of war in the air. I need you here. Not Wittenberg. This isn't a time for reading books."

Hamlet rolled his eyes, which always infuriated his uncle.

"I'm a student. Not a warrior."

The King came over and looked at him frankly.

"We're not like the Norwegians. They pick their kings through force and bribery. We elect ours from those of royal blood. But a king can name his preferred successor. To me you are my heir, Hamlet. A beloved nephew. The only one I have. The only one I wish. You've my trust and admiration. I love you as if you were my own."

Gertrude joined them, wound her arms through theirs.

Hamlet wouldn't look at her. Instead he stared at the cold floor and muttered, "I wish to mourn my father in private. I wish to study..."

"That's enough!" A hard, chiding voice. Gertrude took his chin. "Claudius is your father now. One who adores you. More..."

She stumbled on the words.

"He has more time for you than Old Hamlet was ever allowed. It wasn't his fault..."

"A few months in the grave and you're married. Perhaps my extended mourning makes up for the brevity of yours."

Her eyes flashed with anger.

"We own this land. We're the shepherds of our people. The rules are what we make them, and they come with heavy duties. You must learn this, or the king's favour will not be enough to put the crown on your head when he is gone. And you must learn it here. Not in Wittenberg."

She removed her hand, unwound her arm.

"I'm your mother. I beg you... I pray for you to stay. For a Danish prince to flee the country at a time like this. It would look bad, Hamlet. You'd throw away your own reputation for a month spent wrapped in dusty books?"

The King held out his hands, beseeching.

"And I plead too... As your monarch. As your loving uncle."

"I wouldn't want my mother's prayers to go unanswered. After all I am a loyal, dutiful son."

"Of course you are!" Claudius clapped his hands happily. "Honest and fair. I can only guess at the sorrow you feel. But remember... he was my brother too, much loved. A fierce and warlike man. I'm not like him, I know. God made me more the diplomat than the warrior. Words are my armour, and what pass as my weapons too."

He smiled and felt Hamlet's arm.

"I know you think of yourself as a bookworm. But you've your father's blood in you. I've seen you practising with a rapier. It's there and perhaps one day we'll need it."

A thoughtful expression crossed his face.

"But if I can negotiate a settlement...Your father slaughtered Norway out on the ice for herring rights and land that will scarcely grow barley. There's room to haggle. There always is."

"And lose these clothes," his mother ordered, tugging at his black sleeve. "Smile once in a while. Be pleasant to the court. There's a fine line between mourning and melancholia. Don't overstep..."

"I wouldn't want my mother's prayers to go unanswered," he repeated in a dull, plain voice.

"That's my boy," the King declared.

But though Gertrude smiled she stayed silent.

Back in his room Hamlet found Yorick at the window.

"You again? Get out."

The little man didn't move.

"But where am I to go, Prince? It's dead boring out there. And no one but you gets my jokes."

"I don't laugh at them."

"You understand them and that's what counts." Yorick clambered down from the ledge and waddled over to Hamlet at the desk. "Cheer up. It might never happen."

"What?"

"Whatever makes you think you've the weight of ten worlds on your shoulders."

"Maybe it already has happened."

"Ah. So we're feeling suicidal, are we? Excellent."

Hamlet glared at him.

"I'll have you arraigned for witchcraft, imp."

"And then who'll you talk to? Yorick will do just fine by the way. But if it's any help..."

He hunted in his suit, came out with a pocket knife, held it out in his right hand, bowed and flourished the blade with his left.

"Take it. Nice and sharp. Want me to run you a warm bath too? Recommend a suitable vein?"

"Go away."

Yorick came round and stared up into Hamlet's face.

"No. I won't. Not until you're frank with me."

"About what?"

"Your problem."

"The problem? All the world knows the problem."

The jester chuckled.

"All the world's got problems of its own. Enough to concern it without worrying about yours." He raised a finger. "Oh! I remember now. Your father's dead. Denmark's like a beautiful garden gone to seed and weed. And as for your mother...." He raised himself as high as he could manage and said in a theatrical voice, "Frailty, thy name is woman. Who said that? Search me. I suppose it fits Gertrude actually, but once you've seen one courtly lady..."

"Don't push it."

"But Hamlet, dear boy. Pushing's what I'm paid for." He sat on the floor, cross-legged, like a pupil in school. "That god of yours would be mightily pissed off if you topped yourself, you know. As I'm sure those clever theologians in Wittenberg told you."

Hamlet jabbed a finger at the door.

"Tonight she'll be with him again. Sweating away in their filthy, incestuous sheets! While I lie here listening..."

Yorick shook his head.

"Strictly speaking that's not incest, is it? Also I think you'll find the king and queen get the finest bed linen in the whole of Denmark. You could just ask for another room. Somewhere a little along the way. Besides..."

A knock.

"Get that."

"I'm a jester not a bloody servant," Yorick muttered and slunk into the shadows.

Three men there. Barnardo and Marcellus, castle guards. And Horatio a Danish student Hamlet knew from Wittenberg.

"You should be back in Germany at your studies," Hamlet told him. "Like me."

"I came for your father's funeral, sir. It seemed only right."

"You're sure it wasn't for my mother's wedding?"

A moment of embarrassment. None of the men would look at him.

"There wasn't much time between them," Horatio agreed eventually.

"Close enough they could have used the same banquet for both. Sometimes I feel I still see my father round this grim place..."

"Where?" Horatio asked. "When?"

"In my mind's eye. Where else?"

Barnardo stamped his fist against his chest.

"He was a damned good king. A warrior. He stood up for Denmark."

"My father was a man. Nothing more. Nothing less. I won't see his like again. Nor you."

They looked at each other as if afraid to speak.

Then, almost in a whisper, Horatio said, "My Lord, I think I saw him last night..."

"Saw who?"

"The king. Your father."

Hamlet closed his eyes.

"I pay a jester for jokes. Not students and sentinels..."

"This is no joke, my Lord," Barnardo cut in. "Three nights we've watched his spectre on the castle walls. Last night Horatio joined us and saw it too. A figure just like Old Hamlet. Full armour. Helmet up so I saw his pale face, his grizzled beard. It was the king as we knew him... after a fashion. Though on his face there was pain and grief and horror."

Hamlet came close, looked into their eyes.

"And did he speak?"

"Not to us," Horatio answered. "He looked as if..."

The words fled him.

"He looked as if he was looking for someone else," Marcellus said. "We're just guards and a humble student. He was the King of Denmark. A great lord doesn't come back from the grave to talk to the likes of us."

Horatio nodded.

"We felt you should know."

"And tonight... you think it'll walk again?"

"Like clockwork," Barnardo insisted.

Hamlet took Horatio by the collar.

"How many others know?"

"Not a soul, sir. Only you. And we three."

"Keep it that way. Go about your business. We meet again after dark."

After they left Yorick crawled out of the corner. Stood before him, arms folded.

"Is this wise? I mean..." He brandished the pocket knife. "God or no God I thought you'd made up your mind. At least as much as you ever do..."

The prince snatched the blade. Found a soft pear from the previous summer. Lay on the bed cut off a few chunks and gnawed at them, thinking.

Laertes threaded the last strap through the buckle of the trunk, pulled it tight and nodded for the servants to take it.

"You're leaving now?"

A woman's voice.

She stood in the doorway, simply dressed in grey, long blonde hair up in an ornate knot: his sister, Ophelia. Not now, he thought and looked away, trying to conceal the fact that he'd wanted to slip out unnoticed.

"Yes. The ship's waiting."

"When will you be back from France?"

"At the end of the spring term."

"Not till then?"

She sounded genuinely surprised, even a little hurt.

Laertes shrugged.

"If this Norwegian business turns nasty I'll be back sooner. But I could do with a little less drama for a few months. I imagine you feel the same way."

"Meaning what?"

She was, he supposed, beautiful. Skin pale as milk, hair like spun gold, and eyes the silvery grey of a young salmon's flank, candid, open and inviting. Too much so.

"I'll write. We don't have time to talk now."

"We had time before but you've been avoiding me for days," his sister shot back, stepping in close so he couldn't avoid her fixed, determined gaze.

Two servants were lifting his trunk between them, then heading for the door.

"I said... not now, Ophelia."

She hesitated, listening to the porters' footsteps in the stairwell.

"Is this about Hamlet?"

"Of course it is."

He seized a satchel and checking the contents irritably.

"You don't like him."

Even when they were children she'd had a talent for drawing out of him things he'd rather not say.

"I think you like him more than enough for both of us. Don't you?"

For a second he thought she might slap him. She did that often enough when they were young too.

"So what?"

"So what? So people are talking. There are... rumours."

She laughed at that.

"I don't care about castle gossip."

"You should. You will."

"Really? Why's that?"

"Because he's Prince Hamlet, Ophelia. *Prince*."

"You think I'm not good enough for him? Our father's Lord Chamberlain here. Not a swineherd..."

"Exactly." He snatched her hand and held it. "You're making him look like a fool. Me, too."

She twisted out of his grip.

"I've hurt your pride and standing, dear brother. And our father's. How thoughtless of me. This is absurd."

"Would it be absurd if the King orders Hamlet to marry some Norwegian princess in order to patch up an old quarrel? Leaving you..."

"Leaving me where? Leaving me what?"

"Damaged goods." His voice was just above a whisper. "Another man's castoff. Or perhaps his secret mistress. A whore on the side..."

She did slap him then. He took it without comment and when he looked at her again her cheeks were red, her eyes shining.

"I'm going to miss my boat."

He stepped round her but hesitated in the doorway.

"I'm simply telling you what others won't. You're my sister. I love you. I'm sorry we didn't get to spend more time together. When I come back things will be different. Like they used to be. I hope..."

She came over. He felt the soft pressure of her hand on his arm, but when he started to reach for a last embrace she pushed him gently into the hall.

"Go," she said, smiling sadly. "The tide will be turning."

"CAN'T BELIEVE you're going through with this nonsense. There's no such thing as ghosts."

The dwarf sat on a bench by the windows in the prince's quarters, picking at his nails with a small dagger.

"You know that, do you?"

"Did you read all those books in Wittenberg? Or just stare at the pages? This is the modern world, Hamlet. Not the old one where gods and ghosts walked everywhere as if they owned the place. You're the clever one. Prove me wrong."

Hamlet looked at the clothes he'd put on at the behest of his mother: green velvet pants, scarlet waistcoat. The jester giggled, shook his stick of bells in the air. Stroked his own blue and yellow harlequin suit, smiled a supercilious smile.

"Not just me they make dress up and look like a moron, is it?"

"My father lives in here." He tapped his head. "I see him. Hear him. Is that proof?"

A snort.

"No. That's memory."

"What's the difference. Don't you remember yours? Isn't he still alive there somewhere?"

The jester got up from the seat, waddled to the window, made a short sideways leap to the stone ledge, pointed through the leaded glass.

"My father's down there. In the graveyard. Bones and rotting flesh." A brief, sour look. "Head cleaved from his body. While I was doing the endless rounds of European courts at his behest. Not that..."

"Why?"

The little man hopped down, went to the sheets at the end of the room, tidied them up into a roll, stuffed them in a cupboard.

"You sleep here too, don't you?" Hamlet asked him.

"When I feel like it. You know how bloody cold this place is outside the royal quarters? No heat. No decent grub. No women either, except they've got beards." A nod at the window. "Beats me why the common folk love you. Maybe it's your looks."

A long evening before Horatio's arrival. A fork in the road perhaps. A journey to nowhere.

"I want to know..." Hamlet whispered, almost forgetting for a moment there was another in the room. "I dream things..."

An ugly, distorted face in his vision.

"You want to know what, boy? How the world began? What brings it to an end? You're Prince of Denmark. The next king if you're lucky. Look at me..."

Hamlet turned away.

"Look at me!"

A cripple. A hideous dwarf. Fat, twisted limbs. A face no woman could love. Little bells tinkling as he walked his crooked walk through the corridors of Elsinore.

"What do you see?"

"A midget. A man all the same. Your father was a kindly soul. With a soft voice. When I was a child and troubled he'd tell me stories..."

"Old Yorick. Young Yorick. Old Hamlet, Young Hamlet. Old Norway, Young Norway. Flaming hell... can't you lot think up any names of your own?"

"Young Norway's name is Fortinbras. He..."

"As was his father's if you knew! And the young one'll come over from Sweden with his army and have your guts for garters given half a chance. With good reason too. There's a tale..."

One hour. The Queen and her foul bed mate were at supper. Probably furious that he wasn't with them. A unified family front.

"Tell it then, jester."

"No. You demand answers you know already. You pose questions that needn't be asked. It's outrageous."

Hamlet laughed.

"But I'm the Prince of Denmark. And you're a low-born fool. I command it."

Yorick toddled over to him and peered in his eyes.

"Is that so?"

"It is."

So he told the story anyway. Because that was what he did.

Close your eyes. Know your place. Watch. Listen to the ghost in your ear.

There's a January gale that shrieks and moans all round this bleak, bare corner of Danish rock. Smell the dry hard tang of winter. Look on a world of ice and snow and blood.

Behind you sits Elsinore's towering grey castle. Before it the Øresund, a narrow channel of frozen sea dividing two nations.

On the ice shapes move. Two groups of shivering fur-clad figures shuffling back among the packed drifts, making a circle for themselves. Denmark and Norway, one nation each side.

This is a battleground now, a fleeting stage set for the smallest of wars.

Amid cheers and the rattle of weapons two giants in gleaming armour step forward from the throng. Like shining monsters they circle one another, broadswords flashing, grim-faced behind helmets that reveal nothing but grizzled beards and taut cruel mouths set for violence.

Old Hamlet for Denmark. Old Fortinbras for Norway. King against king, dancing the bloody dance of single combat, fighting for the frozen land and the fish that swim beneath them.

Inside Elsinore logs crackle and spit from the smoky flames of a fire grate beneath a vast sooty chimney. Somewhere a woman weeps. This is the castle's grandest chamber, the king's own. Shields on the wall. Heavy red velvet curtains the colour of dried blood. Three arrow-slits carved into cold stone. A vast ceremonial window that leads to the triumphal balcony overlooking the waters below.

The midwife they found in the hovels that lean along the shoreline teetering over the mud. Next to her a stiff-backed courtier, Polonius, tugging uselessly at his sleeves. At the foot of the bed the king's brother, Claudius, smooth cheeks, smooth hands, never touched by battle. By him the grim-faced medic, Swedish, black clothes, blank face, cold heart.

All eyes on Gertrude, Hamlet's queen, naked legs akimbo, writhing in agony on soiled and sweaty sheets as her husband gives battle on the ice outside.

"Do something!" the brother cries. "We brought you here for this..."

Her thighs stretch open. No royal modesty here. Her belly's fit to burst. Blood and broken waters leak onto Cambric linen. Look close – you know you want to. See. There's the briefest sight of an infant's reddened scalp. A hidden life to come.

The physician shakes his grey head.

"If the child's afraid to be born there's no forcing matters. If it's scared of the light. The world it faces..."

Clumsily, trembling with fear and fury, Claudius unsheathes his dagger, threatens. The doctor glares back, unimpressed.

"No man can cure death. Even for a king. It's too late to rip the infant from her womb.' He shrugs. 'Besides, if her husband falls to Fortinbras..."

He looks round the room, at each of them.

"Elsinore, all of Denmark will belong to Norway. Everything the land contains. Fortinbras is a decent man but a king above all else. If this is a son of Hamlet's he'll run his sword through its little heart anyway..."

The Queen screams. The knife, a slim, slight diplomat's weapon, slices the cold air.

"He's alive now," the brother says. "And so's Gertrude..."

From the window comes a loud and violent racket. Shouts and cheers. A familiar tongue, that of Norway.

Outside the tallest, greatest of the two lies on the packed ice of the Øresund, legs sprawled, as awkward and defenceless as his wife in the royal bedchamber above.

"This is for property," Fortinbras roars above him. "For land me and mine own by right..."

"The earth belongs to those bold enough to seize it," Hamlet snarls on the packed snow then wipes blood from his beard, removes his helmet, shakes greying locks in the harsh January sun.

His sword lies an arm's length away, next to it a battle axe.

"Retreat," Fortinbras orders, and edges the tip of his broadsword towards the man's throat. "Take your pride and your warriors back to Elsinore. Cross the Øresund no more. The land you've stolen shall be mine. Be satisfied with what you have. Do this and live. Do this and we'll be friends, not foes."

The sharp blade withdraws. Silence between the two of them.

"If I wished your life I'd take it, Hamlet. I've no designs on Denmark. No hunger for a bloody and unnecessary war. No...'

A high-pitched feverish wail breaks his concentration. The warrior looks up at the walls of Elsinore.

"Go home. Be with your wife. She's more use to you than my barren fields or the herring beneath us."

The long and armoured figure on the ice glances towards the castle's grey walls. Listens to the faint and agonised moans of a woman in the throes of labour.

Inside close by the bed Claudius hesitates, sheathes his blade. The midwife grabs his sleeve.

"Either the babe comes out or both will die." She glares at the doctor. "He knows it too. Why fetch a damned Swede for the Queen of Denmark?"

"It was the King's wish," Polonius interrupts.

Claudius casts him a sharp glance.

"And whatever my brother wants..."

The woman walks to the doctor's bags, rifles through bottles and envelopes of powder, hears Gertrude's shrieks grow louder, finally finds a pair of French forceps, long hooked arms, shiny silver.

"They keep these things secret. But a midwife sees." She holds up the instrument. It's the colour of a warrior's breastplate, of the weapons beyond the window. "I can use them too. The baby may perish. The Queen for all I know." A hard, wry smile. "Then me I guess..."

Claudius looks at the stricken woman on the sheets. His brother's bride, her brisk rude vitality fading with each racing minute. The loveliest woman in Elsinore. Had he been three years older and monarch in Hamlet's place...

"Do nothing and you'll be burying both before the morning," the midwife repeats. "Give me leave and I'll let her husband judge me. Or Fortinbras. Whichever."

A silence broken only by Gertrude's shallow, unsteady breathing. Her eyes are closed. The scarlet scalp within seems no larger. There's a rattle in her throat, not the sweet, calm loving voice he cherishes.

"Do it," Claudius orders and she's there in an instant, opening the jaws of the silver weapon, forcing them into place around the half-hidden gory head, starting to tug.

Gertrude wakes. Her mouth opens. This scream is the worst and he won't forget it.

The brother strides to the window, looks down at the small circle on the frozen sea. The battleground. His King lies lost on the ice, Norway above him, blade in hand. Talking. But not for much longer.

"We can negotiate," Claudius whispers. "I'll beg and plead and give Fortinbras everything he asks for."

So long as she may live, he thinks. So long as...

Shouts and arguments. The Swedish doctor has intervened, snatched the forceps from the midwife, elbowed her away. As Claudius watches the man in black thrusts the implement so far inside Gertrude she screeches like a prisoner caught on the rack.

"This creature refuses to be born," he mutters then heaves at the silver handles with all his force, pulls and roars as much as the woman on the stained and sweaty sheets.

For a moment Claudius feels faint. It's as if the room itself is made of nothing but flesh and blood and pain. Then, steadying himself against the wall, he dares to look. To hear.

Two screams that will never leave him. One a voice he loves, the second a shrill wail, bawling at the world beyond the warm dark womb.

The physic's knife flies down, severs the red, writhing cord that joins the baby to the mother.

"Give it to me," Claudius says.

He seizes the hot damp form in his arms. Walks to the window, steps out onto the balcony, into the icy gale blowing from the Øresund.

"See this! See..."

A cunning, articulate man. Words rarely desert him. He reaches for them as protection, comfort, the way Hamlet his brother seizes at weapons. But now this is all he possesses. A bloody infant boy.

A new life. That small, eternal miracle.

The Norwegian looks up from the ice, caught by the cries of the man on the castle balcony. Swift as a wolf on the frozen Øresund Hamlet moves, dashes for the axe, hurls it upwards. Finds Fortinbras in the groin, doesn't wait to see more as he climbs to his knees, retrieves the broadsword, swings it round, one certain movement.

A warrior always. There's no need to look. The blade hits home between helmet and neck, cleaves the head of Norway's king straight off his shoulders, sends bloody beard and helmet skittering across the ice.

Hamlet rises. He raises his gory blade, voice booming, turns to the cheers and greetings of his men.

On the balcony, shivering and miserable, Claudius grips the king's child.

Hamlet it will be called too, after the father. As Fortinbras named his own boy, now orphaned, revenge brewing in his infant breast, a circle ever-turning.

A scarlet stain spreads across the icy Øresund. A roaring man swings his broadsword round him.

New-born, in the arms of Claudius, eyes blinking at the too-bright day Hamlet's son sees the world he's entered and shrieks at its bright and bloody form.

Yorick finished his tale. Thirsty, a little downcast, he clambered to his feet and poured himself a cup of wine.

"Is it true?" Hamlet asked. "That my uncle was there when I came into the world? That he loved me from the start? And Gertrude?"

"Don't you remember?"

"Only gods recall their own births. I'm no god."

The jester frowned.

"It's a story my father told to me. That's all. Perhaps they change across the years."

A sound at the door. The dwarf scuttled into the corner, not wishing to be seen.

Horatio stood outside, his face pale.

'Soon the thing moves on the ramparts.' He grasped his sword, a wariness in his eyes. 'You need to see it.'

Hamlet rose to his feet, placed his hand on the hilt of the man's blade.

'We've no use for that, if it's what you say. Perhaps we should brandish a bible instead.'

From the curtains in the corner the softest sound. Laughter.

Ophelia was twenty one. Polonius, her father, was in the employ – the ownership – of whoever held the throne. A dedicated man, loyal to the crown. Given ample quarters on the floor below the royal family themselves. He deserved sympathy, support. Demanded it too. Ophelia's mother died giving birth to her, just fourteen months after she'd delivered her first child, Laertes. Her daughter should have been married long before like most of the Elsinore girls. Instead Ophelia became her father's proxy wife, administering the servants, seeing his washing was done, the food was right, their warm and spacious apartment kept in order. It was at the back, overlooking the meadows and the winding, sluggish river that ran down to the icy waters of the Øresund as if wishing it would never get there.

She understood that feeling. Remembered when she'd escaped into that grassy paradise with Hamlet, dreaming they might both be free. That was a long time ago. When she was one more castle maid. A title never to be recovered.

Her father's food could only be served at her hands too, as it had been, he told her, by her dead mother.

The man provided. The woman obeyed.

Cloth in hand, holding the warm pots from the kitchen, she came through with the meal. Winter fare. Salt herring, carrots, broth. He could it eat for weeks on end and never complain. Perhaps he didn't even notice. The mind of her father was on affairs of state always, even when she entered with the dishes.

Polonius came to the table, still thinking about business. She could tell that from the pleasant, interested look on his face. Then he saw her and let the mask drop. He checked his pocket watch, an affectation he had picked up on a visit to Germany years ago. He was never without it. In the silence she could hear it ticking.

The big chair was his. He took it, tasted the food without a word of thanks. Let her begin and chose his moment.

"I saw the way you looked at the Prince this morning, child. Don't do that."

Ophelia bridled at the remark.

"Your tone's hard, father. I deserve better."

He pushed the plate to one side.

"I'll decide what you deserve. Hamlet's a dangerous man to be near." He tugged on his white beard, a gesture that always annoyed her. "Unstable, perhaps. Though maybe it's an act. Hard to say. All the same I tell you..."

"I'm not a child!"

He had cold grey eyes and they fixed on her now.

"Child. Girl. Adult. What does it matter? You're a woman under my roof. My flesh and blood. You go where I tell you. Do what I say. You belong to me..."

'I do not..."

The look on his face silenced her. Only twice had Polonius struck his daughter. But those two times were of such severity they haunted her still.

"You're goods and chattel in this place. Remember that. Stay away from the Prince..."

'We live within the same bleak walls, father! How...?"

"If I say you go nowhere near him... don't dally with him in the meadow... sneak into his quarters like a harbour whore..."

She knew she was blushing. Feared the words to come. This had never been spoken between them. In her heart she still hoped he didn't know.

"I don't warrant such vile accusations."

"You don't allow him between your legs again. If that child of yours had lived..."

Ophelia stared at him, aghast.

She refused to cry in his presence. Had for years. Even now that was possible. But only by silencing the screaming voice inside.

Then he laughed.

"Yes. I know. For the love of God, girl. I have spies in every place in the known world. Do you think I wouldn't have them in Elsinore? Do you truly believe none would see you naked with him by the river banks in summer? Flowers in your hair? Playing that bloody lute and singing your stupid songs?"

The old man speared a piece of herring on his knife. Took a bite.

"You're too naive to understand discretion. And he's too much his father's son to know the need for it. Well?"

Her hands clutched the wooden table. No words. No way to leave him either.

He put down his knife and glowered at her.

"The one thing I don't know is this. Did you lose the bastard child deliberately? Or by accident?"

That she would answer, but it took an effort.

"I lost the baby when the old king died. I think perhaps the shock..."

Polonius pushed his chair from the table, rolled back his head and howled with laughter.

Wiped his eyes after a while. Looked at her and shook his head.

"Two good deaths in a single night, then. If only day could be so profitable."

"Father..."

"Don't weep! I despise that." He jabbed a finger at her. "You've heard him bawling for that savage he called father. Have you heard a word of grief for your bastard brat?"

"He doesn't know. The Prince had no idea I carried his child."

Her father didn't seem to hear.

"Stay away from Hamlet or I'll cite you as a lunatic and send you to the madhouse without a second thought. I don't want more bastards in this castle than we have already..."

"I will not be ordered..."

His arm swept the table. Plates, glasses, knives, cutlery, broth and fish scattered across the rich carpet.

She stared at the food, the shattered glass and crockery.

"I'll call the servants..."

"No servants, Ophelia. You'll deal with it, not them. I'm offended a child of mine could be so selfish."

The finger again, the cold and icy look.

"And you shall do my bidding or pay the price."

There was a knock on the door. She went to answer it, glad to get out from under his stare. A courtier was there, one she'd seen visiting him in his quarters of late. Voltemand, a civil servant from Copenhagen. A good-looking man and he knew it. He always looked at her in a way she didn't like, a knowing smile on his smug face.

"You have a visitor, father."

"Perhaps I came to see you," he told her with a wink and a smile.

She glared at him.

"Why would you do that, sir? I heard you had a wife and children back in the south. Don't they miss you?"

"Copenhagen's a long way, lady."

He reached out and felt the fabric of her dress between his fingers.

Her father was watching and didn't say a word.

"I'll leave you to your business, whatever that may be."

She retired to her bedroom. There she had the servants fetch hot water to fill the copper bath before the fire. Then she locked the door, found the rose essence Hamlet had given her the previous summer, one of several gifts from Paris.

The perfume came with such memories. She took off her clothes, climbed into the water and tried not to weep.

Hours they waited, long into the next morning, freezing on the icy, dark battlements, cloaks around them, marching from the chapel tower to the vaulted roof of the Great Hall, peered round each corner, seeing nothing.

"If this is some prank..." Hamlet grumbled late into the long night.

"We know what we saw," Horatio replied and the other two with them nodded.

The prince paced the ramparts, looking everywhere.

"You all saw it? The same thing?"

"Yes, my lord," said Barnardo.

"And it looked like...?"

"Your father, said the other sentry. "A shadow of how he was in life."

Hamlet had first raced to the battlement with a quickening pulse. quicken. With fear, certainly. Dread too. But also something like a cold excitement. His father was found dead in the royal garden from a strange seizure brought on by a bite from a stray adder. Ever since Hamlet had wandered round like a half-drowned man. The clean and icy wind blowing in from the Øresund had felt like fresh air in failing lungs. And then... tedium and disenchantment.

"It always comes this way?"

"Not always," said Barnardo. "Last night it went into the tower there..."

He pointed, and then his face changed, his eyes fell and the old soldier's hand made the sudden sign of a cross.

Hamlet spun around and saw the apparition, standing in the doorway they had just passed.

His father, in armour, staring at him alone.

Time stopped. The world and all that was in it fell away till there was only the prince and the dead king alone in the night, their eyes locked upon each other.

For a long and awful moment nothing happened. The apparition stood frozen in the shadowy doorway, grey hair waving around its deathly face, unblinking eyes burning like embers. Then it raised one slow, gauntleted hand, and crooked a beckoning finger.

Without a second thought, Hamlet took a step towards it.

An arm on his shoulder. Horatio held him back.

"Don't, sir! We've no idea what it is. You don't know what it wants."

"Then I'll ask it," Hamlet said and shook him off.

Another stronger arm tried to keep hold him back.

"My lord!" muttered Barnardo. "It might be a devil. Come to seize you."

"And it might be my father, come to speak to his son. I wish none of you harm. But I swear I won't vouch for the good health of the next man to lay a finger on me."

The guard's hand withdrew. The cold night air seemed to gather around Hamlet's heart. Yet he felt calm and his mind was certain.

"I'll speak to it. Stay here."

It was as if the apparition heard. It stepped back into the tower and began to climb the stairs, great sword trailing noiselessly behind it. For all the warnings someone snatched at Hamlet's cloak as he left. He shrugged them off and followed after the phantom, to the winding spiral staircase.

Together they climbed in silence, the only light in the passageway the eerie glow of the spectre itself. Step by step they ascended to the topmost turret. Only when they were outside, with the whole castle laid out below them and the black sea on three sides, did the ghost turn to face him.

At that moment the thing seemed to inhale the bitter wind and changed from unearthly spirit to what might once have passed for a man. The pearly light which seemed to emanate from him faded. Beneath the silver moon the face was older and more real than before, so that for Hamlet it was almost like seeing his father in the flesh.

With that some of his composure failed and he felt the grief and horror mount inside him.

"I am a creature of the night with only moments in this place," the spirit said. "Do not fail me now."

It was his father's voice, commanding, cruel almost. Nothing spectral about it.

"Listen and prepare yourself to revenge what was done to me."

The mailed hand pointed at him then, a frank accusation.

"You know already, don't you?"

"Know?"

"I was bitten by no snake. Except the viper who now wears my crown. And occupies my bed."

"My uncle...?"

"My brother. Claudius. A clever, jealous traitor. His poison poured into my ear as I slept so that the body showed no mark of violence. My brother whose crime has given him all I once possessed: my life, my throne, my queen. You cannot know the horror of my condition, unnaturally cut off by my own flesh and blood, sent to my eternal judgment before I could prepare, weighed down by ancient sins which must now be burned away through endless years of torment."

"What must I do, sir?"

The spectre seemed to smile. It was a familiar look, knowing, testing, almost mocking, and a part of Hamlet recoiled from it.

"No one knows this secret. No one suspects. Except you, my son. You loved me once. You know what you must do."

"And... my mother? She was a part...?"

"Leave her to God and the thorns of her own conscience. Ask no more for..."

The ghost stopped, tipped his head up as if catching a scent on the breeze. An expression on its face Hamlet failed to recognise at first. So unexpected was it. The spirit was afraid now. The soft glow was flowing through it again and as the radiance grew stronger the spectre seemed to tighten as if suffering an inexpressible pain.

The clenched jaws opened in a rising grief and then, like an echo from across a mountain gorge, Hamlet heard its terrible cry of anguish and suffering.

"Father..."

So many questions. So many fears.

But the light was spreading through the armoured figure like fire until there was nothing left but eerie phosphorescence. Then, in an instant, it faded to nothing. The cry lasted a fraction longer before it was borne away on the wind. After that... the cold and unforgiving light of dawn.

# The Play's the Thing

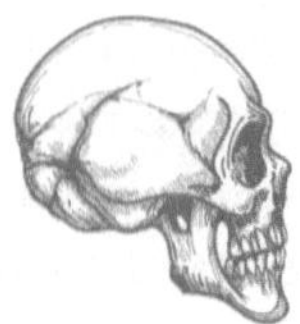

Three days later Ophelia sat in her room, sewing idly, mending her father's clothes. Eyes straying to the window. The river was frozen. The trees bare of leaves. Winter had Elsinore in its relentless grip, and it was so cold she wondered if spring would ever come.

There'd been few words that morning at breakfast. He'd taken the food from her, given some orders about the housekeeping and the servants. Left matters at that.

But Polonius needed to say no more and knew it. He had her secret. The failed clandestine affair. The lost child. He thought he knew everything, but in that he was wrong, though the knowledge only made Ophelia's private grief more painful.

She stabbed at the sheet on her lap. The needle missed, stuck into her leg. A gasp of pain. Ophelia lifted the soft damask fabric over her knee, looked at the pale flesh just above, saw a tiny pearl of blood begin to grow on her skin.

Stood up, dropped the sheet, dabbed at the wound with a spare length of thread.

Then looked and saw someone at the door, leaning against the frame, watching her avidly.

Hamlet walked in and closed the door quietly behind him. Ophelia forgot the sharp needle, stiffened her back, held up her head defiantly.

"My father says..."

He was on her then, strong hands lifting the fabric higher, fingernails brushing lightly against her thighs.

"The Lord Chamberlain insists..."

Hamlet pushed her against the wall. Held her there, tight against the fabric of the one tapestry she owned.

"Not now, Hamlet," she whispered. "Not here."

"Says who?"

"Polonius. And I must obey him. As you..." She shook her head. A stupid thing to say. "As you must obey the King."

"Says who?"

Ophelia folded her arms, looked him in the eye. The dreamy, wistfulness she'd loved when they were in the woods by the river was gone. Now he looked hard of heart and manic.

His fingers briefly brushed her stomach.

"You were plumper before, lady. Or so my mother says. She thinks you're sick. Wasting away. And all since my father died. Why? He was mine not yours. With you there's a reason to argue for a necessary boundary of grief."

She didn't answer.

"And yet..." He stood back, put a thoughtful finger to his chin. "You look much the same as I remember when I went off to Wittenberg. My mother..." He paused and said this very carefully. "Perhaps she's mistaken. Or lying."

Close again, he stroked her flaxen hair, moved it from her cheek.

"Slender. Charming. Beautiful." His eyes were laughing, even if the rest of him seemed wrapped in misery. "Willing. That was a splendid summer, Ophelia. Did I learn more from you? Or you from me?"

"I never touched another man!"

His hand briefly stroked her cheek.

"I could tell you I was a virgin too I suppose..."

"And in Wittenberg?"

He did laugh then.

"In Wittenberg mostly I read books." A shrug. "Or sleep. And sometimes dream."

"My father has commanded me. I mustn't see you."

"Why were you fat before? And thin now? Or is my mother lying? Again."

"Stop this."

He touched her shoulder tenderly.

"No. I won't. I'm your... beloved, aren't I? Prince of Elsinore. I'll do what I damned well like. If I fancy a roll with the chief counsellor's daughter I'll have it. Whether he's willing... or she..."

"This isn't you!"

There was a madness in his eyes then.

"Do you think you know me, lady? If so you're a better judge of character than I. If..."

"I had your child!"

He blinked, recoiling as if struck.

"What?"

"I had your child..."

He shook his head, squinting at her as if trying to make sense of a code or foreign language.

"It died," she went on in the silence. "*He* died."

Another long stillness, but in it Hamlet seemed to freeze. His eyes which had been momentarily full of pain, hardened.

"I lost the baby," she went on, desperate to finish the story now, "the night Old Hamlet passed away. There was a commotion in the castle. They said there was a viper loose. For a while my father seemed terrified. Perhaps he thought the Norwegians had come too..."

A sly, sarcastic nod.

"We blame the men from Oslo for everything, don't we? I had a child? Was that a man from Oslo's doing too?"

"Yours! Two months. Perhaps three." Her eyes drifted to the window. "A gift from the long summer. I lost it. I thought no one knew except a nurse I used. Who's now in France at my command. Yet my father seems to have spies within the fabric of this bloody place..."

Hamlet jabbed a finger at his bare chest.

"Why didn't you tell me? I had a child and you kept me ignorant."

That goaded her.

"What was I to say? You were beside yourself with grief for your own loss..."

"It was mine!" He stopped, thought. Closed his eyes. "Ours. So what got rid of it? A potion from your French bitch? Or a...?"

Her hand flew at his face and slapped him hard.

"What kind of love demands the life of another? A child at that?"

"Danish love, my sweet. Can't you smell it?"

"I lost the baby through grief and fear and... and shame."

He had his hand to his cheek, as shocked as she was.

"And if I'd carried it? What then? Would you have married me? Or paid for the bastard to be raised elsewhere out of embarrassment? While you took a more suitable noble lady for your wife? Because a fallen woman could never be your queen now, could she?"

His fingers gripped her throat. Any tears she had were gone.

"I would have wed you. Without a second thought."

She dragged herself from him.

"But only if I was a virgin. Your family would have demanded that. And there's the problem, sir. What you... what we wanted... ruined the game. I was your summer love and grateful for it. It was more than I expected. And if I could have kept that child I would have loved it all the same."

"So that's two murders then."

"Two?" she asked. "What madness is...?"

She stopped. There was a new look to him, and something there she'd never witnessed before.

"Don't hate me, Hamlet. I beg you."

"You could have been my queen."

At that she laughed.

"What me? Your secret mistress by the water? I'm too easy. Too lustful. Spare me the compliments." She pointed at her breast. "Queens aren't made of this."

He stepped back, staring at her with those cold, hard eyes.

"You had no faith in me. In us."

His face was blank, his voice level. But she could hear the rage within him, trapped like a wolf inside a cage.

He retreated to the door. Without another word, he was gone.

ACROSS THE ØRESUND, in a makeshift encampment behind Helsingborg, Fortinbras sat in his commander's tent, listening to the Scottish warlord Gregor go through the numbers.

A thousand Norwegian foot. Four score knights on horseback. Two hundred and fifty bloodthirsty foreign mercenaries, the only battle-hardened warriors he had. Supplies for a week's campaigning, no more without support.

"Could you find more hired men? Quickly?"

Gregor was a gruff, ginger-haired giant. The leader of the mercenaries. Veteran of a host of campaigns throughout Europe. He scratched his head and asked the question Fortinbras knew was coming.

*How much?*

"You know the coffers are empty, Scotsman. They get paid out of booty and what they can find."

The giant laughed until he shook.

"No offence, sir, but my comrades rarely get off their arses without a penny in their hand. As for plunder... it's Denmark. Pretty as their women are there's not much worth nicking outside Elsinore except herring. And we're drowning in them already."

The Norwegian took a sip of the cold, sour beer. Even that was running out.

"We could take Elsinore with these men. And hold it too. Claudius is quaking in his bed. Sending begging messages to my uncle..."

"I believe that's called diplomacy. It's his trade."

"And warfare's mine. My uncle will be dead before winter turns to spring. He won't stop me..."

The Scot smiled.

"But he won't send you more men either, will he?"

"Get me over there and I'll give you half of Jutland."

Gregor shrugged his shoulders.

"Give me the ships. Or a thousand sets of wings and I'll do it. There's that small matter of the Øresund. I know you could spit from one side to the other if the wind's in the right direction. But it's too far to bridge or for men and horses to swim. If..."

Fortinbras got to his feet. He was thirty. Three years old when his father died and his uncle Magnus was elected to the throne. That was the way the crown worked in Norway. The man the nobles liked – or feared most – became monarch.

"If I can take Elsinore they'll make me king of Denmark and Norway together. And then..."

"This is all a matter for diplomats, Fortinbras. Men like Claudius over there. Not soldiers like me. Nothing..."

"I pay you to fight, Scotsman! Not to argue with me."

The giant got up, walked to the open door of the tent. They had camped on a hill overlooking the small port below. The slender strip of water lay beneath them, placid on this bright, calm winter's day.

"I've served with the best of them. Learned from them, too. One of the finest, a condottiere from Milan, told me something I should never forget. We're mercenaries. We're not paid to fight. We're paid to win."

"And?"

"Only fools die for nothing. Not us. If there's a chance of seizing Denmark and getting rich from someone's coffers we'll take it. But if it's just a matter of sitting here freezing our balls off..."

He thrust his fists in his pockets. Gazed at the distant blue horizon.

"Scotland's lovely in the spring, lord. I've got women over there. And kids. Wouldn't mind seeing them. For a little while anyway. Until I'm bored."

Fortinbras shoved him out of the way. Stretched out his arm, pointed at the distant shape of Elsinore across the water.

"Twenty seven years ago the Øresund froze. My father died there on the ice. Through Old Hamlet's treachery. Did you know that?"

Gregor tapped his ginger head.

"Got half the history of Europe in there, mate. Not much room for anything else."

"The sea froze! My father had his entire army across there, beneath the castle walls. Could have taken Denmark like a wolf seizing a lamb if that bastard hadn't talked him into single combat. While Claudius watched from the bedchamber of his queen..."

The Scotsman looked interested finally.

"If it freezes, we can walk across. Gregor, will you be with me? Will you lead my men?"

"If it freezes like you say." He looked up at the clear blue sky. "But will it?"

"I don't have mastery of the weather. Just money. Men. And you."

Gregor sniffed, wiped his nose with his sleeve.

Then shivered and pulled his fur cloak around him.

"We'll give it a month at most. After that it's Perth for me and mine."

~

Polonius was in his study, listening to reports from two of his spies. Violent men his daughter knew and feared. He mixed with them so easily, always had. And yet to the court he could appear the most gentle and urbane of lords.

Voltemand, the man from Copenhagen who had been dispatched to the royal court in Oslo, was there too, eyeing her as she walked in.

Back already. She wondered if that was good news or bad. She loathed politics.

Her father glared at her when she entered, told her to wait outside until he called.

An hour it took and when the spies came out they were grinning and counting out gold pieces in their fingers. One of them held up a coin, winked at her. Made a coarse gesture and asked, "Up for it?"

Ophelia laughed in his face. Watched his hand rise.

Voltemand was behind them, struck him hard with the back of his hand, then fetched a knee to his groin and sent him gasping to the floor.

"Offend this lady again and neither of you will leave Elsinore alive."

The one who was still standing looked terrified.

"He thought she was a servant girl," the spy said, then kicked his compatriot hard to make the point. "Didn't mean nothing."

Voltemand smiled at her.

"The Lady Ophelia's no servant. Too lovely for that."

She pushed past him.

"You flatter me without purpose, sir. No good reason at all."

Her father was at his desk, poring over papers and maps. Books open in front of him. Danish, English, Latin. Military tomes from what she could see.

"Don't walk in on me freely again," he said without looking at her. "Not until we're done with all this business. We're as near as dammit in a state of war. I've affairs to manage that shouldn't reach a woman's ears."

Finally he put aside his quill and documents. Checked his watch for no reason other than to show he owed the damned thing. Glared at her.

"After all I said last night... did I waste my breath?"

"Father?"

"Hamlet visited you. In your room. When you retired there this morning. It was a brief encounter. Raised voices. Afterwards you were flushed and near hysterical. The way feeble girls are in love..."

"You do not know!"

"If I can't stop you rutting I'll dispatch you to a convent. Or marry you off to a farmer."

"He came to me. I didn't want it. Any of it..."

"But you let him..."

"He wanted nothing more than to talk to me. He's distressed. I've never seen a man in such pain. Perhaps his mind's adrift or something. I don't know."

Polonius looked interested. He got to his feet.

"You think he's mad?"

"I'm not a physician. Just a feeble girl..."

His hand struck her cheek, hard enough to bring up a blush.

"Don't mock me, child."

She didn't cry. Refused to. But she held her fingers to her face.

"The prince is sick. He needs help and comfort. Perhaps if you told his mother ..."

"You're saying he did nothing?"

"I am."

Another blow. She took it, stared at him.

"You're lying."

"I fear he may harm himself. Or others. There's a violence to him I've never seen before. I tell you this because you're my father. And the king's adviser. What you do with it, sir..."

"If he presses himself upon you again keep him interested. Keep him on the hook. Let's see what happens. That's my wish."

"It's not mine. And I..."

His hand was raised a third time.

"Best hit me somewhere private, sir. Unless you want him to see."

"You're an insolent child. Do as I say."

"If you'll tell the Queen he's sick I'll do it. And report back to you with everything. Like a spy so you can love me."

He looked at her with interest then.

"Don't fail me, daughter. There's a price for that. You wouldn't like it."

HAMLET WAS TOYING with the penknife again.

"I've been giving some thought to this weapon of yours."

The dwarf looked up, interested.

"And which way are you pointing the blade, Prince?"

"That seems to be the question, doesn't it? Such a little thing, the pressure it takes to push the tip of a good dagger through flesh."

"Makes a mess though."

"Of all kinds," Hamlet agreed. "Perhaps this is easier."

He reversed the knife so that its tip pressed softly into the skin of his own throat.

Yorick watched him, unimpressed.

"Probably. Still a bit bloody. No thought for the poor bastard who'd have to clean up after you."

"That's all that worries you?" Hamlet asked, still holding the blade against his neck as if testing it.

"Pretty much. What do you want? A few home truths? A sermon on despair, the unforgiveable sin against the holy spirit? I could maybe rustle up a few woodcut prints showing the torment of those damned for suicide if that would help."

"Seems unlikely." Hamlet removed the knife and looked at his face reflected in the blade. "Still, not much of a reason to live, is it? The fear of being punished for killing yourself? I thought God was supposed to be full of love and forgiveness."

Yorick tugged on his long, untidy hair.

"I'm sorry. Have me we met? I'm the king's underpaid jester."

"I know."

"Then why are you treating me like a priest or – worse – a philosopher? If you wanted reflections on the nature of the universe and your place in it, you should have stayed in school. You want fart noises and cock jokes, I'm your man. If it's sympathy you're after talk to your chum Horatio. Or Ophelia."

"I'm done with Ophelia."

"Or she's done with you."

"Amounts to the same thing."

Yorick grinned.

"Not the same as rejection though, is it, Romeo?"

"It doesn't feel anything at all."

"Oh.," The jester drew out the single syllable. "So that's the pose of the day, is it? Fine. You're a man of iron. Of stone. A stoic of pure purpose, undistracted by feeble human emotions. You'll make your father proud yet. Were he not dead..."

Hamlet turned quickly on him, the knife sweeping out towards the dwarf so that he jumped back and ran away, cackling.

Then stopped at the door, looked serious for a moment.

"So let me understand this, Hamlet. Neither of us has room for error. A spook on the battlements says your father was murdered by your uncle. And the game is... what?"

"I play the fool."

"That's my job, not yours."

He poked Yorick's harlequin jacket.

"The mad fool. The lunatic. The king's deranged stepson. More to be pitied than feared. Ignored. An embarrassment to the court. And so... invisible... I bide my time..."

He stopped. Yorick cocked his head to one side.

"And...?" He waved his hands for more.

"I think. Got a better idea?"

A pause then, "Not at the moment I'll admit. But if this is the game, you need to play your part to the full. As if you mean it. No point in shrieking at the walls in here. Mingle. Mooch." He slapped Hamlet's leg. "Look at things that aren't there. Weep. Sigh. Groan. Groaning's always good. And do it..." His stubby arm pointed at the door. "Out there. Where they'll all see."

A hard nudge with a bony elbow then.

"Quite futile trying to prove your madness to me, sunshine. I know it only too well."

Hamlet grabbed at his cloak.

The jester dodged him, rubbed his hands together in glee.

"And now I'm off to exercise my third best talent, after telling ribald stories and juggling."

"Which is?"

A bright, broad grin. "I'm going... snooping."

Claudius sat at his desk, peering at a shag-edged roll of parchment on which a map of the country and its neighbours had been etched and shaded in colour. A series of dated notes had recently been written in.

"The Lord Chamberlain, my liege," said the page at the door.

"Good. Send him in."

He went back to his examination of the papers, barely looking up when Polonius entered.

"I've been tracking Fortinbras's movements." He tapped a circle of red ink. "We've heard nothing for days."

"May I?"

Polonius sidled over to the desk and ran his fingers over the map. Then the old man reached for the quill, dipped it, and added a new red circle – just across the Øresund.

"So there's only that narrow puddle of water between us?" the King asked, rising from his chair. "You're sure of that?"

"Absolutely, my lord. Though this is not what I came to report."

There was something in the old councillor's tone.

"Which is?"

"A delicate matter, my liege. It pertains to your..." Polonius hesitated. "To Prince Hamlet."

Claudius tapped his finger on the map.

"A Norwegian army on our doorstep's more pressing than my nephew's misery."

A pompous smile broke on the old man's face.

"Stability at home is never more important than at times of diplomatic crisis."

Another easy adage. Half of what he said sounded like an old wives' motto.

Claudius frowned.

"Very well. Out with it. What's my beloved nephew done now?"

"It's not so much what he's done. More what's happened to him as a result. It involves, I'm ashamed to say, my daughter. The two of them have been... involved."

Polonius let the phrase hang in the air.

"Just how *involved*?"

"Too much for a caring father and a virtuous household to be comfortable with. Illicitly, behind my back I fear she... seduced him."

Claudius laughed at that.

"It's always the woman when there's blame to be apportioned, isn't it? Is this affair common knowledge? Or can we keep it quiet? They're young. She's beautiful. He's a handsome lad, too. It's understandable. But I'll need Hamlet betrothed to a foreign princess one day. If there's a girl who'll have him. I can't have gossip. It has to stop."

Polonius nodded.

"It has. Only those in my employ know of it. A serving girl who's now far from Elsinore. And the guilty parties themselves. That's it."

"And you're sure this is done with?"

"From the moment I learned of it. Unfortunately the prince is mightily distressed by my daughter's rejection of his company. He has become... unbalanced."

Claudius shook his head.

"Lovelorn, you mean?"

"No. Much worse than that. You've seen for yourself. His behaviour has become erratic and unpredictable. Ophelia, finally showing the duty she owes to me, reports that his...*dealings* with her show him to be unstable. Prone to violent outpourings of emotion which, apart from being unseemly about the court, may – I fear – turn dangerous."

"Dangerous? To whom?"

Polonius licked his dry lips and stared at the King.

"To himself in the first instance. To those who are – or seem to him to be – involved in his misery too I imagine. My daughter. Myself. Even others who are unconnected to this matter but against whom he wishes to bear a grudge."

Another phrase left floating in silence.

"You mean me?"

"The prince has spoken openly of his dissatisfaction with the circumstances of your coronation. The haste of your marriage to his mother. He is neither rational nor reliable, and I'm afraid that some desperate act of violence is not beyond him. The odd death of his father from a snake in winter." A smile. "We never did find that viper, did we?"

"No," the King snapped. "As if I need this now. What do you propose?"

Polonius produced a notebook and turned to a page marked with a red ribbon.

"We double the guard on your royal person. We surround him with those we can trust to relay his words, his thoughts directly to us. Ophelia may be one of them."

"Is there anyone you wouldn't use as a spy, Polonius?"

A diplomatic smile.

"Not if they're needed. She'll do as I tell her."

"What about friends of his? Drinking mates. Find out which of them can be bought."

The old man nodded and made a note.

"But not that chap Horatio," Claudius added. "He worships my nephew. Those two you sent to Wittenberg to watch him when he first went out there? I forget the names. Sycophantic little turds, always dressed to the nines."

Polonius scowled.

"Rosencrantz and Guildenstern. Minor nobles. They never earned the pittance I paid them. They can start now. I'll have them here by tomorrow."

"Your daughter and two so-called friends. Is that enough by way of spies? Can they handle a distraught young man like Hamlet?"

"We'll see. I believe so."

The King returned to the map.

"Good. And keep this between us. No word to the Queen. She's... easily upset."

He stabbed a finger on the narrow stretch of sea in front of them.

"If that freezes..."

"It won't."

"Your spies can read the weather now, can they?"

"No." Polonius stared at him with a sour face. "But there's plenty of men in the harbour who can. Ship's captains. Your admirals. Fortinbras won't find his way here that way."

"I hope you're right."

Polonius smiled.

"I am, sir. I warrant it."

~

INCHING along the Elsinore road between town and castle were a pair of horse drawn wagons loaded with a dozen men and an assortment of crates and trunks. English actors touring the continent. The public theatres were closed for the winter, so they picked their way around the surrounding countryside, playing in the stately homes and palaces whose owners didn't threaten to set the dogs on them when they came calling. It was an uncertain way to make a living, and Richard Burbage, the company's veteran thespian and unofficial leader, had already voiced his dissatisfaction about their current excursion.

"Three days through snow and ice with a wind that could cut you in half," he remarked, "and for what? So some lackey can greet us at the gate and tell us to piss off?"

Kemp, the clown, the only person who had been with the company long enough to stand up to him, shrugged.

"Might go all right."

Burbage glared him.

"You think so? Because what a new king wants, what an *unpopular* king wants, a monarch being watched by every foreign power for signs of weakness, a rogue Norwegian army on his doorstep... what a king like that desires most in life is to watch a play."

"Might lighten his mood," Kemp suggested with half a smile. "Christ knows they could use a little entertainment."

The road inclined as it snaked up to the fortress. The wagons' wheels began to slip on the frozen cobbles so that the actors had to dismount and shove. One of the boys who played the women's parts slipped and fell flat on his face in a muddy ditch. The hired men guffawed, but Burbage shot the boy a murderous look.

"When we reach the gates, stay out of sight. And the first thing you do if we get inside is scrub your damn clothes spotless. I don't care if you have to stand naked in the snow while you do it."

The boy nodded, chastened, and Burbage relented a little.

"You know your lines, boy?"

"For what, sir?"

"*The Malcontent, The Spanish Tragedy, Friar Bacon...*"

He ticked them off on his fingers.

"Every one."

Burbage wasn't sure he believed him.

"You'd better. Another performance like that one last week and I'll beat you till you can't stand up straight. You hear me?"

Kemp shot him a knowing look. They both understood Burbage wouldn't hurt the lad. Audiences could smell fear and terrified boys on stage were nightmares to work with.

"Maybe they'll turn us away," the actor said. "I heard that Prince Hamlet was home for his father's funeral. Or his mother's wedding, I suppose."

Burbage just shrugged. They'd performed for the prince two years before. Apparently Hamlet liked the theatre. Some of the servants said he took parts in plays at school. A friendly ear inside Elsinore might be what they needed to get their foot in the door. And with it decent food, a warm bed for a night or two, and a fee that would see them through the end of the month.

The grim outline of the castle loomed over them.

Kemp's mood was growing gloomy.

"Never much liked this place. It's creepy."

Burbage grinned.

"Not here to like it, are we? We're the bringers of theatre. Supplying imagination to the gloomy Danes. The harbingers of joy... Oh God..." He scowled. "What were we thinking when we took that ship here, Will?"

Kemp smiled.

"Something about all the world being a stage. And we're just players in it."

The old actor roared with laughter.

"Oh yes. That!" He turned to yell at the hired men struggling with the wagons in the mud. "Push at it, you lazy bastards. Put a little colour in your cheeks. The King of Denmark awaits us."

Then, more quietly, "It could be worse I suppose. We might be playing for the Welsh."

~

WHILE CLAUDIUS SURVEYED the two young men Polonius had delivered, Gertrude sat by the table in the study, lost in her thoughts.

The tall visitor was Rosencrantz, skinny, lean and weasel-faced, sly-eyed. The diminutive one Guildenstern, tubby and with a fawning manner and even more garish clothes. Both wore new-fangled pistols on their right hips, short swords on the left. Neither looked as if they knew how to use them.

Minor nobles from Aalborg in Jutland. Impoverished, ambitious, stupid.

"I'm grateful you could get here so swiftly," the King said.

"A monarch's desire..." Rosencrantz replied then winked at his fat companion.

"Equates to his subject's duty," Guildenstern added. "May I say, on both our parts, your majesty, that never has Elsinore looked finer, yourself in better health, the Queen more lovely, the nation more secure. Were the Almighty himself to occupy the throne..."

"Yes, yes," Polonius snapped. "That's taken as read. Do you know why you're here? Have you heard rumours?"

They twitched nervously.

"Rumours?" the tall one said. "You mean about the Norwegians?" His hand went to the flashy new pistol. "Did you... did you bring us here to fight?"

Claudius scowled and cast Polonius a vicious glance.

"By the looks of you those things on your hips are no more than jewellery. No, no fighting for you my fine mannequins. You're friends with my nephew, Hamlet?"

They smiled and looked relieved.

"Oh, yes," Guildenstern replied.

"Like a brother he was to us in Wittenberg," the other went on. "For which we shall always remain both grateful and honoured. That a prince of the realm should deign to mix with fellows such as..."

Gertrude stared at them.

"I heard you spent most your time in brothels and taverns, sirs. Are you saying you took my son with you?"

The edginess returned.

It was Rosencrantz who spoke.

"When I say we were friends, my lady, I may have overstated the case. We know him more academically than socially. That would be improper given the difference between our respective stations." A glance at Polonius. "But we reported back all the same. As the Lord Chamberlain requested."

"So you met him in the hallways now and again?" she asked. "Between lessons?"

The fat one leaned forward.

"Also on occasion outside. In the courtyard. A polite and pleasant student. More bookish than us, I'll agree. A finer prospect for the Danish throne it's hard to imagine..."

"Except for you, your grace," Rosencrantz broke in hastily. "Long live your majesties, and good health attend all your..."

"Shut up!" Claudius barked. "Be silent and listen."

They were quaking then, their shiny pistols tinkling against their silver brocade belts.

"Hamlet isn't himself. He's always had a solitary, introverted nature. A tendency to the reclusive..."

"Truly I never noticed that," Guildenstern began to say only to be quiet when his neighbour gave him a look.

"He takes more note of his inward thoughts than the world around him," the Queen explained. "It's a temporary affliction made worse by his father's death affecting a sensitive nature."

"Sensitive," the fat one agreed.

"He needs company. Familiar faces around him. Reminders of his happy student days." She glanced at Polonius. "We were told there was no one in Denmark he better admired in Wittenberg than..." Gertrude looked them up and down. "Than you."

"And Horatio," Guildenstern conceded, shame-faced.

Gertrude nodded, pleased that they weren't totally without self-awareness.

"What do you truly want of us, madam?" Rosencrantz asked. "If it's within our power we'll surely give it. If not we'll do our best."

Gertrude leaned forward from her chair and begged them, "Be his friends, sirs. Lighten his day. Ride with him."

"Riding? We're pretty good at that."

"Go hunting." They fell silent. "Fill his hours with pleasant activity. An intellectual young man needs something to occupy him. Otherwise his mind will dwell on dark and unnecessary thoughts."

The tall one bowed and flourished his hand.

"Your highnesses ask that which you are entitled to command. On behalf of us both we give ourselves up to your wishes..."

"And freely lay our services at your feet," the fat one finished.

Polonius stepped in front of the pair and gave them a small black book.

"Keep close to him. When he speaks stay silent and listen. Then afterwards write down what he says and bring it to me."

They smiled and took the notebook.

Claudius waved at the door.

"That's it!"

"They're idiots," Gertrude said when the two were gone. "Hamlet will see through them in an instant."

Claudius got up and wandered to the window, stared out at the grey sea and Helsingborg across the water.

"The crown needs idiots from time to time. We'd be lost without them." He pointed at Polonius. "Make sure they do their job."

"As if I'd countenance otherwise," the old man replied sourly, joining him at the window and peering down to where men and wagons had gathered at the main gate. "Are we finished here? It seems there are other matters needing my attention."

"Oh look!" Yorick scampered across the room, threw himself on the floor at Hamlet's desk, rested his cheek on his right hand, grinning madly. "There I was thinking the dear boy would be out there sighing and groaning. All the time he's back in his bedroom, reading booky-wookies again. What a fine and noble student. All those miserable grey Germans in Wittenberg will love you."

He scrambled to his feet, snatched the leather volume from Hamlet's fingers.

"The meditations of Marcus Aurelius. Stoic stuff. Anything saucy in it? A touch of rumpy-pumpy?"

"Bit heavy for fools."

"True. Though that statue of my father out in the hall, sitting stark naked on a tortoise..."

"What about it?"

The jester found the frontispiece, showed it. A line engraving of the Roman emperor on his great horse, hand raised to the crowd in front of him.

"See the resemblance? That's where Old Hamlet got the idea. Your father's way of taking the piss out of mine. You lot do that quite a bit. Have you thought of getting a dog? They always cheer people up.'

"No."

"I've never fully trusted people who don't like dogs. They rarely turn out well."

Hamlet grabbed for the book. The clown withheld it.

"Not till you tell me what good this is, child. And what you plan to do with all this dry and pointless knowledge. Waste your time thinking or something?"

The prince leaned back in his chair, nodded.

"Maybe. What's wrong with that?"

"Old saying round here. You know what thought did? Followed a muck cart. Thought it was a funeral. Doing stuff." He raised his fleshy fist. Parried with an imaginary blade. "Being a man. That's what counts."

He handed over the book.

"A touch of rumpy-pumpy in the night. We all require that." A smile. "Even you." A nod, a wink next. "And the Queen of course."

Silence. The jester folded his arms.

"There's a question on your face, Prince. Care to voice it?"

Nothing.

"Let me guess. You're asking yourself... does she know something she's not saying?"

He jumped onto the desk, sending the books there flying.

"I mean... eleven weeks after your old man pegs it, snake bite in the garden, poison dripping out of his ear... whatever. Dead's dead. Who cares? And there she is. In your uncle's bed. Happy as a lamb in spring. Lord knows we hear that every night, don't we?"

Hamlet extended a hand and prodded the front of the jester's harlequin jacket.

"There are limits."

A grin.

"Aye, Prince. But do you know what they are? Three months. Most people would say that was a decent enough space for mourning. That a widow's got a right to happiness too, even if her only son don't want it. And your uncle... Nice man, Claudius. Bookish like you, though a bit more diplomatic with it. Not like your father..."

"My father was a king!"

The little man laughed at his fury.

"If by that you mean he'd lop off your head for nothing more than a sideways glance... I suppose he was. Didn't get him into Heaven though, did it? There he is, stuck in that place your friends in Wittenberg don't think exists. Purgatory. Waiting for all his foul crimes to get burned away or a ticket out from you."

A snigger.

"Unless it's not your father at all. But a demon up to mischief. An imp whispering in your ear. As if you need another one of them."

Hamlet looked at his library. The day book he kept for his own thoughts. In Wittenberg these things made sense. They were the rules and boundaries set for an ordered life, one ruled by logic and the law. But in Elsinore, behind the castle's dank, cold walls, they seemed like nothing more than props for a pointless play. Devices that sought to hide the truth, not reveal it.

"Did she know?"

"Why ask me? I've no more idea than you. We're not going to find out either, are we? While you sit here scribbling and whining like a monk in solitary confinement there's devilment on your doorstep."

"I told you. I've been playing my part."

Yorick grinned.

"So have I. Good news, Hamlet."

The prince turned away from his books.

"Which is?"

"Entertainment! The splendours of the theatre. Well... a bunch of travelling actors if you can call that splendid. Here to perform whatever tragedy the court chooses to ask of them."

He bent his head, gross ear comically listening.

"Any ideas, Prince?"

"A tragedy. Perhaps..."

"No! Shush!" the clown cried. "I've a better idea."

Not long after Hamlet was born the Queen had demanded her own quarters. Marriage was a duty not a choice. Not with her first husband anyway. Grudgingly Old Hamlet had allowed her an adjoining apartment. After all, she'd delivered what he wanted: a son. There she could find some peace during the day and rest when he had to work – or carouse – late, though only if he gave her express permission. Most nights when he was home she was to wait for him in his chamber. There was never any argument about that.

Claudius was easier in everything. She was allowed to come and go as she pleased, to pick her own servants, arrange her own time.

She knew that Polonius heard every sigh and whisper in the castle anyway and would relay what he heard to her husband. There was no need to keep her close. Old Hamlet did that out of possessiveness only. To let the world know she was his.

Three months dead, interred in a cold tomb in the castle chapel. A lifelike statue of him, fierce in armour, long sword in hand, stood above his stone coffin.

She hadn't followed his interment closely. Men and women died. Sometimes quickly. Sometimes slowly and in agony. Hamlet was on his own, reading alone in the royal garden when it happened. Cold by the time the servants found him. A snake had bitten him, they said, though it was late in the year for adders and no one ever found the creature. Just a king, eyes open in terror, puke around his mouth, stiff and dead on the autumn grass.

Perhaps it wasn't a snake at all. Sometimes, she thought, men just died and no one knew why, even if the doctors felt they had to offer some explanation to save face.

Still the sight haunted her. She'd never witnessed such a death. Never seen fear and horror like that on his ruddy and frozen face.

There was a madness within the man. She'd come to understand as much not long after they married. Her husband possessed a hard, unyielding fury against the world that rose without warning, full of anger and violence, brought about by nothing she could guess at.

When she first saw that red anger inside she'd tried to argue, to comfort him, to reason. To be the good and loyal wife. It was a week before she could come out of her room; it took that long for the bruises to heal enough to be covered up with powder. And all the time he'd tried to drag her into public. To show her beaten, swollen face and proclaim to the world, "This is mine. Behold what I've done. That proves it."

And Hamlet was his offspring. No doubt about that. Sometimes she saw in her slender, sullen son his father's eyes. Bleak. Cruel, even, sometimes. Unrelenting in their fierce thirst to leave a mark upon the world.

If that crazed blood had been handed down...

This dark reverie was interrupted by a rap on the door. Claudius stood there smiling; in his right hand a single white rose.

She laughed straight away. He'd had the ability to amuse her from the very beginning, long before she realised there was a look in his eyes that unsettled her. Interested her, too.

Gertrude walked over, sniffed the flower, looked at the stem. He'd removed the thorns already.

"Where on earth do you get a rose in Elsinore in the middle of winter?"

"Don't you want it?"

She took the flower from him, kissed his cheek. No bristles. No beard. A clean-shaven man with a kind and amiable face. Scheming. She didn't doubt it. But he was a diplomat by training. It was only to be expected. And if he'd lacked those skills perhaps neither of them would have managed Old Hamlet's death, the marriage, the succession so easily.

"Where did you get it?"

He looked grave.

"It struck me a while back that you didn't seem yourself. I wondered if this was because you regretted marrying an unworthy man. Which would be understandable..."

She closed her eyes and whispered, "Claudius, my sweet..."

"So I sent a ship south. To Africa. I told them not to return until they'd bought the most precious and beautiful flower they could find. And to bring it back to Elsinore so I could possess two such wonders..."

Gertrude laughed again.

"They braved storms and pirates. Half the crew died of disease or combat. The cost to the treasury will require numerous measures of fresh taxation..."

"Liar!"

He shrugged.

"Only about the flower. It came from some gypsies who turned up at the gates. Where they got it...?"

She sniffed the bloom.

"What are we going to do?"

"About Fortinbras? We make sure his uncle keeps him on a short, tight leash and that's the end of it. If I have to throw a little territory or money their way I'll do it. If..."

Her hand went to his arm.

"I meant about Hamlet."

Her husband fell quiet. She could picture him with her son when he was a boy. Claudius and the jester Yorick had been the only men in his life when Hamlet was young. Both kind and interested, friends to a troubled child whose own father largely ignored him. Saw him as too bookish, too weak and intellectual to be of much interest.

"We do what we've always done. We treat him with love and patience and generosity. And hope that one day he'll once again return us with the same... No... What do I say? He loves you, Gertrude. Don't doubt it."

"Sometimes I see his father in his eyes. There's a fierceness. An instability..."

"Then we'll make him whole again."

She ran her fingers down the rose's delicate stem.

"I hate the idea of spying on my own son."

"You're a loving mother. Of course you do."

Gertrude shook her head.

"The old man... Polonius. I feel he watches us all. Every minute of the day. It's as if he inhabits the fabric of the castle somehow."

"My sweet..."

He reached for her hand.

"You're going to tell me it's necessary."

"It is."

"And Hamlet? Will these fools of Polonius's see something that will cure him?"

"If they don't I'll find someone who will. He's my flesh, my blood as well."

But he's his father's son too, she thought again. More than Claudius appreciated.

The King bent down and sniffed the flower.

"Summer's fragrance in bleak midwinter. I've no need of it. Not if I have you."

The sight of his kind face cheered her. She laughed and kissed him on the cheek.

"Words. You're so good with them, my dear."

"They're all I have, love. I pray they're all I need."

Polonius sat back in his desk chair and considered the young man who stood so stiffly in front of him.

"Leave us," he said to the guard, waiting until the door latched closed and they were alone. He took out his watch, checked the time, noted how the young man stared. Such fine instruments were rare in Elsinore. "So, Reynaldo. You've been with us, what? A year?"

"Eleven months, sir."

Polonius nodded.

"And in that time you have worked in the buttery and, most recently, in the armoury, yes?"

"That's right. Mainly accounting. I'm good with numbers, they say."

He smiled nervously, then looked down, fearing he had sounded arrogant.

" And you have some languages." It wasn't a question. He was consulting a note book. "Latin and French."

"I attended the Canute school. On a guild scholarship."

"Most impressive. And your French is good? Be honest, boy. I've no time for empty claims."

"Almost fluent. I had an aunt from Rouen who came to live with us..."

"Very well. Do you know my son, Laertes?"

"Not to speak to. I've... I've seen him in the castle..."

"Would he recognize you if he saw you?"

"I don't see why..."

"Very well. You no longer work in the armoury. You work for me."

Reynaldo looked around, his eyes wide.

"Thank you, sir." He couldn't hide the tremor in his voice. "In what... what manner of work?"

"An easy, pleasant task. You'll go to France. You will take up lodgings close to my son's school. Follow his movements, his activities, his friends – that is most important – and you will write to me weekly with a full account of everything he does."

"Everything, my lord?"

"That's what I said. Who he's seen with. How he spends his time. What people say about him. That last is also most important. How is my son reputed? Is he considered studious, respectable, trustworthy? Or is he a gambler, a drunk, a frequenter of whore houses...?"

"I'm sure your son would never do such things."

Polonius sighed and glared at him.

"I don't care what he does, you fool. Only what he's thought to do. Reputation is all."

The young servant hesitated, then asked, "And if I'm caught?"

"They'll hang you as a spy."

Reynaldo swallowed hard and looked at the man in front of him.

"And if I say I would prefer to stay in employment at Elsinore? Doing my duty here?"

"Then I'll look at your book-keeping and find reasons to hang you for thievery here. Any more questions?"

Terrified the young clerk shook his head.

"Good. Gather what things you have. I'll find you a ship. Be ready to leave when I tell you."

~

Burbage had known warmer welcomes for his troupe. The Lord Chamberlain had seen the players' arrival from one of the upper windows and made a point of sending one of his minions to say that their services were not required "at this time."

The actor had watched the look of smug satisfaction on the doorman's face when he came back with the news. Then he played the only card he had left before the sentries started forcing them back over the bridge.

"Prince Hamlet sent for us personally. He won't be happy if you thugs lay a finger on artists like us. He's an intellectual fellow, after all. Many's the time we've discussed Petrarch and Dante together late of an evening..."

This was not strictly true or, as Kemp later pointed out, even slightly so. But it did the trick. The doorman sent a kitchen boy up to the prince's quarters, closing the door in their frozen faces while he waited for confirmation. When he stuck his head out again, the sour look of disappointment on his shiny mug said it all.

They left the larger boxes in the courtyard and followed the kitchen boy up to the Great Hall where they found Hamlet dragging benches aside with a manic energy to give them room to play.

"We're in your debt, my lord," said Burbage. "Polonius wasn't for bringing us in."

"Not what you'd call a man of culture, our Lord Chamberlain." He stopped the actor mid bow and shook his hand. "All the way from England, then?"

"Copenhagen actually. Via Hamburg and Amsterdam. It's a European tour. So many royal houses request our presence these days." Burbage wiped his brow, then Kemp, sarcastically, did the same. "It's hard to keep up with demand frankly."

"Wherever you came from you're welcome. All of you."

"Too kind, my Lord," said Kemp.

The Prince wore a fixed, determined smile.

"Hardly. You'll earn your keep."

There was something a little frantic about his manner that Burbage hadn't seen before. Perhaps, in spite of his sober black clothes, he'd been drinking, not that he had the smell about him.

"We're used to singing for our supper," the actor said uneasily.

"How about killing for it?"

The Englishmen exchanged nervous glances.

"My lord?" Burbage asked.

Hamlet put an arm around his shoulder and whispered in his ear.

"I was wondering if you might stage *The Murder of Gonzago*."

"Oo," Burbage grumbled. "That old chestnut? We haven't performed Gonzago for six months or more. Not so much call for tragedy these days. Comedy's the thing." He looked into Hamlet's eyes and wondered what he saw there. "It's the way things work, Prince. The more miserable the world, the more the audience craves a bit of laughter. We've got some good stuff too. Had the Germans rolling in the aisles and that's not easy."

Hamlet's mood shifted.

"So what use are you? What kind of actors if you can't brush up a play you've done a hundred times in time for tomorrow night? We're not fond of amateurs in Elsinore."

"It's not that we can't do it, my lord," Burbage answered, fighting to keep a hold on his temper. "I just thought it was a little old fashioned. Everyone already knows the story for one thing..."

"Then we'll change it." Hamlet's hostility vanished as quickly as it came, replaced by an instant, agitated enthusiasm. "I'll write you some new speeches. That'll freshen it up a bit. Give things an edge. If..." A sly glance. "If you're up to learning new lines that is."

Kemp butted in, "We mastered Doctor Faustus in two mornings. Devils and all."

"No devils here. Not on the stage anyway. I can get you copies of the play from the castle library if you need them. You can have the new speeches by nightfall. Good enough?"

"More than adequate," Burbage agreed, forcing a smile.

"In the meantime..." The prince leapt onto one of the long tables, striking a theatrical pose. "Give me a speech."

A grumbled murmur went round the company

"We're auditioning, my lord?" asked Kemp.

Hamlet thought for a moment then snapped his fingers.

"If you want paying. Remember that play you did at the Swan last year? About the last days of the Trojan war?"

"*Ilium*?" Kemp muttered putting his hand over his eyes.

"That's the one! There's a part where someone tells the story of the soldiers coming out of the wooden horse, and Pyrrhus hunting down old Priam."

Burbage stood back, bowed, flourished his right arm.

"I know it, sir. Every word."

He closed his eyes, half a recalling of the lines, half dramatic effect, and paused as the rest of the company sat down to watch.

Then there was a loud commotion in the hallway and a man's angry voice boomed through the hall.

"Who's behind this? Get these scum out of here. I expressly said they weren't welcome!"

Polonius, the Lord Chamberlain. The man whose fingers were on the purse strings.

"Oh bugger," Burbage whispered.

Hamlet was on the old man instantly, twice as loud.

"And I... told them they were!"

The players fell uncomfortably silent as Polonius, red faced, marched into the room.

"Far be it from me to contradict the wishes of the prince..."

"Well shut up, then!" Hamlet yelled, leaping from the table to confront him. "You're nothing more than a jumped-up clerk in the presence of artists. Take your ledgers and your notebooks and sit in silence. Or get out."

"Hosting common players," Polonius began, officious and irritated, "is hardly a suitable activity..."

Hamlet drew his sword and held it front of him.

"One more word and I swear I'll trim that goatish beard of yours and stuff a pillow with it. So what do you say? Ready to let the man speak?"

Polonius's back stiffened.

"If you wish it."

"I do."

Then he gave Burbage an encouraging nod and the actor, this time pausing for only a second, began.

"Pyrrhus didn't break stride," he recited, eyes flashing around the watching faces. "Anyone who got in his way felt the edge of his sword. Each step took him further from the wooden horse and deeper into the city which was already ablaze, and when someone stood in his way – man, woman, or child, they got it in the neck. By the time he found Priam, Pyrrhus looked like a devil, dripping blood from head to foot. A monster.

"The old man spies him, but he's already exhausted and can barely hold his sword. He starts to beg for mercy, but Pyrrhus just keeps coming, muttering the name of his father, Achilles. Well, when Priam hears that name, he knows he's a dead man. Pyrrhus hasn't just stumbled on him by chance, and he's not looking to capture the old king for ransom. Achilles was dead, killed by Paris, Priam's son. Pyrrhus is there for revenge, a father for a father."

"This is too long," Polonius grumbled.

"A common perception," Kemp agreed. "All talk, isn't it?"

"Out!" yelled Hamlet. "Both of you!"

Polonius looked affronted, but clearly didn't care to listen to any more, of the play or the abuse. He got to his feet and stalked off. Kemp, sulky and unsure what to do, went to the back of the troupe and stayed there out of sight.

"Get to the bit about Priam's wife," Hamlet ordered. "Come to Hecuba."

Burbage braced himself once more, then told the rest, the story of the old queen rushing through the ravaged and blazing city, clad in nothing but her night gown, looking for her husband. He told of how she came upon him, Pyrrhus motionless, sword raised over the fallen king, as if listening to Troy collapsing all around him. For a moment, she thinks he will be merciful, but then the sword comes down, over and over again, and she can only watch and scream, and cry.

It was a moving speech, one the actor delivered with great skill. As he described the awful scene, tears started to his eyes and began to trickle down his cheeks.

"Stop," Hamlet cried. "That's enough."

He took a step towards the actor and studied his face, fascinated. Slowly the rest of the company got to their feet, watching, as spellbound as they had been by Burbage's performance. Hamlet raised one hand to Burbage's cheek and touched the trace of his tears, testing it between his fingers then studying his fingers with something like awe.

The other actors shifted uncomfortably. Then the moment evaporated and Hamlet began applauding loudly, hooting and cheering until the others joined in, and Burbage – slightly alarmed – recovered sufficient composure to take a bow.

"Good work, man. Very good. I'll run up on those new scenes and then you can rehearse *The Murder of Gonzago* for tomorrow night."

"Scenes?" Kemp objected from the back of the crowd. "I thought it was just a couple of extra speeches."

Hamlet sought him out, prodded him in the chest.

"I told you to leave, sir."

"But my lord! You heard our master? You saw his tears? Who could walk away from such a performance? Such an artist at his very peak?"

Burbage fingered his collar and beamed proudly.

"No man of feeling," Hamlet agreed. He looked round at them. "Make sure my new words are delivered with such force, I beg you."

"Tears?" Kemp demanded. "You'll be wanting tears too?"

"Do they cost extra?"

Burbage wiped his cheeks with his sleeve.

"No, Prince. Since it's you I'll chuck them in for free."

The Scots were getting restless. Two days running Gregor had been sniffing round the tent asking for news from the ailing king. Fortinbras had stonewalled him. But the Scot knew. Letters had come from Oslo demanding he stand down his troops and send the foreigners home. Claudius, the Danish king, was promising gifts. A little land. A little money. And Norway was willing to be bought off for a pittance.

Again.

Mercenaries were always dangerous when they were bored. The encampment outside Helsingborg had few of the amusements they craved. Only a handful of women. A meagre supply of beer. They needed a fight and the chance of plunder. Without that they'd soon be off. Or worse taking their prizes from the locals.

Maps on the table. Fortinbras studied them, thinking of numbers and deployments. The tent flap opened. The big man from Scotland was there again.

"Did I ask for you?" the Norwegian wondered.

"Just come to say goodbye."

Fortinbras leaned back in his chair.

"You've been paid, Gregor. You and your men. Handsomely from my own pocket. You were hired for a campaign..."

'Aye, sir. That we were. But since there is none..."

That got no response.

"And since your uncle's deeply pissed off with you coming all this way and shaking your sword at old Claudius across the water there..."

The Norwegian frowned.

"He is? It's news to me."

Gregor laughed, shook his head and pulled up a seat.

"You know, mate... I'm very fond of you. Honestly. We all are. Even though you're a lying bastard when you want to be."

"You should never call a prince of Norway a liar. That way lies bloodshed."

"Call it what you like then. Your uncle sent you sealed orders. They turned up with that messenger we saw this morning. I know what they say."

"Court business. Nothing of interest to you."

"He told you to stand us all down. Every last soldier of fortune. All the men you've conscripted from your estates. This..." The Scot gestured at the tent. "Well, it's been an unprofitable adventure for us lot I must say. They said Claudius's court was a fine one, full of riches just waiting to be lifted. Guess we'll never find out now, will we?"

Fortinbras pulled out a fresh map, drew an imaginary circle around one of the nations there.

"Poland. You know it?"

"Can't say I do. Is it warmer than here?"

"Much. They grow grapes and make good wine. The women..."

Fortinbras winked, made an obscene gesture.

Gregor laughed.

"You're a lying bastard."

"Twice you've said that, Scotsman. No more. Not if you want to see your home again."

The smile disappeared from the soldier's bearded face.

"What about Poland?"

"My uncle has asked me to divert our attention from Claudius. For the moment. The Poles have been making warlike noises for some time. There's an internal dispute within the ruling family. If we back one half against the other we've been promised land, money... whatever you feel like pillaging from the losers' cities."

The Scotsman's heavy scarred fingers ran over the map.

"Rich are they?"

"Very."

He nodded towards the sea.

"As rich as our friend over there?"

"No one's as wealthy as Denmark. Old Hamlet was a parsimonious crook. He taxed the life out of his people and never spent it on anything but soldiers and whores."

Gregor considered this.

"Minded as I am to remember your words about lying, sir, I must say this doesn't quite tally with what I've heard from a few people who ought to know."

Fortinbras jabbed his finger at a stretch of land well south of their present position.

"As part of our settlement with Claudius we'll be allowed safe passage through his territory here. From Malmo to Copenhagen, across the straits. If you want a ship back to Scotland you can find one there. You'd have to go to Copenhagen anyway. Claudius will never let your warriors use his port here."

The Scotsman nodded.

"That rings true."

"Because it is. The choice is yours. Either way it makes sense for you to accompany us to Copenhagen. Once there take your ship home if you like. If not... should the fair ladies of Poland catch your fancy... come with us there."

The man had a bold, hearty laugh. Fortinbras listened, liked what he saw.

"We strike camp in the morning, Gregor. Slowly. There's no great rush. The Poles are still arranging their own loyalties."

"And we get to Copenhagen... when?"

'When we wish."

He was the most experienced mercenary Fortinbras had ever employed. A veteran of campaigns that would fill the history books. No fool.

"And in Copenhagen if we find that, for some strange reason, we need to make our way north to Elsinore. Not all the way to Poland... how long will that take?"

Fortinbras got up from his seat, walked to the tent flap, opened it, looked out at his army.

"Two days. Three at the most."

The great castle stood across the water, a hulking shape in the winter sun.

"It's a formidable place, Scotsman. They say Elsinore has never been entered by force in all its history. I understand your reluctance..."

"I've toppled bigger than that. Don't play those games..."

"No games. So you're with me?"

"For now." Gregor nodded at the fortress across the Øresund. "And I want a look in that place too. If there's half a chance of it."

HAMLET HAD SAT at the table in the hall, head in his hands, lost in thought until Burbage's company realised he'd say no more. Then, with a few puzzled words, they had shuffled awkwardly out. For a minute or more after they had gone Hamlet said and did nothing.

Then he spoke softly.

"I know you're there, fool. You can come out now."

Yorick rolled grinning from behind a drape at the far end of the room.

"You spot everything, don't you, Prince?"

"Did you watch the whole thing?"

"Heard enough, thank you. Tragedies. I don't know what you see in them. Give me a bit of cross-dressing, mistaken identity and ribald banter any day. If it doesn't make you laugh, what's the point?"

"You saw what happened to Burbage, didn't you? As he described Hecuba's grief and horror at her husband's murder. You saw? He cried!"

Yorick blew a raspberry.

"Of course he cried. He's an actor. It's not emotion. It's a trick. You just stare really hard till your eyes water."

"No! He was weeping. For a woman who's been dead – if she ever existed – for a thousand years or more."

Yorick yawned.

"This is all so very moving. Where's the nearest toilet?"

"So what would he do in my place? How would an emotional man like that react if the spirit of his own father charged him to revenge his murder? If Burbage can get so passionate about a woman..."

"I'm slow today, Prince. Your point is...?"

"Can you imagine the play that would come out of that?" Hamlet got to his feet and took up Burbage's stance, eyes shut.

"Well... I can imagine he might skip the play altogether and simply kill the chap who did it."

Hamlet glared at him.

"But what if he's wrong? If it's your mistaken identity for real? And the ghost's a liar? Or not a ghost at all? Some kind of devil sent to lead the avenger into damnation?"

The jester scowled.

"You're a rational, modern man, Hamlet. You surely don't believe in devils."

"I didn't believe in ghosts either."

"Fine." Yorick beamed at him. "I'll play along. What new scheme do I smell a-cooking now?"

"This. Tomorrow night I'll have the actors play Claudius's crime right in front of his eyes. Every detail as the ghost reported it. Then we'll see, won't we? The guilt will be all over his face. Maybe my mother's too. Then we'll know. Then we'll act."

"In which sense?"

"What do you mean?"

"You'll act, you say. Meaning you'll take action and slit his throat? Or act in the sense of perform? Put on another of these little plays you like so much? A touch more make-believe to pass the time?"

Hamlet glowered at him but said nothing.

"Right," said Yorick. "That's what I thought."

~

The following day the castle was as quiet as it could be with a bunch of noisy, argumentative thespians going about their business. Hamlet wrote the new scenes for Gonzago and gave them to Burbage with directions. After that he stayed in his room, thinking, sulking, fiddling with his new-fangled pistol, practising with his rapier.

The jester was nowhere to be seen. Nor was Ophelia and he felt a touch guilty about how he'd treated her the day before. Around midday his mother came to see him and asked how he was. Didn't listen much to the answer. Didn't stay when he grew silent and unresponsive.

He ate little except bread, drank nothing but water. Then in the afternoon, before the sun set, there was a break in the weather. Hamlet went to the stables, found his favourite horse. A piebald stallion called Zeus. Claudius had given him the mount when he was ten, saying it was a present from his father, away on a campaign against the Poles.

Even at that age Hamlet hadn't believed his uncle, though he'd wanted to. Old Hamlet never gave anything away lightly or without reason. And there was no point in handing his son an expensive pedigree horse newly imported, Claudius said, from France.

He was a brave mount, full of spark and character. As a teenager, Hamlet had spent many hours on his back, riding through the woodlands around Elsinore, galloping through fields, leaping hedges.

Later he'd lifted Ophelia into the saddle and led her quietly, discreetly into that same forest for different, more private purposes. By that stage Zeus was getting slow, wheezy and easily tired.

On this day there was nothing godlike about him at all. He was old. Not yet broken, not ready for the final, quiet ride to the slaughter yard. But the years were eating at him visibly. Even so, when Hamlet approached, his grey head bucked up, a delighted whinny came from his throat and his tail swished in welcome.

The stable hand came up. A young lad Hamlet hadn't seen before. The boy patted Zeus on the back, fed him some straw.

"I bet he was a fine one, sir."

"The finest," Hamlet answered.

"Of his time. In his day. They're like us, aren't they? Bold and so full of life for a while. Like it'll never leave them. Then one day... not so quick as they were. And the next a little slower."

Zeus nudged the boy for more straw. The bond between them was obvious and affectionate.

"He's your favourite."

"That he is. Always has been since they took me in here a year ago."

"Why's that?"

"He's a lonely old soul, that's why." Another slap. Just a touch more hay. "Don't you eat too much old, lad. Then you'll get fat and sick. And slower than you are."

"Lonely?"

The stable lad pointed at the castle keep.

"He was the prince's horse. Hamlet. Had him from when he was a boy. Present from his dad, the old king."

"Is that so?"

"That's what my master told me. Young Hamlet loved this big, grey rascal. Used to ride him everywhere. Every day." He laughed. "They may be kidding me here but they reckon now and again he used to come and muck him out too. Would sleep with him in the stable if old Zeus didn't feel too well."

He shook his head.

"Imagine that! A prince who mucks out horses. Who cares. Shame is he's been in Wittenberg for a couple of years, studying. And when he does come home it's nothing but tragedy, is it? Poor bugger..."

Hamlet snorted.

"I heard he was a cruel and selfish bastard..."

"I will not listen to that, sir! Whoever you might be. My master's lived here all his life. He reckons Prince Hamlet's the best of them all. A fine young man. Bright as a button and strong too. Upset over his father now, but who wouldn't be? I lost mine when Old Hamlet went to war over Jutland. I know what it feels like. And that young prince didn't just lose a dad. He lost a king..."

Hamlet patted the horse on the neck and said, "I'd like to take him out."

The lad's cheery disposition disappeared.

"This chap's not yours to ride, now is he?"

Hamlet reached into his purse, took out a couple of gold coins. As much as a stable hand like this would earn in a year.

He held out the money.

"But he's not yours to ride, sir," the lad repeated slowly.

"And if I told you I was the Prince?"

The boy gulped.

"Then I'm dead, aren't I? And asked for it."

Silence between them.

Hamlet walked to the horse's head. Looked into his grey eyes. There were cataracts forming there, like milky glass. But Zeus could see him. He was sure of that.

"He's too old for the saddle," the stable lad said. "The master keeps on saying we should do him a favour. Take him you-know-where. But I tell you..."

His voice was breaking.

"When I come down in the morning. Feed him. Water him. Deal with his business. This old fellow looks at me and smiles. I swear he does. So I walk him out of them gates and let him nibble some grass down by the meadows. If there's grass there that is. And if not we just wander around a bit. Then I bring him home and that's that."

His calloused hands went to the horse's head. Zeus neighed, yellow teeth showing.

"Whether you're the prince or not you can't ride him, sir. He's not up for it and he'll never be again. I'm sorry. And if in any way I've offended..."

"You haven't." Hamlet placed the coins in his hand. "But you will have these."

"But..."

"And no arguments!"

There was a commotion by the gates. The lad stuffed the money in his jerkin pocket.

Two men in fine robes were dismounting near the keep. One short and fat. One tall and slender. Both familiar.

"Lot of coming and going at the moment," the stable hand said. "People reckon it's for these players who turned up. They're putting on a show."

The lanky one turned and stared in Hamlet's direction. He seemed embarrassed for a moment then waved, called out the prince's name.

"It is you, isn't it? Me and my big mouth."

Hamlet held out his hand. Got a puzzled look in return.

Then the stable lad took it and grinned.

"Enjoy today, my lord. I hope it eases your pain."

"That's lifted a little already." He had found their names now. Rosencrantz and Guildenstern. Two students who'd followed him to Wittenberg where they were never close but rarely distant.

The spies of Polonius, he thought. An employment joined but never left.

CLAUDIUS SAT at his desk in his study, Gertrude by the window, staring down into the courtyard. Polonius silent in a chair, awaiting instructions.

"These players," the Queen said. "I heard my son's been speaking to them."

The old man grunted.

"At length. I wish they'd never come. The boy has no need of any more fantasies in his head. I detest these theatricals. They demand good coin for nothing but acting! Pretence! Nothing worthwhile."

She stared at him.

"Everyone likes a little amusement from time to time, Polonius. Don't be so dry. No wonder your daughter seems so miserable every time I chance upon her. I met her this morning. She would scarcely look me in the eye."

He glanced at the King.

"Ophelia's upset about the attentions of your son. I apologise on her behalf. He can be quite... persistent."

"Hamlet's distraught. It'll pass."

"He's mad," Claudius said without looking up from his maps and letters. "Show her."

Polonius took a piece of parchment from his coat and held it up to the light to read.

"To the celestial beauty and the idol of my soul, the most beautified Ophelia."

He shook his head and swore.

"What a filthy phrase. Most beautified... what does that mean? And this?" He stabbed his finger on the page. "In her excellent white bosom. Filth."

She snatched the paper from him.

"You say this is from my son? To Ophelia?"

"Who else?" he snapped.

Gertrude ran over the lines, reading them in a soft, shocked voice.

"Doubt thou the stars are fire; Doubt that the sun doth move; Doubt truth to be a liar; But never doubt I love."

She handed it back.

"Most of us wrote something like that when we were young. Perhaps... later too." Polonius looked baffled. "Though not all I imagine."

"These are the words of a prince to my daughter. Had I known this illicit affair was on the cards I would have stamped it out immediately. Be assured of that."

"And now you have and you claim he's mad." It wasn't quite a criticism, but it wasn't the commendation he expected.

Claudius shook his head.

"You think this has more to do with the girl than his father?"

"Perhaps. He doesn't talk to me much anymore. It's almost as if I'm a stranger. If his heart's set on Ophelia we should allow it..."

"A man of noble standing wouldn't fall so far over a mere girl of the court," Polonius scoffed. "There's more to it than that. Sometimes he walks round the castle – four, five hours at a time, talking to himself. He's been heard in his room, chattering away as if he's got company. My men have noticed. If..."

"Discover the root of this," Claudius ordered. "Diagnose the sickness. Treat the cause. Hamlet's my nephew and my preferred heir. A fine young man worthy of that honour. I want him back."

Polonius put a finger to his cheek.

"If we find him in the lobby... I could arrange for my daughter to be there. I'll set her loose on him. Tell her to be affectionate and welcoming."

"And?" Claudius asked.

"And then you and I can wait behind one of those tapestry hangings. We'll listen..."

"You've already set those clowns Rosencrantz and Guildenstern to spy on him!" Gertrude cried. "Now you're going to do it yourself?"

Polonius looked at the king.

"If you want the cause of the malady..."

"Arrange it," Claudius ordered.

"He's there," the queen cried, pointing out of the window.

The two men walked over to join her. In the courtyard below, dressed in black again, Hamlet paced to and fro, a heavy book in his hands.

"Leave this me," Polonius said. "I'll talk to him and gauge the state of his mind. Then report back here immediately."

THE BOOK WAS IN GERMAN, a tedious philosophical tome. Once he'd read such works avidly, listening to the words of his tutors, taking notes. Now they seemed irrelevant. A real world was swirling around him, one full of dangers and possibilities. A realm more mutable and insidious than he could ever have imagined before.

He strode around the courtyard trying not to shiver, knowing he would be seen. Madness was an inward mask. It hid itself from the victim. The insane saw themselves as lucid, just as criminals so often believed themselves wronged and justified.

And he was bait. Soon Hamlet saw his catch, Polonius wriggling on the line.

"How's my Lord Hamlet?" the old man asked cheerily as he approached.

"Who?"

"Hamlet. Prince of Denmark."

"Oh him? He's well I believe." He felt his arms and legs. "Yes. Well enough. Is he yours then?"

Polonius smiled.

"Pardon?"

"You said *your* Lord Hamlet. If he belongs to you perhaps you ought to take ownership. The man's been behaving rather oddly of late."

Polonius gathered his cloak around him.

"Do you know me?"

Hamlet squinted and peered at him.

"Of course. You're a fish, aren't you?" A laugh. "No. Stupid of me. A fish*monger*. That's it."

The Lord Chamberlain shook his grey head.

"No, sir. Not me."

"What's wrong with fishmongers? They're honest enough..."

"Nothing," Polonius interrupted brusquely. "But I'm not one."

"Honest, you mean?"

"A fishmonger."

Hamlet tucked his book under the arm.

"You're full of riddles, I must say. Do you have a daughter?"

"I do..."

"Is *she* honest?"

"As much as any woman."

"Not a lot, you mean?"

Polonius smiled.

"If this is madness, Prince, I have to say there's method in it."

Hamlet pointed at the sky.

"You see that cloud? The one shaped like a weasel?"

Polonius looked up.

"Yes. Very like a weasel. What about it?"

"I think it's more like a whale."

"So... so it does."

"Or a lobster."

Polonius looked again.

"Quite right. Exactly like a lobster."

"Or if you squint a little." Hamlet closed his right eye. "Much like a sycophantic old fool, don't you think?"

The Lord Chamberlain came closer and scowled.

"Do you really not know me, Prince? Or do we have one more actor in the palace than we bargained for?"

"A fishmonger. I can smell it. Unless your pretty daughter serves herring for breakfast. Which is it?"

Polonius patted the book and smiled. "I must take my leave of you."

"You can't take anything I'd more willingly give, Sir Herring. Except my life."

Hamlet watched him wander off.

"There is method in my madness," he whispered. "And that tedious old fool can see it."

Footsteps across the cobbles. The tall one and his little fat friend were walking daintily over, smiling, fawning, yipping like little dogs.

"Hamlet! My dear lord!" Guildenstern cried. "Finally we've found you."

"God save you, sir!" Rosencrantz chirruped. "God save us all."

Hamlet retreated from their outstretched hands.

"Not all, surely."

They stared at him.

"By which I mean there are men out there too damned to be saved by anyone." Hamlet's eyes drifted to the castle. "And women too for all I know."

Rosencrantz slapped his companion's shoulder.

"Why didn't I think of that?"

"Such an insight had never crossed my mind," Guildenstern added. "Even the most knowledgeable of tutors back in Wittenberg..."

"How are you, chaps?"

Rosencrantz sighed and nudged his companion.

"See. He does remember us. As well as can be expected, my lord."

"Content," Guildenstern agreed. "One aspires to happiness, but not too much since one would not wish to be disappointed. On fortune's cap we're not the smartest feather. Actually not a feather at all..."

"Perhaps she wears you on her shoe?"

"Feels like it sometimes," Rosencrantz agreed. "Trudging through horse crap mostly."

"Or somewhere around her waist?" Hamlet bent towards them and said behind his hand. "You're her privates."

The two snickered.

"If only we should be so lucky," the little one said with a grin. "We haven't been close to a lady's secret parts in ages." He tapped his belt. "Money you see, sir. Lack of it."

"So what brings you to this prison?"

The two men looked around them.

"Elsinore's a prison?" Guildenstern asked.

"No," Hamlet replied. "Denmark is."

Rosencrantz nodded.

"In that case so's the world."

"Why are you here?"

They shuffled and looked awkward.

"Out of friendship," the tall one answered eventually. "To see you. No other reason."

"Except my uncle summoned you."

Guildenstern stared at his fancy shoes.

"We're just impoverished students, Hamlet. Humble fellows."

"And being humble fellows you can tell the truth. You were called for."

The two exchanged worried glances. Then Rosencrantz said, "It's true. We can't lie to a fellow student. The king requested our presence."

"There! That wasn't hard, was it? And I'll tell you why."

They watched him keenly.

"Just recently I've lost my appetite for life. I waste my time. Nothing delights me. I walk through this grey world and find it barren and full of nothing but despair."

There was a cold, disdainful look on Guildenstern's face at that moment.

"What is it?"

"We're penniless, sir. Our families too. No prospects. No rich wives on the horizon. No future. You've scant reason to feel so sorry for yourself. What have you to complain of next to us?"

"Hush, you idiot," the other one whispered.

A dangerous moment between them. Rosencrantz stared his companion down, then gave Hamlet a reassuring smile.

Across the courtyard some of the actor's men were lugging costume baskets and primitive scenery into the castle.

"There's a play tonight," Guildenstern said brightly. "You always liked the theatre, sir. I remember that in Wittenberg. Surely... surely a spot of theatre will cheer you up a bit."

His hand went briefly to Hamlet's arm.

"You're not mad, you know. Just a touch down. That's all."

Hamlet shook his head and glared at them.

"But I am mad. Who denies it? When the wind's from the northwest anyway. If it's southerly I'm as sane as you."

Guildenstern licked his finger and held it up in the light breeze.

"Easterly. What does that mean?"

"That's for others to judge. You will excuse me now."

"The play?" Rosencrantz asked.

The Prince smiled.

"Wouldn't miss it for the world."

After Hamlet left them the two men went to see Polonius and reported back. Then the Lord Chamberlain found Claudius in his study and related what the prince had said, to him and the men in his employ.

"So what do we make of that?" the king asked.

"He's mad, after a fashion. When he wants to be."

Claudius raised his head from the latest reports from Norway.

"What does that mean?"

"I'm not sure. When I spoke to him he rambled. Told me I was a fishmonger. Talked nonsense about my daughter. The same with those two fools who watched him in Wittenberg. Spies they'll never make but from what they say they think he's deranged too. He wittered on about how Denmark's a prison. Some filthy nonsense, the kind of chat students indulge in I suppose. Whether it was about Ophelia..."

Claudius got up from the desk.

"Am I wasting my time here?" he demanded. "Fortinbras is playing games in the south. Claiming he's headed for Poland, not that I see any sign of it. And here you are, obsessed with my lunatic nephew..."

"It's a curious lunacy, my lord." Polonius paused, tried to find the right words. "A very rational kind it seems to me."

"You mean it's an act? A performance?"

"Perhaps." A shrug. "Honestly, I don't know. One moment he talks gibberish. The next he seems as sane as anyone. Perceptive, too."

Claudius looked round. The door was open. He closed it, came near to the old man.

"You think he suspects?"

The old man stiffened and his hand gripped the king's robe.

"How can he know? By what possible means...?"

"I asked if he suspected. Not whether he knew."

"What's the difference?" Polonius responded in a low voice, one eye on the door. "I gave you the poison. You delivered it. No one else was privy to our intentions. At least..." His eyes moved away from the king. "I've told no other."

"Any more than I have. Hamlet's not stupid. He may never find proof. But if he harbours suspicion... who knows what he could do?"

"He's your nephew. You're the king. If he suspects us we can deal with that. Through exile. A trip to Italy, say. A spell with the Medici in Florence would do him good. Wine, women and art. It might soothe him. If not there are other avenues to explore."

"I will not murder my wife's son," Claudius vowed. "My nephew. I love Hamlet. He was like my own. You know this."

"All the same you wronged him, sir. You killed his father. He doesn't love you."

"*We* killed his father. Who merited it ten times over."

"And had a beautiful queen," Polonius added.

"You over-reach yourself, Lord Chamberlain. Were my brother alive you'd never have voiced a sentiment like that."

"No. And we're both complicit in his death. If somehow Hamlet comes to realise..."

"Keep Rosencrantz and Guildenstern close to him. Get better intelligence out of them than this nonsense they gave you this morning. Make inquiries of the Florentines. Give me options should I decide to take them. And arrange this meeting with your daughter so you and I can watch. With luck he's simply love-struck. And all this nonsense will pass."

"Perhaps."

Polonius didn't move.

"Do we have more business?" the king asked.

"A monarch must be merciful and heartless in equal measure. Old Hamlet knew this. Sadly he lacked the gentle touch to keep the balance. I hope we haven't exchanged one disproportion for the other."

The king grabbed the collar of his velvet jacket, dragged the old man's whiskery face close to his own.

"You put the blasted idea in my head. You found the poison. You told me he was alone."

Polonius met his stare.

"I'm a servant of the realm. It's my role to understand your wishes, even if you don't fully appreciate them yourself."

Claudius pushed the old man away and sent him out into the corridor. Then went back to the maps. Fortinbras was out there, with an army strong enough to take Denmark if he wanted it badly enough.

Perhaps Hamlet was right. The place was a prison, and he the king of nothing more than finite, shrinking space.

"Chess!" the jester declared and started to set the board on a small table beneath the window.

Hamlet didn't move from the bed.

"Come along, Your Royal Slothfulness. Time to sharpen your strategies. Before this odd show of yours."

"They're sharp enough."

"You're just terrified I'll win."

He got up, shambled over to the table, dragged up a stool.

"Pawn to Queen Two," Yorick announced. "Always lull your enemy into thinking you're predictable."

"How did your father die?"

Yorick yawned.

"Not that again? I thought we were about to have some fun."

"Seven months ago I went to Wittenberg thinking I left Elsinore in a fit and happy state."

The little man shook his head.

"You believed that? Really? How depressingly naïve ..."

"One month later your father's executed for treason and I never saw or heard a harsh word between him and the king."

"Or any word. Old Hamlet wasn't a fellow for jokes."

"What...?"

Yorick slammed his bishop on the table, so hard the pieces jumped.

"Why ask me? I spent most of my life shambling from one dingy inn to the next. Touring Europe as Elsinore's present to others. Why else do you think none here but you seems to know me?"

"I did wonder."

"When all this happened I was in Moscow trying to make the Russians laugh. There's an engagement for you."

Hamlet took the piece from his hands and put it back in place.

"On whose orders? Claudius?"

"No."

"The king's."

"Wrong again. It was my father. I imagine he wanted me out of the way. If... Shit!"

He leaned back on the stool, caught the edge of the table with his feet and stopped himself tumbling to the floor. The little man had the agility of an acrobat when he needed it.

"There boy. You made me say it. I can't be drinking enough. This is a shameful lapse. It's all your fault."

He got up, checked the corridor both ways, slammed the door hard shut then came and moved the table as close to the window as it would go.

"My head may mean little to you, lord. But I'm rather fond of the thing. I don't want it stuck on a pike on the ramparts too."

"My father..."

"... was a monster. A vicious, bloodthirsty beast."

Hamlet didn't move, didn't speak.

Yorick folded his fat arms.

"You took that better than I expected. You knew, of course. My father on the other hand..." Beneath his heavy brows the jester's eyes became misty. "He was kind and gentle, a generous man."

Hamlet nodded. "I remember that."

"So you should. When you were a boy he was the one who spent days on end with you. Not the king." He leaned across the table, peered into Hamlet's eyes. "Him and Claudius. A devious cove your uncle. But a man with a warm heart nonetheless. You had the benefit of that as much as anyone. The son he never had. Gertrude the wife he lacked too."

"Tell me, fool, or I will give you up I swear."

Yorick's exaggerated face was wreathed in hurt fury.

"There's no need for threats. You've a cruel and heartless streak in you sometimes. No need to guess where that came from."

"Tell..."

"Very well!" the little man snarled.

He pulled up his knees and wrapped his arms around his shins, miserable and angry at this forced recollection.

"Shortly before I was sent to Moscow my father called me into his room. He'd been out with the hunt and wandered off when they were about to kill a stag. Never liked blood much. Or possessed a talent for direction. So he came upon Claudius together with the queen in one of the royal lodges in the forest. Their particular hunt was a private one and had reached a heated moment. So happily they never noticed him goggle-eyed at the window."

He sighed. Picked up a piece of cold sausage and gnawed on it.

"I told him that if he didn't forget the entire matter immediately I'd be the one who murdered him. Not Claudius. Or Hamlet. Or your mother. One week later he dispatches me to crack jokes to drunken oafs in wolf skins. When I get there I find a letter from him saying his conscience demanded he tell all to the king and he'd rather I wasn't there when that happened. One week after that I get another letter telling me crows are pecking out his eyes on a spike outside the walls."

Yorick took a big and ugly bite of the meat.

"Decapitate the messenger. Originality isn't a royal forte, is it?"

"Claudius..."

"It wasn't Claudius who killed him!" Yorick's eyes strayed nervously to the door. "Too loud, you make me too loud, Prince. You'll be the death of us both. It was..."

"A just and honourable king doesn't murder an honest man for speaking the truth."

The man in the harlequin suit blinked.

"The relevance of that remark being...? Oh to hell with it..."

His stout arm reached across the table, took Hamlet by the collar, dragged him close.

"One last time. Your father was a bloodthirsty tyrant. You sit in grand judgement on your mother because she found love and happiness in the arms of a man who wasn't her husband. Yet Old Hamlet had mistresses and bastards the length of this land and never set foot outside the castle without knowing the name of the next whorehouse along the way."

A dagger came up between them, tight in Hamlet's hand.

Yorick laughed.

"You know that vile statue of my father naked on a tortoise?"

"What about it?"

"It was made by a curiously nasty sculptor from Florence. A man named Benvenuto."

"So?"

"So why keep it after he'd killed the man who modelled for it?"

"Nostalgia? Regret? Maybe he had a change of heart."

"You'd have to have a heart to change. No. It wasn't enough to kill him. That's what I think. He had to do more than take my father's life. He had to piss on his memory too. So there he is. Sitting on a tortoise in the altogether. Not funny. Not charming. Grotesque. A freak. A monster. Forever. Why? Because he'd dared tell the king the hard truth that not everyone loved him. That, your highness, was your father."

"Liar," the prince said but it was barely a whisper.

Yorick scowled at him.

"Why would I invent such tales? What gain is there for me? The facts are simple enough. Your father knew of your mother's affair with his brother. I don't doubt he had plans to deal with it. And the last thing Old Hamlet needed around him was a jester with secrets burning in his heart and a habit of blabbing. I'm afraid we're all like that really. But Claudius has friends here too. He was a powerful man before he ever sat on the throne. It would take time and cunning."

"Polonius?"

"He's the Lord Chamberlain. I'm shocked you've forgotten since you bed his daughter. Or used to."

"Did he know?"

"Search me!" Yorick cried. "Am I an all-seeing apparition too? I'd imagine so. Kings are too high and mighty to be lone assassins. They crave accomplices. But your father was old and despite all the lip service to the contrary a lot of people hated him. A Lord Chamberlain serves the state, not the king. If he were in the picture..."

He opened his big, rough hands.

"You think Polonius was as likely to work for Claudius as my father? Even in matters... of this kind?"

"Murder, you mean?"

Hamlet flinched at the word, then nodded reluctantly.

"I would assume he'd back the most favourable horse to his personal cause. Wouldn't you?"

The prince put the dagger on the table.

"Sorry."

Yorick bent forward and looked up into his eyes.

"Don't forget our respective places here. I'm your clown. Your plaything. Your toy. Scarcely human. No need to apologise."

Hamlet carved himself a piece of meat with the blade. "You're the only friend I've got."

"Flattering but I'd have to say that's somewhat unfair on young Horatio. While I agree I am by far the more entertaining let's not forget I'm nothing more than a joke, a bad one usually. I never do."

He was scarcely listening. Hamlet had picked up two pieces from the table. Black king, black queen. Was running his finger along their wooden crowns.

"My father would have killed them both?"

"In his own time and in a way that would have given him some political advantage."

"And instead, with the old man's help, they murdered him?"

Yorick retrieved the pieces from his fingers and placed them on the board.

"That dread creature you saw on the walls spoke only of Claudius. Your mother's a virtuous woman..."

"I know. I hear her proclaim her chastity every night."

"Perhaps you should ask her," the jester said in a miserable, sullen voice.

With a flick of his finger Hamlet toppled the black queen.

"Perhaps I will."

It was dark now. The players would be getting ready. Time to go.

"Let's take our seats."

The jester shook his head.

"Not me."

"I demand it."

"Demand all you like, sunshine." He stood up, straightened his collar. "I'm a thespian myself. A better one you'll never meet though much under-appreciated. If you want a tragedian's turn I'll give you one..."

Yorick raised his hand and declared in a ringing stentorian tone, "Oh, that this too, too sullied flesh would melt, thaw, and resolve itself into a dew. Or that the Everlasting had not fixed His canon 'gainst self-slaughter! How weary, stale, flat and unprofitable..."

"Quite," Hamlet interrupted. "Suit yourself. I'm going to watch the play. I hope it's better than that."

~

Rosencrantz intercepted Hamlet as he made his way through the gallery, took him into the neighbouring loggia and talked idly and at tedious length about the statues there. Polonius told his daughter to stand close by, then led the king through one of Elsinore's many winding private passageways to hide behind a giant Flemish tapestry of Hercules and his labours.

"This disgusts me," Claudius whispered as they stood and waited. "I'm King of Denmark. Not a common spy."

Polonius took out his penknife and carved tiny eyeholes in the tapestry.

"You wish to know whether it's the girl that ails him. Or something else. Don't you?"

"What else? He can't know about his father. This is grief and grief passes."

The old man stayed silent.

"Perhaps there's more to it than that," the King admitted. "Your daughter. We'll..."

Polonius put a finger to his lips, placed his eye close to the rough back of the fabric.

"Two parents eavesdropping on their children," Claudius murmured. "To what have we been reduced...?"

"To caution and common sense, sir. He's your nephew, not your son."

"As good as..."

Ophelia wore a summer dress. Polonius had made her pick one Hamlet had liked when they were lovers. Leaf green with flowers round the low neck. Her skin was pale. She shivered in the tall castle gallery.

Rosencrantz called farewell. Then Hamlet bumbled in, reading what looked like a script for the play to come. He'd almost walked into her when she said, "How are you, my lord? Better I hope."

The prince stood back, looked her up and down, then peered round the gallery, at the shadows, at the tapestry.

"Fair Ophelia. I hope you remember my sins in all your prayers. Keeping well, are we?"

"Very..."

His eyes ran round the round the gallery.

"Isn't that... spiffing?"

"Don't be mad with me. I brought you these." She had a packet in her hand. "They're the letters you wrote. And the poems. I should have given them back a long time ago. Please..."

She held them out. He laughed.

"What's this? I never gave you anything."

"Hamlet. I know you're not well and there's so much to worry about what with..." She took a breath, abandoning the train of thought. "When you sent me these they had a perfume so sweet I thought it would never fade. But it did. I pray you now. Take what you sent me. Let's put an end to this."

He glanced at her trembling hand and began looking around the room again. When his eyes returned to her they burned with loathing.

"What have you done here, madam?" he growled as he brushed away the offered letters.

"I'm trying to return these tokens of your affection..."

"That's a harsh, chaste tone. Do you merit it?"

Ophelia blushed.

"I only give back what's yours..."

He was scanning the walls, the long corridors around.

"You, too, now, eh? I should have known. Put on a black robe like mine and get yourself to a nunnery. Or better still a whorehouse and spread your legs. At least there no one expects to believe what the women say. Do anything for a few pieces of silver, won't you?"

"What do you mean?"

"It's not about money though, is it? Not for the daughter of Polonius. With you everything's about family. That's where your real loyalties lie. Which means..."

He began walking briskly along the tapestry, punching it with his fist so that the fabric crumpled against the stone behind.

"Where's that cunning bastard, your father? There's an old man's stale stench here!" Then he was singing it like a child at play. "Out, out Lord Chamberlain! I'm coming, ready or not!"

She rushed him to him, took his arm.

"He's in his quarters! Where else would he be?"

Another punch on the wall just steps away from the holes Polonius had cut in the tapestry. His knuckles bruised on the unyielding stone behind.

A glint of an eye through the fabric. Then nothing.

"Are you honest, Ophelia?"

"I'm trying..."

He dragged her to him.

"You see what you've done? Betrayed me. The one person I thought I could trust! So here's this in return. If ever you marry I'll give you this curse. You may be as chaste as ice, as pure as snow, but they'll still damn you, girl. Every man shall cast a stone. Your whore's reputation precedes you. Anyone with half a brain will know you're cheating him the moment his back's turned..."

Ophelia threw the letters in her face.

"For God's sake, Hamlet, there was only ever you! What reason did I give you to think otherwise? How can you possibly...?"

He kicked the packet, scattering the letters across the floor. She looked at them, at him. He was raging now. Out of control.

"I will pray your health's soon restored, sir..."

"God can do nothing for me. You might have once. Your beauty... but then that's not your real face is it?" His voice turned harder still. "Not the one God gave you. You get your little paints out and streak it on: a little shadow around the eyes, a little blush here. That's an important one, isn't it. Blush. Since your real face forgot how to do that long ago. Paint it on. Hide your wantonness with innocence."

"There never was another."

"And when I'm king I'll banish marriage. Send you all to brothels where you belong. Exile traitors. Hang spies. Stab this vile world in the heart and..."

He twisted, rolled along the wall, withdrew his short dagger, gouged at the holes in the tapestry. Once. Twice, where the eyes were.

The blade hit hard stone sparking as it ran.

"Come out!" he roared. "Let me see you in the light."

Ophelia was crying, protesting her innocence again. Claudius could hear her plaintive voice as he followed Polonius into the private passageway they'd used.

Another of the Lord Chamberlain's secrets. He wondered how many more were withheld from him, had been from his brother too.

In the darkness, brushing away the spider's web, they stopped by a torch Polonius had set along the way. The old man's eyes were wild. Frightened.

"He would have stabbed us in the eye if he could."

"Hamlet will blame your daughter," Claudius said. "We left her there with him. And his fury."

The old man scowled.

"I never told her we'd be listening."

"Ophelia's no idiot, man! Any more than he..."

"Hamlet's in love with her. You heard as well as I did."

"Love?" Claudius asked, amazed. "Did that sound like love?"

"It takes many forms I believe."

"That's not one of them. And it wasn't madness either. There's something, some worm eating at my nephew's soul. If..."

"Love, sir," the old man interrupted. "I'm sure of it. After the play let me try again. We'll have him speak with his mother and I'll listen, hidden like before."

"Better I hope. He knew we were there from the outset."

"Better. His mother will get the truth out of him. Then we'll decide how to proceed."

A FIRE BLAZED in the hearth. The torches had been lit and evergreen garlands hung around the frames of the high windows. Burbage watched through a crack in the door of a spacious pantry they'd been given as a dressing room. The players had been ready for over an hour and were getting restless. But nothing would happen till the king gave the order. If he didn't feel like it, there would be no play at all. They'd still get to eat, but their promised wage would be cut in half, and if they were thrown out into the freezing night immediately, it wouldn't be the first time.

Burbage drummed his fingers on the door.

"Any sign?" asked Kemp.

"Nah," grumbled Burbage. "Still eating. Calling for wine. He might have forgotten we're here."

Kemp put his eye to the crack.

"Can't take his eyes off the Queen. Like a love-struck teenager."

"He did marry her," Burbage pointed out.

"I thought that was just, you know, *politics*." Kemp kept his face up against the door jamb. "You know what royalty are like. But there he is... holding her hand and everything. Smiling. Kissing now! I wonder what Polonius makes of it. Winding that damned watch of his. That old bugger doesn't want to give us a penny. And there's our prince too, sitting with his pretty lady."

"Ophelia," Burbage pointed out. "She's Polonius's daughter."

"Lucky girl didn't inherit that old bastard's mug. She don't look too happy. Interesting. More of a play going on out there than we'll have on the stage if you ask me."

"I'd keep your observations on royalty to yourself if I were you, Kemp," Burbage declared. "How long are they going to keep us waiting? God, I miss being at home, calling the shots in our own house. You know how long I've been a professional actor, Will?"

"Rumour has it you got your first job the day after Adam and Eve got kicked out of Eden."

"Not far off. A little respect wouldn't go amiss. Why must royalty make us feel like vagrants and street musicians? If we were playing in front of our adoring crowd in London..."

"Well we're not and they normally chuck cabbages at us," Kemp said, breaking from the door. "Anyway... Hamlet's coming."

The chatter dried up. The troupe of actors stopped lounging, muttering their lines, munching on meat pies, got to their feet, eyes on the door, expectant.

"Ready?" the Prince asked when he came in.

Burbage frowned.

"We're professionals, sir. We always are. What about your audience?"

"They will be when I announce you. You have the changes memorised?"

Hurried nods around the little room.

"And just the lines as written. No adlibbing. And yes, Kemp, I'm looking at you."

The actor made an exaggerated face: shocked and hurt. Then grinned.

"And get their attention," Hamlet added. "Especially in the murder scene."

More nods, and a hush of expectation.

The Prince smoothed his black doublet.

"Right," he said. "We're on."

He nodded at an actor at the back who wore a drum around his neck. The man began to beat a loud, steady rhythm. Hamlet flung open the door into the great hall wide and led the procession out, through the ranks of spectators, past the statue of Old Yorick, a naked dwarf seated on a laughing tortoise, hand outstretched to the open space before the royal dais.

Actors. Audiences. One watching the other, always. Burbage had seen this so often. The look of anticipation, of boredom among some, excitement among others. And then there was the King. A pleasant-faced man, not cruel or infamous like some of the monarchs they'd played for.

He sat at the head of the royal table, playing the part himself. Waving off Polonius when the old man stooped to his ear to whisper something. Determined to see this through.

The Queen had eyes only for her son though she seemed anxious, sitting up stiffly, smiling too widely to show the royal approval her courtiers and servants should imitate.

There was a polite round of applause. Hamlet led the players onto the makeshift stage then flung himself at Ophelia's feet, lay sprawled on the floor, facing the stage, with his head resting on her legs. She looked alarmed, her eyes flashing to her father, but then found a version of the Queen's smile and watched the actors as if afraid to look anywhere else.

Burbage could read his public as well as any man and this was the oddest bunch he'd ever seen. It felt like an audience of one – Prince Hamlet. And a room full of wary actors indulging him and... afraid.

The cagey look on Kemp's face told him he wasn't the only who'd noticed something was up.

Afraid of Hamlet? Perhaps. Burbage understood stage fright: the real and paralyzing terror of being up there, suddenly unable to remember your lines or even what was happening in the scene. He knew the bowel-clenching horror of wanting so desperately to get through a speech, stumble off, hide somewhere no one could see you.

He'd just never felt that subtle, lurking terror from an audience.

Kemp declaimed the prologue, a half-dozen lines of apology and throat clearing to beg the audience's attention.

Then they were off. It went well at first, he thought, watching from the side. Burbage was no fan of *Gonzago*. It was a posturing, ponderous play. Sound enough if you were in the mood for melodrama, but predictable, especially when you could act it in your sleep.

The first couple of scenes passed without a hitch. Then it was his turn to enter, playing the doomed king. And something curious occurred.

Hamlet got up and left Ophelia's side, falling into an awkward pose in front of the stage. As Burbage spoke his piece – a tedious declaration in which the whiskery monarch declared his wife should remarry were he to die – he found the Prince staring at him acutely, murmuring the very lines word for word though he had no script in his hands.

The old queen was played diligently by one of the boys shoved inside an old gown and plastered in make-up. In her protestations of undying love for her husband she went so far as to say that sleeping with another man would be like murdering her current husband.

At that Hamlet gasped with delight and clapped his hand like a child.

Then he started talking. Not the play's lines, like before, but a running commentary, delivered with backward glances to the courtly audience full of observations and pithy remarks.

"Good, isn't it?"

"Great line."

"You think she'll keep her word?"

Each intervention was met with an embarrassed hush. Soon there was a tension a man could cut with a knife.

And then, the scene Hamlet himself had written.

The murder.

Burbage was to lie on his side while Kemp came stalking in and poured a vial of poison into his ear.

The troupe had proved awkward about this in rehearsal. Several actors found it implausible to say the least. But Hamlet had been adamant when a rewrite was suggested. Loudly so. It was murder his way or no play at all. So they did it, Burbage lying there, feeling the thick, cold liquid – treacle in fact – pooling in his ear then running down his neck.

"This is the king's nephew!" Hamlet announced, standing up and pointing. "He kills him for his crown. Then seduces the monarch's wife, a woman of his own blood, who had earlier sworn..."

And that was as far they got.

Burbage was lying rigid, his eyes closed, but he heard the tumult in the hall, the shouting, the scraping of benches and chairs, as one by one the place emptied. He sat up in time to see the king leading the exodus, face flushed with fury. The queen was white, eyes bright with tears.

As they left everyone avoided the prince who pranced around the stage with delight as if awaiting an encore.

A hand caught the actor's arm.

"We will get paid, sir?" the boy who played the queen asked meekly. "I was doing it best I could."

"Not now, son," the actor said in the gentlest tones he'd ever used to the lad.

It was clear to him now. These people knew Hamlet. They were afraid of this odd, unbalanced young man with reason. The prince had just threatened the life of the king, all within a few changed lines of a hoary tragedy.

In the drama in his head he was the murderous nephew. And Claudius somehow a victim to come. It was hardly surprising the king had fled in fury and fear.

Burbage looked at the prince whooping like a loon, flipping over tables, singing at the top of his voice.

In previous years he'd been good, intelligent company. One of the few nobles who combined intellect with energy and a sense of purpose.

"Sir," the actor pleaded. "May we talk a while and..."

But then another hand took his shoulder. A strong one this time, and when he turned he found himself face to face with a burly soldier, Polonius next to him holding out a purse.

"This is half your fee," the old man said, throwing the money at them. "Think yourself lucky you get a penny out of Elsinore." He took out his fancy watch. "If you're still here on the hour I'll have that back and whip every last one of you."

Then Polonius bellowed at the shrieking Hamlet, telling the Prince he'd offended his mother and should go to speak to her immediately.

"Time to depart this particular stage," Kemp said, nudging his colleague's arm.

"Aye," the old actor agreed. "I long for England."

Soon they were outside, seeking cheap lodgings in the town beyond the walls. Glad to get out of the fortress. Bad things were going to happen. Acts of blood and fury, real this time, not imagined.

He wanted to be far away when they started. Assuming they hadn't already.

~

"There," Polonius roared when he saw the players out of the gates and got back to the king's study. "We have it. He knows. But..." His hand went to his forehead. "For the love of God... how?"

Claudius bent over his desk, a goblet of red wine in his right hand.

"What does it matter? You're the lawyer here. What can he do?"

The old man scowled.

"Nothing. You're the king. You *are* the law. Besides... he has no proof. No certainty. If he had why would he arrange this performance? I've seen that damned play before. It never had that scene. Hamlet wrote it. I'm sure of it."

"He inserted it to prick my conscience fool! If you had one of your own you'd know."

The King took a long swig, wished he had time and space to get drunk. That was new. The world was closing in on him.

"Hamlet knows I murdered his father. He thinks that by telling me I'll somehow... respond. Give him opportunity to do the same to me perhaps. Or simply dispatch him to the same place."

Polonius nodded.

"That last's a possibility. I would wish to arrange it the way we did before. Quietly. Without fuss. He's popular with the common folk. They love him for some reason. A trial wouldn't go down well. More likely a sudden and tragic illness that confines him to his room, takes away the power of speech, and sees him off in swift measure. I know the man who can arrange the potions..."

Claudius got to his feet and grabbed him by the scruff of the neck.

"I killed his father because I had to. It was him or us."

"And you've me to thank for that intelligence."

The King was getting sick of this pompous, sly old man.

"Yes. You betrayed the old king so I could murder him and take his place. Thereby saving our lives. Yours too, perhaps." Claudius paused then added, "For now."

"What are we to do?"

The latest numbers for the treasury had arrived. Late taxes and shortfalls in the army left the kingdom in a weak position, too feeble for any coming war.

"The English have been neglecting the tribute negotiated by my late brother. Hamlet will sail there on the first possible ship. He can remain in London until his humour's improved."

Polonius nodded.

"And then?"

"And then I'll see."

"This won't go away. He knows and that knowledge will fester. However long he spends in England."

"We're family, Polonius. A better, closer one than you'll ever understand. And happy once. Perhaps in time again..."

"If I may suggest..."

Claudius slammed his goblet on the desk.

"You have your orders. Send those two idiots Rosencrantz and Guildenstern with him for company. Write the necessary papers to gain him a welcome in the English court. Trade off some of the money they owe us against his keep. If they see him as a hostage so be it. At least they'll treat him well. Here..."

He handed the Lord Chamberlain the royal seal.

"Use this to finish the papers. I've no need to see them once you've done."

Polonius took the seal and looked at it.

"Common practice would dictate the king reads anything that carries his mark. Unless you wish to delegate to me responsibility for..."

"Deal with it! As you see fit. Now leave me. I need some private time to think. And pray."

HAMLET RANGED THE CASTLE. Mad then. Truly. He craved Ophelia's company though in truth there seemed no point in seeking her out. The cruel treatment he'd delivered earlier had a reason. An audience, her father, perhaps Claudius too, there to witness his feigned lunacy.

Yet a part of him had enjoyed uttering those harsh words. It was as the jester said. His father's blood was inside him, and when the fever raged it took a course of its own.

A dagger in his belt. A pistol too. If he encountered Claudius now...

An hour he wandered. Then finally, down a narrow passageway he saw a familiar figure, harlequin suit, seated on a guard's chair, fist beneath his chin.

"Back," Yorick ordered. "Shoo, boy."

"Don't shoo me, clown."

The little man got up and blocked his way. Hamlet realised where his aimless wanderings had taken him. To the anteroom beside the king's chapel. A few steps led down to a small altar richly decorated with statues of saints, precious paintings from the Netherlands and Italy. Gold and silver. A crucifix that often caught the moonlight falling from the stained glass window above.

His father's body had lain in state here. In a sealed coffin to hide the horror of the sight.

"We're going back to your room," Yorick told him. "There we'll drink two flagons of wine, one each. Nothing excessive. Along the way we'll devour half a pig. And I shall recite you an ancient Greek tale. A favourite of mine. It concerns drink, sex and farting. If that doesn't cure your melancholy nothing will."

Hamlet pushed past him. There was a sound beyond, a light too. He could just make out a shape. The king on his knees before the altar. Praying out loud, in a voice he could almost hear.

"This is the moment," Yorick said by his side, voice so soft and concerned it seemed unlike him. "Continue on this path and you may never return to what you once were."

"As if I want that. As if I could."

"Of course you can. You're a prince. An intelligent creature. You have power over your own fate. More than most. If you choose to use it."

"Out of my way," he ordered and crouched by the door, one hand on the dagger, the other on the pistol.

Claudius was muttering in a low, frail tone. A soft and tender voice. Like the one he'd used when Hamlet was young, frightened and worried, alone in a castle his father had once more deserted for war.

The chapel was a solitary, private place. No congregation but the royal family and their bishop. Just the king now.

"Don't do it," Yorick whispered in Hamlet's ear.

"Don't stop me," the prince said and got closer still.

He was mere yards behind the king's back now, almost close enough to hear his garbled prayers. Claudius knelt, hands together, eyes closed before the cross.

Hamlet slid his dagger soundlessly from his belt and took another careful step forward.

Claudius's hands came down. He leaned forward on the cold flagstones, then raised his head to stare at the painting above him: Mary, mother of God, rising to Heaven.

The jester sat beside the prince, arms folded, watching keenly.

Hamlet hesitated, listened. Watched as Claudius raised his hands again, eyes closed.

Lips murmuring a silent prayer.

Yorick clicked his fingers.

"Go on, then. Let's have done with it."

He could. One hand to the kneeling king's face, jerking his head back. The other stabbing him in the throat. A life eking out on the cold the chapel floor...

"And then he goes to heaven," Hamlet whispered. "A villain who kills my father. This is blood for blood. Not honourable retribution."

Yorick screwed up his eyes, waved his hands about in bafflement.

"Excuse me?"

"I can't kill a man on his knees, at prayer."

Quietly he stepped back. Replaced his dagger in his belt dagger. Walked out, followed by the jester.

"Not now. Another time. When he's drunk asleep, gaming, swearing, fornicating with her."

Yorick struggled to keep up.

"Not wishing to be pedantic, old chap, but this seems a touch picky if you don't mind my saying."

The prince moved swiftly along the passage, the jester at his heels.

"When there's no hint of salvation about him. And I know for sure his soul will go damned and black to hell. Then..."

Briefly he clutched at the dagger.

"Then's the time."

The dwarf ran in front and stopped him.

"Hang on a minute. How many times lately have you seen dear Claudius without a brace of guards at his side? That was your chance. The one time you might have reached him without taking a poleaxe to your guts. Not that I'm complaining you understand..."

"For someone who hated my father you're suddenly very keen on seeing me revenge his death."

Yorick shook his head as if to clear it.

"Not at all. I'm just puzzled, Hamlet. All this faffing about. Do you know what you want or not?"

"I'm not my father! I won't spill blood unless..."

He went silent.

"Unless?"

"This isn't black and white, Yorick! It's complicated."

Yorick nodded.

"Imagine all you could achieve if it wasn't. Life would be so much simpler if you didn't have to think things through."

"Then better to achieve nothing," Hamlet answered through clenched teeth. "Wine. Go fetch. I'll even listen to your bawdy tales."

He turned to go. In a rush the jester blocked his way again.

"But I told you, Hamlet. No going back. Not in this direction. There." He pointed. "The queen's quarters. She's been asking for you. After that we'll get drunk for Denmark. If you wish it."

Hamlet moved on through the darkness, angry at himself, at everything around him. Especially his mother. The blood was singing in his ears as he flew down the narrow hallways, shrieking that this was all her fault.

The Queen's closet was a tapestry-hung antechamber that led to her bedroom. Normally a place of maids and ladies in waiting. Not this strange and violent night. At Hamlet's insistent knock, she answered herself. He barged past her, slamming the door behind him, looking around. There was no one else inside. None that he could see.

His mother had pulled herself together and seemed less upset than angry.

"What in the name of God was that?" she demanded.

"What, mother?" he asked with a shrug.

"The play, of course. If that absurd tantrum of yours can be called such."

"That's why you wanted to see me?" A post-show critique? Bollocks to that."

"You forget who you're talking to!"

"No," said Hamlet, rounding on her until she took a step backwards. "I remember who you are. I know full well. You're the one who's forgotten. You're the queen, my father's brother's wife. And, more's the pity, you're my mother."

Gertrude reached back and slapped him once, hard across the face. Hamlet didn't pull away, didn't even flinch. But his eyes flashed, and his hands reached for the dagger in his belt, drawing it in one, swift motion that sent his mother staggering backwards towards her bedroom door.

"What are you doing? Put that thing away!"

Then he heard. A shuffling of feet from the left side of the room. The movement of a man concealed behind one of the wall hangings.

A spy, hiding. This time there would be no hesitation.

"What's this, mother? More rats in the walls?"

"Wait! Hamlet!" she yelled but already he was on the move.

A shape behind the tapestry. He flung himself at it, hitting with all his weight. A groan from behind. Hamlet brought up his knee hard, grasped the struggling figure.

A man. Tall, but not especially strong. Breathing as if elderly. Perhaps it was the king, and this the moment he'd wished for.

The dagger rose in his hand. But...

He'd left Claudius in the chapel on his knees. There was no time to reach these quarters.

No time to think either. The shape behind the fabric was struggling to roll out of his grip. Together they stumbled, tearing the tapestry from the wall as they collapsed to the floor. Hamlet shifted, pinning him, his mind racing, and through the sudden silence he heard the distinctive ticking of a watch.

Second by second, eking out the time.

*Polonius.*

Creeping. Whispering. Plotting. With all of them, his mother, his uncle. All Hamlet's life the Lord Chamberlain had watched them from Elsinore's shadows. What had his part been in the murder of Hamlet's father? What had he done since, keeping Ophelia from him, turning her against him?

In fury he stabbed once. Twice. Then paused, breathing hard, as he pulled the tapestry aside to reveal the white bearded face beneath.

There was blood on the pale lips, a gout of it bursting from his throat.

"What?" Hamlet asked lightly. "Speak louder, fellow."

He put his ear to Polonius's chest, pretended to listen. Looked at his mother, frowned and shook his head.

Gertrude began to scream.

Another day, another world, he might have been struck with horror at what he'd done. Not now. Not here. He pulled the gory dagger from the body and rose to face his mother, sending a thin rain of crimson droplets spattering across the floor.

"Mother?" he said, pointing the blade in her face.

Gertrude fell silent, chest heaving, sobs subsiding as the fear took over.

"Good. Keep quiet." His heart was racing. There was a tang of blood in his mouth as if he had bitten his lip during the struggle. Or perhaps it was the stench of the dead man in the room. "You will listen to me, mother. You will tell me what you knew of this business."

"This business?" she cried. Her eyes wouldn't leave the pool of scarlet that had begun to puddle around the crumpled tapestry by the old man's corpse. "Polonius arrived before you. He wanted to hear our conversation. We were concerned about your sanity..."

"This doesn't concern my health. My father. I want to know what you did."

"I...I don't know what you mean, child."

"Two months you waited! Between my father's death and your marriage to my uncle. Two months. Makes a man wonder, *mother*."

"Wonder? Wonder what?"

She had one hand clasped over her heart, and below it hung a locket. Hamlet snatched the thing from her neck, snapping the chain, then opened it. On one side was a miniature of Hamlet's father. On the other, newly added, one of Claudius.

"I wonder how a woman who wept for this man," said Hamlet, holding the first portrait in front of her face, "goes to this, in less time than it took for the funeral banquet to rot. I've had dogs that were more loyal."

"You knew this before," she said, forcing herself to look at him. "You just killed a man, Hamlet! What's happened to you? This is more than grief. Your mind's infected..."

Hamlet gave a shout of derisive laughter then cast the locket across the room. For a moment he stood there, face in bloody hands, eyes shut, rigid with concentration. Gertrude extended cautious fingers towards him, her tears flowing freely now. But as she touched his cheek he seized her by the wrist and flung her backwards.

"No! You won't treat me like a child. You will *listen*!"

Like a mad beast he roared the last word. She shrank away, hands over her ears, braced as if he would hit her. Then there was silence again, and at last she turned to see what he was doing.

Hamlet was gazing open mouthed into the bedroom doorway, looking almost as appalled as she did.

"What is it?" she asked, trying to see whatever had caught his attention. "What frightens you now?"

"Look," he said, his voice barely above a whisper. "There. You see it?"

She peered again. Still nothing.

"I don't understand..."

"There!" he shouted, grabbing her head and pointing her face towards the doorway. "Look!"

"I see nothing!"

"My father!" Hamlet screamed, jabbing a finger at the shadow. "In your bedroom, wearing his old robe. As he was in life. As he is in death."

Gertrude fastened her gaze on Hamlet's face.

"There's nothing there, dear Hamlet. Nothing, my son. You're sick."

"Look at him!"

"This is a disease of the mind. I understand," she said, glancing sadly at the body of Polonius. "He was right. He said you were ill... I should have listened."

"You've come to demand why I haven't done it yet," Hamlet whispered, staring straight ahead of him. "I tried, but... I will do it. I swear, sir. I swear..."

Her hand fell on his arm and stayed there.

"There's just the two of us in this room," Gertrude said calmly, reaching up to stroke his face. "Who do you think you're talking to?"

He was looking at her again, with a new concern.

"Sorry, mother. I didn't mean to frighten you. Truly..."

One last look in the bedroom and then he nodded.

"He says I should leave you to your grief. The king's going now. I wish you could see him. It might make you remember who you are."

"What do you want me of me, son?"

"Pray," he answered with a shrug. "And when Claudius asks you to join him in his bed, say you're...sick. Which you are, even if you can't see it. Stay away from my uncle. It would be for the best."

He kissed her on her tear-streaked cheek and then moved to Polonius's blood daubed body. At the sight of it, something of his former mood returned.

"I suppose I'd better lug this old meat out of here before it turns more rancid than it was before. No rest for the wicked, eh?"

He grabbed the corpse by its ankles and dragged it from the room.

"Night, mother!" Hamlet called from the hallway. "Sleep well."

# A Sea of Troubles

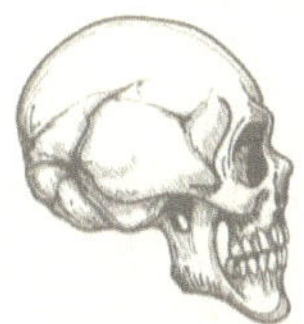

The morning following her father's death Ophelia received a visit from Voltemand. After a few casual words of comfort he talked to her about the funeral, wanting to know how she planned to pay for it. For some reason the man's eyes wouldn't quit the apartments. Once he left she locked her bedroom door and tried to think. Not about mourning. That might happen sometime in the future. Out of duty, little more.

But she needed to think about loss and rejection, how best a woman might deal with them.

The servants were gone. Fussing around a corpse. Negotiating with an undertaker. Arranging hymns and pulpit eulogies. The pain and the confusion in her head still hadn't diminished one whit.

Her mind was on the Spanish wheel-lock pistol she'd stolen from her father's weapons drawer in his study early that day. A heavy complex weapon, locks and levers, brackets and cogs. Laertes told her a famous Italian, Leonardo da Vinci, had invented the device to protect the Florentines against their foes. A quicker, surer way of killing a man than any blade in history.

Then, one bright morning that lost summer, her brother had taken her into the wood behind Elsinore, a place she associated with love and

Hamlet, and shown her how to work the thing. Talked of sear arms and pyrites, mainsprings and a mechanism called the dog.

All she remembered was the loading. Gunpowder in the pan. A ball in the barrel. Arm. Pull. Fire.

In the forest Laertes taught her how to hold it. Laughed as her arm jerked back and she yelped with surprise and more than a little pain from the sudden and unexpected recoil.

He roared when out of the ash tree ahead the brown shape of a sparrow fell before them, all feathers, blood and mangled skin tumbling to the leafy carpet where, not far away, unknown to him and all the castle, she and Hamlet came to make sweet love. Ophelia had been horrified that she'd taken the little bird's life, however unintentionally, and never touched the gun again.

Remembering that distant time she took out the weapon from beneath the sheets, held it, looked at herself in her mirror. The long gun in her hand. Her body slimmer now the baby was gone.

It was hard but she tried to remember what her brother had taught her. There was a waxed box of powder, some round lead balls that fitted the muzzle.

She played with them. Put one where she thought Laertes had said. Held the weapon in her hand. It wasn't so heavy. Not so difficult to manage either. A man, hit full and close by its force, would go from waking to dead so quickly.

It was not within her nature to wish him pain or anything but love once he'd given that in return. More so than Polonius, her father. A cruel, distant man who'd treated her as servant and chattels, another pawn in the quiet game he'd played within Elsinore's walls.

There was another solution.

Ophelia lifted the wheel-lock, shifted her flaxen her out of her way then pressed the cold metal barrel against her temple.

One shot through the skull and then everything she knew, everything that moved and affected her, would be extinguished. Or rather the memory and consciousness of it would be. The causes would remain, not that she understood them.

Suicide was a sin. It would condemn her for eternity. But so was murder, even a just one sought out of righteous grief.

The revenger always dug two graves, they said. One for his victim.

One for himself. She'd never understood that old saying till now.

Either way she was dead. They'd bury her father later that day, in the cemetery within the castle walls where aristocracy were interred. There was no time to waste. Gossip was rife within Elsinore. The king had lost patience with his nephew. Hamlet would be gone from Denmark before nightfall.

Ophelia checked the powder and the ball again. Found her long black mourning dress and slowly pulled it on. Slid the weapon in the pocket. Walked out into the chilly corridor and turned for the stairs to the royal quarters.

A tiny sparrow was the only thing she'd ever killed, and that by accident, not intent. But this was a changing world of which she was but a small and mutable part.

Hamlet sat in the king's study, opposite Claudius, Rosencrantz and Guildenstern scared on chairs in the corner.

"Another funeral in Elsinore. At this rate, uncle, you should bargain with the undertakers. Perhaps they'll give you a discount for bulk."

"Hamlet..." Claudius began.

"Unless you think they're finished for now. Do you?"

He'd hidden the body of Polonius to begin with. Refused to tell anyone where. It had taken Rosencrantz and Guildenstern the best part of an hour to find the Lord Chamberlain's bloody corpse, stowed in a privy set aside for the royal household. They had lugged it into the common chapel where it would lie until interment.

Gertrude remained in her quarters, refusing to speak to anyone.

"If you weren't a prince, nephew, and still loved by the people, I'd have your head off before sunset," the King said. "No trial. No questions asked or answers given."

Hamlet shook his head.

"But I am. So what's the problem?"

"You slaughtered a faithful servant of the crown!"

He shrugged.

"An accident. Could have happened to anyone. There I was enjoying a private conversation with my mother. I heard someone skulking behind the tapestry." He pointed at the maps on the king's desk. "It could have been a Norwegian spy. Or an assassin. I can't believe you dragged me in here for a bollocking. I rather thought I'd be on the receiving end of your gratitude. Especially after that play I gave you last night. I do hope the old man paid those actors properly."

He caught Claudius's eye.

"They read their parts well. I contributed more than a little to the tale by the way. In case you hadn't heard."

The king summoned the pair from the corner. They slunk to his side, looking rattled.

"Before you murdered him I had Polonius draw up documents of travel. We'd already decided it was time you left Elsinore for a while."

"We? So you and the old fool worked as a pair, did you? In everything? Surely not. He was just a servant."

"Don't be impertinent! Or so disrespectful. The man's dead, at your hand."

Hamlet shrugged then yawned.

"I'm surprised you don't promote me. Polonius would have."

Claudius looked away, his jaws clamped shut.

"You'll go to England." He glanced at the two men next to him. "Rosencrantz and Guildenstern will accompany you."

"As jailers?" Hamlet asked, eyeing them with suspicion.

"To ensure your health and safety," Rosencrantz said meekly. "We pray for your return to happiness, lord. But if the king commands..."

"If the king commands you'll wipe his arse."

The two shrugged as if this was obvious.

"There are private diplomatic discussions to be had between our realm and the English crown," Claudius told them. "To do with tributes."

"I'm a tax collector now, am I?"

"No. You're a murderer."

"What's that these days, sir? Men die at the hands of others all the time."

Claudius turned to Rosencrantz.

"I'll have the warrants of passage brought to you. They bear my seal so keep them safe. Show them to the officers of the court who will greet you in the English harbour."

"When?" Hamlet demanded.

"On the next tide."

"I want to speak to my mother."

"Well she doesn't wish to speak to you. I've discussed this with the Queen. You go with her good wishes. But after last night... she's still upset."

Hamlet stormed to his feet. Rosencrantz clutched at his sword in terror.

"She's my mother!"

Claudius stood up and faced him.

"You must leave these shores immediately. I've sent word to Laertes. He's in Lübeck dealing with court business before he goes to France. The lad knows of his father's death. When he gets here he'll understand the circumstances. I'll do my best to deal with him, but not with you around."

That calmed him a little.

"Nothing makes up for losing a father."

"I know. I lost mine. It happens to us all."

"Though the circumstances may differ. And I may return when?"

"When it suits our interests. When you're fit and well. These gentlemen..." He gestured to the pair from Copenhagen. "They will communicate your condition. I will follow it most carefully. As will the queen."

"Can I take the jester?"

"What?" the king demanded.

"Can... I... take... the... jester?"

"A jester? For pity's sake, Hamlet, what do you need a jester for? Be on your way."

"I want my fool!"

Silence in the room. Claudius gestured at the door and went back to the papers on his desk.

Then Guildenstern said, as cheerily as he could, "We'll find us a nice boat, Hamlet. How about that?"

"You've got two fools already," Claudius said without looking up from his work. "That should be enough for you. Get out of here the lot of you."

~

Yorick had vanished. Rosencrantz and Guildenstern were sorting Hamlet's things into trunks. A few clothes. Some books. The weapons he was allowed.

He left the pair in his quarters, thought about going to the queen's chamber, forcing his way in. Trying to... understand.

The ghost had been there the previous night. His father's shade or something like it. The spectre had urged him on. And things from the grave saw everything. It must have known Polonius was complicit in his murder. Must have protected Gertrude, too. Since she lived and might so easily have perished under Hamlet's furious hand.

Down a dark corridor, halfway there, a slight, slim figure stepped out of the shadows and stopped him.

He saw the face. Pale and beautiful. But different somehow. Lost and a little crazed like him.

"I owe you an apology," he said, honestly. "I was rude to you yesterday, Ophelia. I meant it, but for a reason. And the reason wasn't you. Not really."

Wild-eyed and lovely she had her hand in her black dress. He wished he could roll back time and take her to the forest again, the two of them locked together beneath a perfect blue sky.

"You slaughter my father and apologise for petty insults?"

Out of the dress her hand came. In it was a pistol, one of the new Spanish types, he thought, not that he knew much of powder weapons. Swords would do just fine.

Ophelia stabbed the barrel at his chest.

"Your father killed mine," he said. "And never apologised at all."

"What?"

A long silence between them. When she shook her head her hair moved like August straw and he knew how much he'd lost. Her eyes were on his, the pistol seemingly forgotten though it still pointed squarely at him.

Hamlet reached down and took the gun from her fingers, too easily. Then laughed.

"Oh love. You haven't a clue. Here." He moved the mechanism, corrected it. "And here."

Then returned it to her hand.

"What do you mean?"

"I mean we're fools, the pair of us. Polonius schemed with my uncle to kill my father. By putting put poison in his ear. The play pricked what passes for his conscience. The way he reacted shows his guilt as clear as the light of day." He closed his eyes for a moment. "That and a few other things."

"You know this?"

"As much as I know that every word I wrote in those letters you threw back at me was true."

He placed his fingers on her shoulder, touched the warm flesh of her neck. She didn't recoil.

"They tell me my father was a cruel man. I never noticed. Or never allowed myself that pain. Perhaps sons don't. For his final years I was in Wittenberg, apart from the summer. And that I spent with you." He looked at her. "Was it true?"

"All men are cruel."

"But a few have love inside them too. Did he?"

No answer.

"Did I?"

"Once," she whispered. "And then you were mad. Or pretending to be."

"Pretending? I abandoned you. I walked away and..."

So many conflicting thoughts and desires. Perhaps he could smuggle her onto the ship. Take her with him to England. Though what might happen there...

He took her fingers, pointed the gun barrel at his chest.

"Shoot me. Have done with it. I deserve no better. I murdered your father yet I couldn't kill my uncle. I don't know why. Perhaps that, too, was an odd, unwanted love. He was kind to me once. Still was until today."

His hand moved, found her hair.

"As you were always."

A sudden stern commanding tone to his voice.

"Shoot me and have done with it. No one will blame you. And somewhere my sad shade will weep with gratitude."

Her fingers didn't move.

"I hate you."

He smiled.

"Then do it."

Ophelia sighed, didn't look at him. Her hand came away and with it the gun.

Abruptly Hamlet snatched it from her, thrust the muzzle to his neck but she was on him in an instant, pointing the barrel into the darkness, pulling at the trigger.

A snap, a spark, a puff of smoke into the shadows. Then nothing.

The Prince rolled back his head, laughed, almost cried.

"I even fail at this. The most helpless, hopeless, useless man in all the world."

She took the gun from him.

"True," Ophelia agreed. Then looked at him and found herself laughing briefly too. "Here we are, me about to bury my father. You headed for England and exile. Acting as if this were somehow... happiness."

His hand went round her waist. He pulled her to him.

"If there's time we'll give one another joy again. The briefest but greatest there ever is and in your arms..."

Her fingers flew to his lips and silenced him.

"Time abandoned us the moment you left me last summer."

"Perhaps there's a watchmaker in London. With a mechanism that will let me wind back the months..."

Her eyes grew damp.

"And then we go through this misery again."

He glanced down the passageway.

"There must be somewhere..."

"A part of me came to kill you, not to love you."

"Not much to choose between them, is there? Ophelia..."

There was something in her eyes he recognised. The quick cunning she used to hide them in the woods.

"How long will you be in England?" she asked.

"Not a minute more than I can manage. Though how I can find my way safely back to Elsinore..."

Her hand touched his cheek.

"The people love you, Hamlet. They recognise a good heart when they see one."

"What use is that? I'm a murderer now. Of your own father..."

She rapped her knuckles on the wall.

"The only things set in stone are these. Perhaps Elsinore is more open to change than you imagine."

Hamlet gazed at her.

"My sweet. It sounds like you're plotting. How very unladylike."

"You think? I am my father's daughter."

He shook his head.

"This is a dream. I'll be in England. And everything I've attempted here has come to little more..." He could barely look at her, "...than the murder of an accomplice. Not the villain himself. I'm captive to the wishes of the King now. If he..."

"Hush!" she ordered. "Be quiet and listen to me. I've access to my father's papers now. His records. Everything. What if somehow there were evidence? Proof of what he and Claudius did?"

He looked interested.

"Then a judge would throw it out, since the judge would be the King's."

"But if you were to hold it. To publish it. The people do love you. They have no great affection for your uncle, especially with Norway's army at the door. If you were to prove he killed your father. And perhaps reach an accommodation with Fortinbras along the way..."

A quick and pretty smile. It broke his heart twice over.

"Who knows? Perhaps you could come back to wear the crown," she said.

"And you my queen. There's a dream worth having. Claudius would take your pretty head in an instant if he heard a word of it."

"And what's that worth?"

"Everything if we're together.".

"And nothing if we're not. Oh, damn..."

She threw the pistol into a shadowy corner.

"I hoped you'd be horrid to me again. That would have made things so much easier."

He shrugged.

"That's possible if you want it..."

"Take me somewhere," she sighed, reaching for him, hands in his hair, mouth fighting for his. "Quick, before you go."

THERE WAS a man Gertrude didn't recognise in the king's study. Lean, about thirty, of average height, with a black velvet jacket and trousers, an intelligent handsome face, a trim dark moustache in the Italian fashion.

He was the new Lord Chamberlain, Claudius said. Voltemand, a man who'd spent the last few years in Copenhagen overseeing the harbour dues. He came from a trusted family, one that had once provided captains for Viking ships and now produced treasurers and tax collectors.

Gertrude took one long look at him, glanced at Claudius and asked, "Do we need to be so hasty?"

Voltemand smiled then nodded.

"A good question, madam. Polonius is not yet buried. Perhaps it would be more decent to wait a while." He glanced at the king. "To interview other candidates. It's important you make the right decision. In the meantime... I will perform whatever function you wish."

"That makes sense." She took a seat, hoping it wasn't so obvious she had acquired a dislike to the man already.

"No need. You're the Lord Chamberlain and that's that," Claudius replied.

The king waved a letter at his wife.

"It was on his recommendation that we had Voltemand send messages to Magnus in Oslo, to keep young Fortinbras in check. A fine job he did too. I have a note here from Polonius advising I promote him to the highest position available by way of reward. If the old man placed sufficient trust in our friend here that's good enough for me."

"Do I have any say in the matter?"

"No. There may be a war coming. To say nothing of the mess your son's left for me to clean up."

She looked at him coldly.

"I am your wife, the queen and Hamlet's mother. Would it not have been at least good manners to have told me you planned to send him into exile?"

Claudius sighed.

"It would. I'm sorry. It was a hasty decision. Polonius pressed it upon me. Had I reflected on it this morning I would have reconsidered. But the circumstances have changed somewhat..."

"You're a poor liar, sir."

He glared at her. Voltemand shifted awkwardly, looking at the carpet, trying to smile.

"You, my lady, should know your place," Claudius said without feeling. "Hamlet will go to England with Rosencrantz and Guildenstern. They have instructions to deal with matters of state in London. Problems over tributes and taxation. The kind of tedious civil affairs a prince like Hamlet should be concerned with if he's to wear this crown one day."

Gertrude got up, stormed over, jabbed a finger in his face.

"Don't play games with me. He's sick, Claudius. If this journey will cure him..."

"Travel and an absence from his troubles should surely ease his mind," Voltemand said easily.

"Do you know my son, sir? Have the two of you ever met?"

"I've watched him from afar, madam. He's a fine young man who will one day make a worthy king I'm sure. Once this present ailment has left him."

"How long?"

"A month or two no more," the king said. "If there's an army on our doorstep... it depends upon his state."

He took her hands.

"I want him back. I want him well. We need him here. He's popular, the object of some sympathy now. More than Polonius ever was from what I hear."

"No one likes the man who holds this position," Voltemand observed cheerily. "If they love him the job's not done well."

"Wise words." Claudius took a set of keys from his desk. "These are for Polonius's quarters. His offices. All his records. His staff works for you now. Judge them as you see fit. Fire any you feel merit it. No need for recourse to me."

"That was his home too!" Gertrude cried. "A few hours dead, not even buried, and you give it to a stranger. What about his daughter? Where's she to live?"

Claudius stared at her, angry now.

"Polonius was a servant of the state! The realm stops for no one. Not even a king. This is what he would have wished."

"The king knows what dead men desire now, does he? Are you coming to the funeral or not?"

They rarely argued. Never in public. Or with such venom.

"You will represent the crown, I'm too busy with matters of state. Voltemand and I..."

"And what of Ophelia? Do I tell her she's homeless once we've buried him?"

Voltemand came over. He looked sympathetic, concerned.

"I've seen the lady now and then, when I've visited Elsinore. Also this morning to discuss the arrangement of the service. She's naturally much distressed. With good reason. I would never wish to put her to further pain, my lady. The apartments are of some size. Until there's an acceptable alternative it seems sensible, so long as she's willing, that she keeps the rooms she has. And the servants. I'll make my own arrangements. It will be of no inconvenience to me. Very much the opposite."

He smiled then and she knew for sure she loathed him.

"I have a niece in Copenhagen much the same age. These girls, even with the losses Ophelia has borne, can become weak and feverish in the head. They imagine things. Have fancies that delude them. If I can be an uncle to her, help guide her back to a happy, contented state. Perhaps one day..."

He shrugged.

"It would be good if we could find her a noble husband."

"She's about to bury her father!"

The smile again.

"Of course. But there will be a tomorrow. And a tomorrow after that. The future comes on whether we ask for it or not. Better we bury our parents than they bury us. With a little affection, some understanding and a little patience these juvenile fevers of the mind... perhaps one day she'll laugh at them. As will your son."

Gertrude was lost for words.

"Tell her at the funeral," Claudius ordered. "If she's not content with the idea..." He glanced at the papers on the desk then his wife. "Do something else. You must excuse us. There's business to be done."

~

HAMLET HUNTED up and down the jetty. The captain of the little vessel was getting restless. So were Rosencrantz and Guildenstern, and the small team of soldiers they'd brought to make sure he sailed with the ship.

Finally the fat one came up and tried to look commanding.

"The tide calls us, sir," he announced. "If we don't heed its cry your father will be furious. At you. At us. Please..."

"I'm looking for my companion. A little man. The jester. Yorick. Have you seen him?"

Guildenstern rolled his eyes.

"Your father said nothing about a jester. It's only a small ship. There's not much room..."

"He didn't say I couldn't take him either."

Up and down the cobbled pier he marched, shouting the clown's name. No response. Blank looks from those around, soldiers, sailors, fishermen bringing in their herring to be gutted, salted and sent for smoking by the woman in the harbour huts. It was a cold clear day and the Øresund had the aroma of winter: salt with ice behind it, and a touch of sharp, raw fish.

He hadn't seen Yorick since the previous night. There was no sign of him in Hamlet's room. No news of the jester anywhere in the castle. The mention of his name drew blank looks. Had Claudius agreed to see him Hamlet would have asked if the fool had been dispatched back to foreign lands , the kind of life he'd led before his own father's sudden execution.

Finally, at the end of his tether, he found the harbourmaster. An old and decent man, with a ginger beard and fierce blue eyes. When Hamlet was young this man had taken him out on the channel in a sailing boat, giving the boy his first experience of the sea.

"I'm trying to find Young Yorick," Hamlet told him as the man oversaw the unloading of baskets of fish, still flapping, from one of the small coble boats the locals used inshore. "I want him with me in England. Have you seen him?"

There was a look in the harbourmaster's eyes he couldn't read. Puzzlement, confusion, embarrassment.

"Claudius wishes you to go to England, my lord. Do as the King asks. Let's have no nonsense. The ship must sail now or the tide will keep you back another twelve hours or more. The weather..." He looked at the blue winter sky. "It's set fair. The wind's good. It won't stay that way. It never does. You need to depart, sir."

Hamlet looked around the harbour, then back at the towering walls of Elsinore. His childhood home.

"To leave Denmark? For England?"

"If what they say about Fortinbras is true," the harbourmaster replied, "perhaps it's for the best. You're more scholar than a warrior, aren't you? And from what I hear you need some respite from this place."

"Because I'm mad?"

He didn't like making this good man feel awkward.

"They say you're not well."

"And there are good doctors in England? Better than here?"

"I'm a servant, Hamlet. Nothing more. I've my orders. If you're not on that ship shortly those soldiers..." He nodded at three men in armour, watching him, hands on swords, at the foot of the quay. "They will put you on it. Whether you go easily or not."

"I want Yorick. I want my jester. Not the king's two idiots for company..."

The harbourmaster closed his eyes, exasperated.

"Don't make a scene. The people here like you. They know you have a kind heart. They wish you well. But if they should see you sick in the head..."

The soldiers were coming for him now.

"If you're forced onto that vessel like a criminal going to justice it won't serve you well when you return..."

"When I return? You think that'll be soon?"

The men arrived, stamped feet, hands on swords. Stared at him.

"What do you want?" Hamlet asked.

"The king demands your presence on ship," the tallest said. A fearsome-looking man with a battle scar across his cheek. "One way or another."

Hamlet had his dagger. His pistol. More scholar than warrior? He might show them otherwise. He could fight them right there. And if he was lost in a bloody and pointless scuffle here on the dockside, what difference would it make?

But Ophelia had put an idea in his head. A dream. A hint of possible redemption.

"Is my baggage on board?" he asked.

"All three trunks," the soldier said.

It seemed a lot but then he hadn't packed himself.

"We're going now," the man added. "You can walk or we can lug you."

Hamlet clapped the harbourmaster's shoulder then pointed to the fishwives in the huts.

"Tell them to go lightly with the salt but smoke them well. I'll be back before you know it and wanting some of their wares."

For the first time the man smiled.

"I'll do that, sir. And look forward to the day."

Rosencrantz and Guildenstern followed him on board. The gang plank was pulled up, then the anchor. The sail rose and the wind caught it. Slowly, yet picking up speed, the little barque pulled out onto the Øresund, was soon midway between Elsinore in Denmark and Helsingborg in Sweden, heading north, out to the open sea and England.

From afar the castle looked like a sprawling stone monster, slumbering on the hill above the port. Somewhere within those walls Ophelia was burying her father, a man he'd murdered. Somewhere Claudius plotted. Of that, and little else, Hamlet felt sure.

The congregation in the castle church was small and there principally out of duty, not love. When he lived Polonius had a constant stream of visitors to his door. But they were men who wanted something, seeking advancement not friendship or company. Ophelia knew him to be a cold and solitary man. An employer of spies and minions, neither of whom were known to mourn their masters.

And what of his daughter? Who would mourn her when the time came? Her mother had died in childbirth. He'd never tired of reminding her of that, as if it were her fault somehow. Not that Polonius ever spoke with much affection about his late wife. There was no portrait in their quarters, no letters, no sign of fondness between them at all.

Men and women lived and died, mostly without consequence. That was one of his many, oft-repeated aphorisms. And now he was a corpse in a simple pine coffin, borne by paid bearers out of the chapel into the bright day. A quiet ceremony on the King's orders. He wanted no fuss, no gossip, no trouble.

She followed the procession in silence. The graveyard was at the seaward end of the castle, manned by a couple of sextons who went about their business with surprising good cheer. That morning she'd talked to them, tipped the more senior for the best plot he could provide, left them setting their spades to the hard brown earth.

Something the man said had stayed with her.

"You're lucky, darling," the sexton chuckled taking her coin.

"Lucky? Why's that? My father's dead."

"Well everyone's dead in the end, love. But you and yours get buried inside the castle walls. Along with all the other posh folk. Nowhere better except the royal crypt and that's just for their highnesses, ain't it? We mere mortals..." He punched his fellow gravedigger on the arm. "They chuck us in the ground outside. Down by the water's edge. Where wolves and badgers can come and dig you up. And not much to mark your grave either."

The other one spat in the bare earth.

"If you're dead it don't matter, you dolt."

And then the two of them laughed.

If you're dead it didn't matter all, she thought, as she watched the coffin bearers come to a halt, gently place their grim cargo on the ground, listen to the words of the priest and watch him scatter the earth.

She closed her eyes and thought, "He never loved me. Never said a kind word. I was one more pawn to be shuffled round his chess board. A player in a game, nothing more. To be sacrificed if needed."

Held by black bands the coffin was slowly lowered to the base of the grave. The sextons reached for their spades and began to shovel the hard, dry Elsinore soil, pebbles rattling as they found the plain, unseasoned pine of the casket.

A hand on her shoulder. She looked. Saw the lined, unhappy face of Gertrude.

"You can cry if you want," the Queen said.

"But I don't."

She handed Ophelia a handkerchief. It wasn't true. Tears were rolling down her cheek, unwanted, without a thought. She took the fabric, wiped them away. Realised she didn't want to watch this pointless ceremony any more.

"May we speak?" Gertrude asked. "Frankly. When you're ready."

"I'm ready now, my lady," she said and the two of them walked away from the black mourners and the small choir paid to sing a final hymn.

In the shadow of the main gate they stood shivering.

"Is he gone?" Ophelia asked.

"Your father? Of course..."

"I meant Hamlet."

The queen took her hand and led her up the steps to the battlements. The day was so clear they could see smoke rising from chimneys in Helsingborg across the water. A small ship, white sails billowing with the lively breeze, headed towards the broad open water called the Kattegat which led to the North Sea, and then the world beyond.

"My husband... Old Hamlet..." the queen said, hair blowing in the wind, "used to say this narrow stretch of water was Denmark's treasure trove. It's the only way for foreigners into the Baltic. All those rich states they call the Hanseatic League. The English, the French... anyone we choose must pay tribute to pass the channel."

"I know. My father told me many times. Is this an occasion for a history lesson?"

Gertrude stared at her.

"You've a sharp tongue on you when you wish it. There are those in this castle who think you a feeble-minded, willing young girl. Not I."

"I asked a question. I was wondering about the relevance of your answer."

"The relevance is Hamlet has gone to England to seek back payment of some of those dues. Money we're owed. Which may come in useful should Fortinbras's intentions be more hostile towards us than he claims."

Ophelia drew her cloak around her, couldn't stop following the distant motion of the ship on the grey sea. The wind had truly filled her sails. She moved rapidly away from Elsinore, from Denmark. Once beyond the Kattegat the vessel would be in waters beyond the rule of law, full of brigands and hostile ships of many nations. The journey to England was commonplace, but not without peril.

"When will he return?"

Gertrude sighed.

"When he's better. When the king allows it. That's all I know." She peered into Ophelia's face. "It would be best if you didn't hold out hopes for him. I'm sorry. If your father was still alive and Lord Chamberlain... perhaps there might have been a match. Not now."

"I could be his mistress."

Gertrude's face fell.

"That is not a position to covet. Believe me."

"So when... if... he returns I'm to leave him alone. And him me."

"That would be best. For both of you. I will be grateful. You won't regret it."

"How do you know that, madam? How can you?"

The Queen glowered at her.

"You should keep a check on your temper and your words, child. This is a time to make friends, not enemies."

That, Ophelia thought, was doubtless wise advice. So she stayed silent.

"There's one more matter," Gertrude added. "My husband has appointed a new Lord Chamberlain. A little hastily it seems to me. But men..."

Ophelia waited.

"His name is Voltemand."

"Voltemand! He's not even an Elsinore man..."

"The king decides! Not you or me. Voltemand it is. By rights he owns your apartments now. They belong to the title, not the man."

"So I'm fatherless and homeless! All in a single day."

"Only fatherless. Voltemand has no objection to you occupying your own rooms, while he takes your father's and the office."

"Such kindness..."

Gertrude watched her.

"If it's any comfort I'm of a similar opinion about the fellow. But you can stay there for a while. I'll help you find other quarters. Perhaps there's a household, beyond Elsinore, looking for a match."

"I can find a man if I want one, madam."

The queen laughed then.

"It's clear what my son saw in you. The two of you might be twins." She placed her arm through Ophelia's affectionately. "Headstrong. Innocent. And so full of life. As was I once. Or so I imagine."

Her eyes were on the horizon too, and the boat working its way across the Øresund.

"But the years wear you down and make you see sense. You have my love and admiration, Ophelia. I will help you all I can. If Hamlet comes back with an English bride... what the two of you do in private is your business. But listen to me; in public... no."

"In the meantime I'm Voltemand's handmaiden. As I was my father's."

"Not at all. That I won't allow."

Ophelia tried to think this through. Time was short. The man from Copenhagen seemed intelligent, determined, thorough.

"Is the new Lord Chamberlain in place already?" In my quarters, I mean?"

"Not yet. I left him with Claudius. They have much business to conclude."

Ophelia nodded.

"So, my lady. May I have a few hours to myself in my rooms? To mourn. To think. It's the only home I've ever known."

"I'll ask Voltemand to give you till this afternoon."

"Will he listen?"

Gertrude withdrew her arm and scowled.

"If Claudius tells him. Will that do?"

Two hours out. Guildenstern had been heaving over the side. Rosencrantz watched, laughing. Hamlet had seen enough of these two already. He retired to his cabin and not long after heard footsteps following down the corridor.

They entered without knocking. The tall one happy, impudent. His little fat friend still green from the rolling sea.

"It's polite to give me notice."

"Oh come on," Rosencrantz replied. "We're all shipmates together now. No need to stand on ceremony."

Hamlet said nothing. The silence unnerved them.

"Are you comfortable, sir?" the little one asked. "We told them to give you the most comfortable cabin. As befits your station."

He looked around at the bunk bed, the tiny table, the porthole window.

"No. I require more luxury. Call in at the next port and find me carpets, fur bedding. A woman."

"There will be no port calls until Harwich," Rosencrantz told him. "The captain has his orders. We've enough provisions to cross the North Sea. Once we arrive in England a coach will take us to London and the court."

Hamlet shrugged.

"Then why ask if I'm comfortable?"

"Out of politeness," the tall one said coldly. "Nothing more."

"I'd like something against the nausea. Not that I have any. But there's a family recipe..." He closed his eyes as if trying to remember. "A raw egg with garlic in it. Vinegar. The blood of a fresh fish. And fried porridge."

Guildenstern's hand went to his mouth and he raced for the door. Rosencrantz stayed and stared at the prince.

"Jokes pall on the ocean, don't you think?"

"Not if they're good ones. What exactly do we have to discuss with the English court? Where are the documents? I wish to study them."

Rosencrantz hesitated, then said, "The formal papers preceded us. We receive them when we're there."

"Then what am I to read, sir? How shall I pass the time?"

The tall man laughed.

"Talking to yourself?" He juggled a finger at his ear. "That's what you do, isn't it?"

"I find I get a better class of conversation that way. Shouldn't you go and look after your friend?" Guildenstern was coughing and heaving somewhere outside. "It sounds as if he needs it."

Rosencrantz didn't move.

"What?" Hamlet asked.

"Ships are great levellers, don't you think?"

"You've lost me, sir."

A long forefinger jabbed at him.

"Don't push your luck. You don't have Claudius or the king's soldiers to do your bidding here. Or us."

Hamlet got up, caught his collar, propelled him to the door.

"I gathered that," he said then dispatched him outside with a boot to the arse.

Back in the Lord Chamberlain's quarters Ophelia rushed about, wondering where to start. Men were clearing out her father's bedroom already, making way for Voltemand's things. But his office remained untouched. That made sense. Nothing would change except the identity of the official who occupied the grand chair by the window, behind the desk that managed the realm.

Polonius had been a parsimonious man, using scribes and clerks reluctantly. Partly this was money. Partly a matter of trust. As much as he could he wrote letters in his own hand, kept records privately, writing up the day's events himself in the evening.

His daughter knew this well. She'd been the one to fetch him food and wine as he worked at the desk under the light of an oil lamp.

But what happened to those records after he'd written them...

She went to her own quarters. In the sitting room stood a small bureau where she wrote. A few love letters from Hamlet remained in the drawers, those she hadn't tried to return when her father ordered it. Private missives, tender, frank and painful on both parts.

Reading through a few she wondered what Claudius, Gertrude or Voltemand might make of these sad, lost sentiments. Then, with a heavy heart, she bundled them up and walked to the fire.

The parchment burned easily, sending a steady spiral of smoke up the narrow chimney.

Love and hope, fear and despair, all reduced to a single grey cloud and a scattering of ash and embers.

She tried to imagine where his little ship was now, then thought again of what they'd discussed before that last brief embrace.

If there were some way she could prove his suspicions, a form of hard evidence, ink on parchment, that confirmed the king's guilt, then Gertrude's kind yet heartless calculation – that she was fit to be no better than wife to a provincial lord, and at best mistress to her son – might prove mistaken. The thing Hamlet yearned for most – a sense of justice – could be delivered to him, and with that would surely come his constant, unwavering love.

At that moment she caught sight of herself in the mirror. Blonde hair, pale skin, fresh face. They took her for a girl, still. None knew that she'd slipped into the woods with the king's son and enjoyed such sweet and secret pleasures there. And almost borne his child.

"They see a courtier's feeble daughter, not me," Ophelia whispered. "Only Hamlet has that talent."

Yet to pry into state affairs was surely dangerous. Treason even. The king had little love for anyone who intruded into his business. And Gertrude had her own interests.

The face in the glass glared back at her.

"I am not a weak and fearful girl."

She walked out into the hall and looked at the closed door to her father's study. So many hours she'd spent fetching and carrying for him there. She could picture it in her head now. The empty chair at the tidy desk. The quill pen, the inkwell, the pot of pounce for drying Polonius's spidery handwriting. Missives that condemned men to death and a nation to war. Or simply changed the plumbing, or the way a farmer might be taxed. All came from there.

His invoices, receipts and business correspondence. He locked the door when he went in, locked it when he came out. Voltemand had his key now. Surely that came with the position.

But there was another. She was her father's servant as much as his daughter. Perhaps more. Each night, on the hour, she had to enter, ask his wishes, fetch him anything he needed.

Hers still sat inside her gown, tied to her undergarments by a ribbon.

Ophelia checked the apartment. No sign of Voltemand or anyone new.

Then went back to the office, looked round nervously. Took out the key and let herself in.

~

The three trunks from Elsinore were stored between the porthole and the bunk. As Hamlet sat on the single seat by a small table he saw the lid of the largest begin to rise. A small, stocky figure stood up, flourished an arm and declared, "Ta da! Rejoice! The entertainment's arrived."

Yorick cast a suspicious glance at the door.

"Those two travelling companions of yours are very hugger-mugger. Do you think they're queer? Riding the wrong horse? Biting the...?"

Hamlet scratched his head.

"I was looking for you everywhere. I didn't know you'd got on board."

"Spur of the moment decision," the little man said climbing out of the trunk. "You should be honoured. I hate boats. They always stink of poo and spew." Yorick looked around the cabin, walked to the door, stared at the chamber pot there, grimaced and held his nose. "Though had I been aware I'd be condemned to travel with the hoi polloi... is this the best they've got?"

"The very best."

"Oh well." The jester clapped his hands, went to the table, picked up a piece of dry ship's biscuit. "You are, aren't you?"

"What?"

"Honoured?"

Hamlet closed his eyes and laughed.

"Yes. Deeply."

The jester did a little dance, grinning from ear to ear.

"Good. Then I have a purpose once again."

"Won't they miss you? In the castle?"

Yorick brushed away the idea.

"Doubt it. I rather feel my career's peaked in Elsinore. Besides the place is no fun without you to bate. Sorry. I mean... amuse."

He crunched on the biscuit, pulled a disgusted face, then went to the porthole and lobbed it out. A fierce cold wind blew in at that moment.

There was the salt tang of the ocean and from somewhere the plaintive cries of gulls.

Yorick came and sat on the bed.

"Let's hear it then. Brief me, if you will."

Hamlet folded his arms, realised he was glad of his company. The little man made him think. Ask questions. Raise doubts in his own head. Without the jester's questioning voice he felt adrift, bereft of direction.

"I'm an embarrassment to my uncle. To spare the court seeing my malady I'm being sent to England with Rosencrantz and Guildenstern for company. There to learn..."

"What?"

"Manners."

"Manners? From the English? Are you serious? What are they supposed to teach you? The finer arts of farting? Bloody hell..."

"Claudius wants me out of the way." Hamlet shrugged. "Perhaps it's not a bad idea." He looked Yorick in the eye. "You saw I couldn't kill him. I had the chance. On his knees in the chapel. Praying. I couldn't..."

"And yet you stabbed an old man hiding behind a curtain." Yorick paused then said very slowly, "By mistake one assumes."

Silence.

"Well, let's call it an unfortunate blunder, shall we? Either way that nasty old bastard's dead."

"I told you. If I murder a man at prayer I go to hell and he doesn't. I don't mind the former. But..."

Yorick put a finger to his cheek.

"We're back with that one, are we? I never realised. Is there a book you can consult that has all the rules? Must be difficult mastering them..."

He realised now the memories had stayed his hand too. When Hamlet was a child it was Claudius who took him to that same chapel. Who sat with him, reading the Bible. Talking about those strange and savage stories, trying to find some sense in them. Telling whispered jokes when the priest's sermon went on and on.

"What if he wasn't praying?" Yorick asked. "What if he was just...?"

The jester fell to the timber boards, on his knees, eyes closed, hands together.

"Dear God... if you're listening, kindly get my murderous nephew out of my hair before he makes me as barmy as he is. Stick the boy on a boat to England. Have those brutes deal with him not me."

His eyes opened, his hand went to his ear.

"What? *What?*"

Yorick frowned.

"Sorry. Nobody listening..."

"It's Elsinore I wanted to murder," Hamlet said in a low and toneless voice. His hand went out, made a tearing gesture. "That damned place. That world. If I could rip its heart out..."

"You with it? Me too? Ophelia. Your mother... everything?"

"Everything..."

Yorick looked up at him, serious in a flash.

"Then that's what your uncle sees. He's an intelligent man. He knows you better than you know yourself. That's why you're on this stinking boat to England."

He got up from the floor and dusted himself down.

"What orders do you carry for the English court? What papers? Let's see them."

"Claudius didn't give me any."

The fool put a finger to his lips.

"Oh, right. That pair of chums he's sent. Rosencrantz and Guildenstern. What do they have?"

"I asked. They said they had none except some papers of passage. The court documents have gone ahead."

The jester bunched his big fists.

"What? He only decided to ship you off last night. How could he have dispatched the papers separately? There's one ship left Elsinore for England this morning and we're on it."

"True."

"Ergo... Rosencrantz and Guildenstern are a pair of lying, toadying bastards. A king doesn't send his heir to a foreign country without sealed instructions. It's unthinkable."

He slapped Hamlet on the arm.

"Time for a new talent, chum. To add to murder and the ripping out of hearts."

"Which is?"

"You need to wait until those two are out of their cabin, puking or eating or mincing or whatever it is they do. And then..."

Hamlet waited.

"Then Prince of Denmark, you must learn to be a thief."

"You, jester," he said, tapping the harlequin jacket. "You..."

"No, sir." The little man strode across the room and sat on the edge of the trunk. "This is your job. Your role in this drama. Your fate. Not mine."

OPHELIA HAD SPENT an hour patiently going through her father's papers. The daybook. The records. The receipts and invoices. There was nothing there but the records of the state. Nor should she have been surprised. Polonius was cautious and secretive by nature. He would never have allowed evidence of black deeds to be found easily.

And yet... he was a pedantic, pompous man too. He would have wanted credit for his actions. Testament to them for posterity. He was too long-winded, too fond of his own voice to allow it to be silenced by something as primitive as death.

There was none of his odd, controlling personality in these documents. She couldn't believe this would have satisfied him.

Ophelia looked at the study. Books on all three walls. Ledgers and records of meetings and decisions, all in her father's careful hand. She'd taken every one off the shelf. Flicked through them as best she could and was close to giving up the fight when something caught her eye.

On the bookcase nailed to the northern wall by the window he kept the most tedious records of all: simple diaries of the comings and goings at Elsinore. Ambassadors received and dispatched. Nobility. Emissaries of the church. The occasional fleeing statesman from elsewhere seeking sanctuary.

A cunning man would hide his secrets beneath the thickest layer of tedium he could find. She snatched off the bottom shelf of books, found nothing. Then the middle. Polonius was a tall, stiff man. Sometimes she'd seen him reaching to ease his back when he finally retired from the office at the end of the night. She found a low stool, stood on it, removed the first few volumes at the top.

There was something behind just visible in the gloom. She got a candle, lit it, looked. Her heart fell. Nothing but a keyhole, small and damaged in the wood at the sides as if by clumsy use.

It was getting dark. She'd no idea how long it would take Voltemand to return. So little time, and nothing to do with it.

Half-running she returned to her room and went through the things they'd given her after her father was washed and prepared for the burial. Personal effects. Clothes, a chain of office, a watch. What she took to be a snuff box, one of the fashionable new items arrived from America via France and Italy.

A set of keys. All familiar, for the doors of the quarters. Then she looked at the snuff box again and saw an odd button protruding from the side. Tobacco was a disgusting habit. He'd always said so. And hadn't the Pope recently threatened sanctions against any who took to the new habit of snuff?

She played with the button. A lever clicked and out of the side came a short brass key.

Back to the office, up on the stool. She reached in, just managed to find the slot, opened it. Put her hand through and took out a thick leather-bound volume that smelled of dust and age and him.

In the dying light of the afternoon Ophelia sat by the window, read and wept. This was his personal diary written at the end of each day. Every hateful thought, every caustic observation. He was here, still alive, full of an irascible contempt for all around him. Old Hamlet, Young Hamlet. Claudius, Gertrude and the members of the court.

And, at regular intervals, entries about his daughter. No love there. No love for anyone, she could see that. Polonius was a bitter, wicked old man who sat in judgement on the world he smiled at and pretended to serve. Old Hamlet, a vicious, cruel king, too bent on domination and foreign adventure to recognise the dissent and perils close to home. His son, an energetic warrior in spirit broken by his father's neglect and reduced to the fey intellectual life of a student. Claudius, an unimaginative diplomat whose sole weakness was a lustful obsession with his own brother's wife. Gertrude, the flawed queen tempted from her lawful husband by a persuasive and gentle suitor.

It was all there, Elsinore in his venomous curt prose. Even, when she read towards the end, the means, the intermediaries, the plan by which the throne would change hands.

She shivered as she discovered the details. Felt a cold hatred for him when she went through the entries about herself. A daughter stayed blind to the darker aspects of family. That was duty. It came naturally. She knew he had no time for her but didn't understand until this moment the contempt and disappointment he felt. She was no cowed, obedient servant as her mother must have been. Every question, every demand and last proof of her own identity seemed to him a rebuke, a denial of his position as father, ruler of the little kingdom behind the doors of their apartment.

And over the years, she now realised, that had turned to hate.

It was dark by the time she'd finished, weary, upset, wishing all this had stayed hidden. Some things were best left unsaid. Here was her father's life, in his own hand, a testament to an existence spent despising others.

She thought of putting the diary back in its hiding place and throwing the blasted secret key in the counterfeit snuff box out of the window, to be lost in the wintry night. But then she'd disappoint another. Hamlet. The one man whose love she truly craved. Now more than ever.

There was a noise beyond the door. She closed her eyes and tried to think. Then she hid the book as best she could beneath her garments, waited for the footsteps beyond the door to recede, left the office, locking the door behind her, and scurried down the dark passage to her own bedroom.

Ophelia flew in, slammed the door behind her, put the book on her dressing table, wondered what to do.

Ordinary things, she thought. Bathe. Get dressed. Take dinner alone. Think.

And never read her father's blasted private thoughts again. That way lay lunacy, a real madness, not the feigned one of an indecisive man struggling to come to terms with a terrible truth.

"My lady," said an amused and confident voice behind her.

Angry and frightened in equal measure she turned. Voltemand stood there smirking by the bed. He'd been there all along.

"These are my private quarters," she snapped. "A gentleman doesn't enter them without my bidding."

He laughed, walked to the dressing table. She stood and blocked his way.

"But I'm no gentleman. I'm Lord Chamberlain. I go where I please. As did your father."

"If I tell Gertrude..."

"She'll shout and scream and make a million demands which Claudius will ignore." He reached for the book. "You keep a diary?"

"It's mine," she told him.

"Judging by the cover you were writing it in the womb."

"Get out!"

His hand rose, stroked her breast, his fingers curled around her throat. Close up, white teeth, neat moustache, cruel smile, he whispered, "You will bid me... enter, Ophelia. I assure you."

He took her ear lobe between finger and thumb, bent down to kiss her. Stopped when the dagger she'd slipped from his belt reached his throat, the point pricking the skin.

"One last time," she promised. "Leave me now. Or there'll be another funeral in the morning. And the king will be looking for his second Lord Chamberlain in as many days."

Voltemand retreated, still smiling.

"The harder the battle, the greater the satisfaction in victory. Another day, my lady. Not far off."

Then, with a flourish, he was gone.

She sat on the bed, shaking. Found a flask of wine. Took a swig. Looked at the leather-bound book. Felt she could hear her father's sarcastic laughter working its way out from the beneath covers.

In a fury she leapt up, ripped out the pages that mattered, hid them beneath her clothes in the drawers, and threw the rest on the fire.

There it crackled and spat and shrieked, burning on the logs and the embers, parchment pages turning in on themselves, blackening into nothing but ashes. In the end there was only the leather cover, reduced to a piece of hard, ebony skin.

This and a rotting corpse in the castle cemetery were all that remained of him now, and somehow they still seemed too much. She had what mattered. And when Hamlet returned they'd use it.

Heading north from Elsinore the waters had been millpond calm, and had stayed so as they neared Gothenburg where they pulled hard west across the Skagen spit, hugging the shore to keep a healthy distance between them and the coast. After that there was only the wide grey-green expanse of the North Sea, bleak, cold and churning beneath them. The vessel tossed relentlessly as the wind picked up, and Hamlet threw up over the side twice. He crawled back to his berth feeling weak and hollow, but the nausea didn't return.

Rosencrantz and Guildenstern took rather longer to settle. They spent all of the second day clinging to the rail, pale and greenish, but too desperate for air to heed the lashing of rain and sea spray. Their fashionable doublets with their slashed silk lining were already ruined, but for once they were too miserable to care. Everything they had been seemed forgotten. Their beards were left untrimmed, their hair tangled, the perfumes with which they usually dotted their throats and handkerchiefs abandoned, as was their clever banter, their elegant gait, their testing out of lines from popular songs... All gone.

They were like people Hamlet had only seen from afar, through the window of coaches or as he passed on horseback: vagabonds who didn't give a tinker's cuss for what anyone might think of them.

All of which made the leather satchel they had with them interesting. Hamlet hadn't noticed it right away because it was small and unadorned. Then it struck him as odd that they would carry it about with them so religiously when everything else was discarded or abandoned to their cabin. He made a point of watching them from a distance, braving the gale and the slick, lurching deck to see if they ever got anything out of it: a tonic for their seething guts, perhaps.

Nothing.

They had it with them the next day too, trading the case between them when they went to piss or puke over the side, never leaving it more than a couple of feet away. It was hard to imagine why such tedious correspondence as warrants of passage would need this kind of care.

"Feeling better, lords?" Hamlet had called to them. "We'll be there in a week if this wind holds."

They didn't respond except to nod miserably. Guildenstern attempted a wan smile, then pretended he couldn't hear over the gale, and returned to staring at the dark, foaming water. They had been too seasick to sleep, and were now close to exhaustion, particularly since they hadn't kept down any food since leaving port.

Tonight then, Hamlet thought. That would be the time.

He'd been serious when he said he hoped the voyage would be brief. These were dangerous waters, and not only because the sea itself was treacherous and brutally inconstant. The trade routes were dogged by pirates, privateers from England often operating unofficially on behalf of their king, others from Ireland or Scotland, sailing from the howling wastes of the Orkneys or Faroe Islands. There had been reports of merciless and efficient Turkish pirates coming up from Algiers...

Hamlet went back to his cabin and watched the darkening sky through the porthole.

"Your chums stumbled off to bed an hour ago," Yorick announced from the shadows. "They looked distinctly peaky to me."

The prince just nodded.

"What if they wake up?" asked the jester. "Will you serve them the way you did Polonius?"

Hamlet gave him a dangerous stare.

"What?" Yorick protested. "It's all right for you to think it but not for me to say? Apologies, Your Travesty. I forget my place."

"I'm not looking to kill anyone tonight. I just want to see their orders."

"Right. But you didn't answer my question. What if they catch you snooping? Embarrassing that. For a prince, I mean. A thief or a clown on the other hand..."

"Are you volunteering to do it for me?"

The dwarf held up his hands.

"Already been there. I told you. Burglary's not in my contract. Besides, I don't have the heart for secret nocturnal prowling or the head for state politics. You're on your own this time, chum."

"Then leave me be."

"Fine. Try not to kill anyone this time, shall we? Accidentally or otherwise."

Hamlet watched him shrink into the shadows, then brooded for another hour. When the darkness seemed complete he went out and began to pick his cautious way across the deck.

~

Two days of listless inactivity and she was bored. Ophelia had sent Gertrude a note asking for new quarters, received nothing by way of reply. Voltemand had lurked, pestered her from time to time in the apartments. But pressed no further. This was not, she felt sure, reluctance or a change of heart. Simply a question of time.

The winds of war were starting to blow around Elsinore. Rumours were sweeping the castle suggesting Fortinbras's forces had no intention of going to Poland, whatever the ailing Magnus in Norway thought. One day soon they would turn north from Copenhagen and march straight to the high-walled castle by the sea, camp outside its battlements and wait for the kingdom of Claudius to fall.

Then midway through the morning, when she was wondering whether she ought to learn to sew as her father had so often demanded, there was a knock on the door. A messenger with a letter newly arrived on a ship from Lübeck across the Baltic.

Ophelia paid him and retreated to her bedroom. The seal on it was her brother's. It appeared unbroken, but then with her father's spies they usually did.

She lay back on the bed and broke the wax, saw the familiar slanted handwriting of her brother, could feel his fury in the words.

*The Inn of The Three Wise Virgins, Lübeck, Thursday*

*Sister...*

*Scarcely am I gone from Elsinore and dread news reaches me here on the way to Paris. They say our father is dead. Worse, I hear the manner of his death. The king may be keeping it quiet – for which outrage he will answer – but I'm told he died at Hamlet's hand.*

*What do you say about your lover now? The murderer of our father? What words of excuse or justification do you have?*

*Or have you finally seen Hamlet for the treacherous lunatic he truly is?*

*I am a son and I know what I must do. Anyone implicated in our father's death – prince, king or whoever, will answer for it with their lives the moment I return. Which will be soon.*

*I talked long with our father about your perfidious, immoral dalliance with the prince. I know – even if you don't – how much it hurt him. The idea that his own daughter far from being the chaste and modest young woman she pretended was nothing more than a hussy for the court.*

*These crimes against him I may one day forgive. But warn your lover of my coming vengeance... and this I swear: your blood will mark my sword as easily as his.*

*Find yourself a forgiving husband. A village idiot somewhere. Or a convent where you can spend your days in solitary silence for all the sins you've committed.*

*Do that yourself or I will command it on my return. In my grief a righteous anger burns. Hamlet shall bear the brunt of it. But you too, should you be rash enough to stand in my way.*

*Our father's dead. I will exact a bloody retribution for his murder. Mark those words. Think on them. Expect me in Elsinore soon. Then we'll have a reckoning, you and me and him.*

*Your brother who once loved you.*

*Laertes*

~

The ship had only four cabins, two for the captain and his first mate, two for wealthy passengers who wanted some vestige of privacy. Rosencrantz and Guildenstern shared the one on the port side. There was no lock on the door, but Hamlet listened for a long moment, eyes clenched shut, before trying it.

It opened with a low squeak. He froze, poised to run if he heard anything from inside. They would never know it was him. They might guess but they couldn't possibly see.

Still nothing. A single sighing snore from the left bunk. Then a creaking groan from the rolling ship itself, far louder than the noise the door had made.

Hamlet took a careful breath and stepped inside, gently pulling the door behind him.

It was close in the cabin, the air fetid with the aroma of old vomit. There would be an oil lamp hanging somewhere, but it had been blown out so the room was utterly dark. He dropped into a squat, cautiously spread his hands and, with infinite care, inched forward, feeling for the ends of the bunks. He found them then, reaching further, the soft, cool flesh of a leg. Hamlet flinched away instantly, sat motionless, waiting.

Whichever of them it was rolled in his sleep, but did not wake.

Pressing on he neared the heads of the bunks, conscious that he was squatting right between the two men. As his fingers swept the wooden boards beneath the bunks his left hand snagged on something. A thin strap. Leather. With a purse-like satchel attached.

Heart thudding he fumbled for the buckle, opened it and felt inside. Odds and ends. A small knife. A ball of twine. A bottle with a stopper, probably perfume. And a letter, the envelope large and stiff, sealed with wax and bound with ribbon.

He took it out, closed up the satchel and pushed it back where he had found it, then crawled to the door. Moments later he was back on deck and walking briskly to his berth, the letter slipped beneath his shirt, pressed tightly to his heart.

~

A DAY SHE WAITED. Nervous. Uncertain what to do. Then she walked down to the harbour, talked to the sailors there. A ship was leaving for Lübeck early the next morning, expected to arrive the following day. Once a vessel had quit the harbour there was no bringing it back. No chance for Voltemand's spies to intervene before Laertes heard what she had to tell him.

It took only money to persuade the captain to take a private letter to the Inn of the Three Wise Virgins. Then she had a long and empty evening to write it. A night in which to be more candid with her distant brother than she'd ever managed in their father's lifetime.

She told the servants she had a headache and was retiring to her bed. Even Voltemand would never dare to disturb her there.

Then, at the small table in the cold room, she took out her quill, the inkwell, and began to write.

~

ON THE OTHER side of the castle in the royal quarters, the king and queen sat alone in an uneasy silence, barely touching the food set before them.

Finally Gertrude leaned over, stole a piece of meat from his plate and said, "Not hungry, sir?"

"Affairs of state," Claudius grumbled.

"Perhaps you should share the burden with your consort?"

"Do you know about wars, madam? About intrigue?"

She laughed.

"We both know plenty about the latter, don't we?"

He got up to go. Her hand stayed him.

"Don't be cold with me, Claudius. We undertook a long journey here. Together."

"Together? You think that?"

"I believed so. Is there news of Hamlet? When will he be in London?"

"I'm only King of Denmark. Not the wind and the tides."

"What will he do once he's there?"

"As I told you! Matters of state. No business of yours."

"He's my son. Your nephew. You said your preferred heir, should the lords wish it."

"The lords... the lords... What they wish and what they say they wish may be two very different things."

She nodded, felt she understood.

"Who schemes against you?"

"Who doesn't? If Fortinbras goes on to Poland I'll be applauded victor for my diplomacy. If he comes here hunting territory... who knows?"

"This creature of yours... Voltemand..."

"...is the only loyal servant I have. Don't get between us, Gertrude."

"And yet I never met the man before. Why is that?"

"Because you are queen and I am king. There are matters which lie beyond your interest..."

"I hurried into this union, Claudius! It helped you to the throne."

He shook his head.

"Was that why we married then? To put a crown on my head?"

"No!" He'd never reduced her to tears, unlike his brother. "We used to share..."

"Like he did? My brother beat you black and blue and all I could do was watch. He bedded anything he felt like. Didn't even look at his own son. And here you are. Questioning me..."

She didn't take her eyes off him.

"I loathed that man. As he loathed me. You know that, Claudius. But ever since the day he died it's as if there's been a poison in this place. Worming its way into our lives. Our minds. Our bed..."

"Then find another! Go back to your old quarters. Where you retreated when you realised what you'd married before. Stay there. I've a kingdom in crisis. Perhaps a foreign army on the way. If..."

"I wear your ring because I love you!" Her voice was too high, too loud. She knew it and wondered if the servants might hear. "Because I believed you loved me. Not a throne. Not a piece of metal..."

"And you doubt that now?"

He looked both hurt and angry then. With a beard and a few scars he might have been his brother. Or himself, seized by the dead man's shade.

She looked into his face and whispered, "There's a venom in this place, husband. I don't know how it got here. Or how we make it go away. But it's among us. I know you feel it, just as I do."

The King nodded.

"Then I'll leach the venom from our veins. And if the blame's mine for some reason I'll take that on my shoulders. This misery..." He leaned back, closed his eyes. "It seems to go on forever. But I will deal with it as best I can."

He got up from the table then and she didn't try to stop him.

"Perhaps it would be best if you thought of quitting Elsinore for a while, Gertrude..."

"I will not leave you! Not if an army's on the way."

He was silent.

"Not unless you ask it, sir."

There was a sadness and resignation in his face at that moment. Defeat too, and that was new.

"I ask nothing of you, wife, except your love. Which in the present circumstances is, I see, a demand too far. Retire to your old quarters, Gertrude. Keep with your women."

"Claudius..."

"I will restore equilibrium to this land. One way or another. If this world is out of kilter I will right it. If not me... then who?"

"The man who made it so," she whispered, watching him intently.

He called for the servants.

"It's been two months since those quarters of yours were occupied. If there's anything you need for them then order it. No need to ask."

~

THE LETTER BORE THE FORMAL, spidery hand of Polonius. In the cramped cabin Hamlet held it close to the candle flame reading the contents in disbelief.

"Well?" Yorick asked. "Let me guess. They're planning to throw you a birthday party and needed the English royal court to lay on currant buns, whores and fireworks?"

"Quiet, fool. I'm busy."

He went through each line again. There could be no mistake. The directions were clear. This was a direct communication on behalf of Claudius to the English king and it contained a simple request. That – in accord with their recent treaties and the state of goodwill between their nations – England should do what Denmark could not without unsettling the stability of the country. Put Prince Hamlet, who accompanied the letter carriers, to death immediately as a material threat to both their nations.

He scanned it one last time, then thrust it into Yorick's hands.

"See for yourself."

The jester read, his eyes widening. For once he looked shocked before that familiar, cunning grin returned and he asked simply, "Surprised?"

Hamlet lay on the bed, eyes closed.

"A little."

"Well I'm not," Yorick declared. "Look on the bright side."

Hamlet got up, puzzled and stared at him.

"I'm in a puke-filled tub on the way to England. Carrying my own death warrant. The bright side?"

Yorick punched his arm.

"The decision's made for you. The gloves have come off. Now you can put away your student act and become your true self." He swept the air with an imaginary rapier. "A man of action. Vengeance personified."

"We have to get back to Denmark," Hamlet noted.

The pretend sword went down.

"Oh yes. That. Might prove tricky. Unless you intend to kill all on board here and somehow steer us back to Elsinore by yourself. Do you know your way around a boat? I don't."

"I'll think of something."

It was a feeble reply and they both knew it.

"And in the meantime?" Yorick prompted, waggling the letter under his nose. "What about this?"

Hamlet rooted around the bottom of his personal trunk and pulled out a velvet bag containing a stick of sealing wax and a gold signet ring.

"My father's. It has the royal court of arms on it and is therefore..."

"The same seal as the one Polonius used to close the letter," Yorick declared, raising a stubby finger. "So you can close it up and they'll be none the wiser. Clever boy!"

The Prince looked at him and sighed with disappointment.

"Is that really the best you can do?"

"Well, yes," the jester admitted. "I mean. I'm the humorous sort. Not good at sneaky..."

"I can change the letter, Yorick! Rewrite it. *Then* reseal it. And the English will never know. Nor those two treacherous halfwits either."

Yorick considered this.

"Blimey. You're born to this. What are you going to say?"

Hamlet didn't answer. He plucked out a pen, an ink bottle and a piece of plain parchment then began to write. When he'd added the final instruction for the English king the jester read through it and stared at him with horror in his eyes.

"Isn't that just a touch excessive? In the circumstances? I mean, I know what I said about that pair but..."

Hamlet folded the letter back into the original envelope then reached for a candle and the wax.

"Ah the power of princes," the jester sighed. "To determine the fate of ordinary men with a few lines of ink on parchment and a royal ring."

"They had it coming," Hamlet muttered and dribbled the red liquid across the paper.

*Elsinore, Thursday*

*Dearest Brother*

*Know that I love you. Know that what I speak now is the grim truth, and that if any but you see it I shall be dead before you return to Danish shores.*

*Yes, Hamlet killed our father. Yes, it was a cruel and shocking deed. But before you sit in judgement on the prince understand this: he, like us, is wronged. By our father, by Claudius. Perhaps by his mother too – that I cannot tell.*

*Since his death, prompted by Hamlet's suspicions, I have found proof in our father's private papers. The necessary pages I've kept; the rest destroyed, for my own safety and for the sanity of our family. We both knew our father for a secretive, callous man. Our duty to him does not make us blind. He hated me. You he found lacking in the mettle he expected. Do not ask for details. I've read his most private thoughts, set down in every last detail. In time I hope to forget them. Perhaps remember those rare moments when he seemed to love us, or at least showed a little respect.*

*If only the largest crime that could be laid at his door was that of a neglectful parent...*

At this point Ophelia broke off, went to the door and checked there was no one near. When she returned to the page the words there seemed so meagre and inadequate. Hers had never been a close, frank family. But now the paucity of her prose seemed to damn them as much as the knowledge she had to impart.

She retrieved the quill.

*Here is the greater crime, brother. It's set down day by day in his own hand, from the inception to the act. Not long before Old Hamlet died, the jester, Yorick, saw Claudius and Gertrude together in a hunting lodge in the forest. He informed the old king. In return for his honesty, Yorick was executed, to keep him quiet it seems. Our father was summoned by Old Hamlet and ordered to plot the further downfall of both of them, the king's brother and his queen. There was to be no trial, no public accusations. Both were to be murdered quietly, by poison in the case of Gertrude and by a hunting accident for Claudius.*

*This is set down in the familiar hand we both know, signed by Polonius, written in the dry and unemotional fashion with which he managed the realm.*

*Perhaps it's to his credit that he told the king he'd organise the deed then did the very opposite. I am an innocent in politics. I only knew Old Hamlet to be warlike, surly and cruel. But I never understood the hatred and the fear he generated in his own nobility. Our father did and appreciated how this might be used to his benefit. So instead of organising their murder he told Claudius of the plot that was afoot, and between them they planned the killing of the king instead.*

*It's all here in black and white. How Polonius took advice on poison from a nobleman named Voltemand in Copenhagen, whose wife, being Italian, was familiar with potions from the Medici court. How he paid this creature for the substance and the instructions on how to use it. And how Claudius himself performed the deed, pouring the foul mixture into Hamlet's ear while the king was numb with drink, then blaming the death on an imaginary viper within the castle walls.*

*There. You know it now. Believe me, brother. For this is true. I can show you the pages, the cost of the venom, the instructions on how it was to be administered. The concessions Polonius demanded from Claudius in return for gaining the support of the nobles for the throne when it fell vacant.*

*Every word I read in horror, understanding it to be true.*

*Hamlet also knows and this is why he is as he is. A murderer. A man bent on vengeance. Much like you.*

*A son who has been wronged. An innocent cheated by his own father. A decent man struggling to know which way to turn in a world that is falling into bloody anarchy and chaos. Also much like you.*

*Do not be hasty in your actions. Do not mention a word of this to any soul about you. We live in perilous times, where right and wrong, good and evil, meet each other in the dark night and fail to recognise themselves for what they are.*

*I am your ever-loving sister. Come back to Elsinore. Stay your sword till we have spoken. Hear me out, brother. Mark my words.*

*And then...*

Ophelia stopped writing, lost for what to say. Everything she thought certain in the world now seemed false and treacherous. Every inch of Elsinore full of danger.

*Then between us – as brother and sister! – we will decide what's to be done. Beware of this Voltemand above all else. He is a sly and crooked man, and has seized our father's old position, given to him by Claudius for reasons you must now understand full well.*

*And when you've read this letter burn it. That is the last thing I demand until we meet.*

*Your loving sister.*

*Ophelia*

~

Replacing the envelope in Rosencrantz and Guildenstern's leather satchel proved far easier than stealing it. The darkness didn't bother him since he knew the layout of the cabin. The two men remained sound asleep throughout. In a minute it was done. If he was honest, Hamlet was glad that it was still too dark to see their faces. They had, after all, been friends of his once. Acquaintances, anyway. If they hadn't betrayed him they might have had nothing to fear.

As he closed the cabin door behind him he turned to find himself face to face with the first mate, a huge, weather-beaten man with a mane of red hair. A moment of tension and fear, trying to think of how to explain what he was doing.

Then the sailor stepped around him and kept moving with such urgency that Hamlet sensed something was wrong. And it had nothing to do with dignitaries stealing in and out of each other's cabins.

On the deck outside someone was yelling.

"What's happening?" Hamlet called after the man.

"Don't know yet," said the burly mate. "Looks like we have a ship on our tail. I suggest you get under cover, sir. Leave this to us."

Still he followed the man outside. The rain had stopped. The beginnings of dawn were showing in the east. Hamlet tracked back to the stern, where another crewman was gripping the aft rail and staring into the greyness behind them.

"Where is it?"

The crewman said nothing, but pointed a gnarled finger to a shadowy vessel cutting through the breakers.

"No lights," the man said.

"Which means?"

"Don't want to be seen, do they? Probably been tracking us for hours. Even days. Now they're closing."

Ships. He knew so little about them.

"Can we outrun them?"

The sailor snorted and have him a filthy look.

"You got a weapon, sir?"

"A sword. In my berth."

"I'd find it if I were you," the man grunted. "We got pirates calling."

In Elsinore the ship's captain was barking at his men impatiently when Ophelia hurried back to the harbour. It was barely daylight. What looked like the last goods were being hauled onto the small trading vessel. The man glared at her and shook his head when she came to the foot of the gangplank and held out the sealed envelope.

"You're late, lady. And so am I. Should I ask the tide to wait too?"

"Your ship's not yet laden, sir. You wouldn't be gone yet whether I'd got here earlier or not."

He grinned.

"You are a smart one. And the money?"

She held out the purse. There was a man close by she recognised. Reynaldo, a bookkeeper who often spoke with her father. Why he should be on a ship going south she couldn't imagine...

"You're not going to get me into trouble, are you?" the captain asked. "They hang spies here. In Lübeck too. Hang people who carry their secret messages too."

Ophelia laughed.

"Do I look like a spy?"

"If you could tell a spy from the way they looked they wouldn't be spies, would they?"

"This concerns a simple, emotional issue written in confidence," she insisted, holding out the envelope. "Nothing more. A matter of the heart."

He grimaced.

"I may be a ship's captain, love. But I know enough to understand emotions are rarely simple. It's to your brother, isn't it?"

He was wavering. She'd no idea what else she could offer. The last crates were on board. The ship's mate was calling for the remainder of the crew to get on board.

"It's to Laertes, yes. Son of Polonius. The master of spies here. A man whose authority you'd never dare question if he was alive. Will you carry it or not, sir?"

He sniffed and took the envelope.

"You're a pretty one. I'll say that. Best get hanged for beauty, eh?"

She handed over the purse and thanked him.

The captain turned to his crew and bellowed, "All on board who wants to travel. Anyone who don't can bugger off now."

The young bookkeeper hurried down the gangplank ahead of her. Perhaps dealing with paperwork, she reckoned.

Then Ophelia retired to the shadows of a warehouse by the quay and watched the wooden trader raise sail, heading out into the flat waters of the Øresund. One day and she'd be at the foot of the Baltic in Lübeck and Laertes would have her letter.

She stayed long enough to see the ship turn and head off on the southerly wind. Then she returned to the castle, locked herself in the quarters, knew how hard it would be to wait for an answer. And if none came?

There would be a stratagem for that too. She found more paper, and began to write.

So caught up in the act she never once went to the window, never saw a swift customs cutter leave harbour to chase after the trader's vessel, a man in black in the prow, watching as the two vessels closed.

Hamlet's ship was small and meant for commerce, not battle. There was only a pair of small, crude cannons for defence. He watched with sour apprehension as these were brought to the stern and loaded with chain.

"Aim for the rigging!" roared the captain.

Slowing the pirate ship down was their only chance of escape, and it was a slim one. Now that the sun was higher they could see that the enemy vessel was sleek and trim, high in the water and arrayed along its side with serious artillery.

"Why aren't they shooting?" asked Guildenstern, pale with fear.

"Because they want the ship," Hamlet told him. "They're going to board us."

The first cannon blast missed entirely. The second cut a rope or two and slashed the edge of one sail. Still the pirate ship came on hard, nosing away as it got close so that the two vessels were side by side only twenty yards apart. The sky darkened. Hamlet looked up to see a dozen or more grappling irons raining down on them trailing ropes. They scraped along the deck, shedding splinters, then snagged fast. Men opposite, faces visible, grim and violent, heaved and the two ships ground together, the sea beneath them spouting, as the boarding planks slammed down and climbing nets flew across.

The pirate ship's rail was suddenly a mass of bodies vaulting over and streaming across, clubs and cutlasses and axes in their hands.

The captain was cocking a snaplock pistol, grim-faced.

"What are our chances?" Rosencrantz asked.

"If they take the ship they'll kill us all and chuck us in the briny. That answer your question?"

"I meant what are our chances of fighting them off."

The captain took a deep breath and glared at him.

"The only chance is if we cripple their sails. Then we might get away. If it comes to a pitched battle we've had it."

He shook his head and aimed his pistol at one of the brutes who was crossing the nearest boarding plank. There was a cry, a curse, a rush of air and then a crossbow bolt was sprouting from his chest. The captain fell backwards, dead before he hit the planking.

Rosencrantz and Guildenstern backed away. Hamlet dropped to the corpse, snatched up the pistol, aimed and fired in one quick motion, felling the closest boarder who tumbled screaming into the sea. Then he snatched out his rapier and stepped up onto the plank.

The blade was too long for deck fighting but out here, where he had room to thrust and couldn't be hemmed in by enemies with cutting swords, he might do better. One more step along the plank, out over the dark water. The next pirate brandished a pair of hatchets, hesitated, roared and ran at him. Hamlet held his ground, dropped the tip of his sword under the wild axe parry and lunged precisely, pulling the blade from his heart before he fell.

There was a space behind the man. Without thinking, Hamlet ran forward, spitted the next pirate on his sword before he was halfway along the plank then leapt onto the enemy deck . The pirate crew was intent on boarding the trader, not being invaded itself, and in the smoky hue and cry of battle Hamlet found he had gone unnoticed.

He returned to the man he'd killed and took from his bloody hand a battle axe with a broad half-moon blade then moved on to the nearest mast and started hacking ropes.

Behind him the battle was a chaos of screaming and shouting. From time to time there came the flat crack of a pistol but mostly it was hand-to-hand combat. Beyond the crash of metal against metal there was little to distract him. Another rope he slashed with his sword, and then the next. With the third a spar came swinging free and the wind fell from the sail.

Finally that got the pirates' attention.

Two men came for him. The first he met with the axe, leaping and swinging so that he caught the raider just above the elbow. The man crumpled to the deck, screaming. Hamlet turned to face the other, dragging his rapier from its scabbard, advancing on him, shoulder first, as if they were in fencing school. The pirate grinned at that, and came on slashing with his cutlass.

Hamlet gave ground, caught the squat weapon on his sword in his right hand as he swung the axe with his left. The pirate saw the blade too late, and as he flinched away it caught him in the side.

Another down and no one else near. He went back to work on the rigging, moving to the central mast, cutting at everything he found. A rope whipped past his head. The mainsail seemed to deflate like an old balloon.

Instantly the ship groaned as its momentum stalled. Two of the boarding planks were yanked back and fell into the sea with the men still on them. The nets tensed and it was suddenly clear that the merchant ship was breaking free. On the other side the sailors were breaking from the pirates in order to cut the grappling lines.

"Back to the ship!" shouted one of the pirates, Irish by the sound of his voice.

Good idea, Hamlet thought.

But in his case easier said than done. As he scanned the deck for a point to cross there were only pirates coming towards him. He grabbed one of the hanging ropes and started running for the side, leaping out over the water only for the long sweep to swing him back to the pirate vessel in a broad arc.

Then the ships parted. The trader rocked into the wind and freedom. Hamlet looked down, knowing he'd never reach it. Knowing, too, that if he dropped into the water the pirates would watch him get ploughed beneath their hull.

Death had rarely been far from his thoughts these past weeks. But never like this.

Then he heard a cry. His name.

"Hamlet! Prince! Oh... Hamlet! Dearest sir..."

Not Yorick. This was a long, wavering cry full of anguish and despair. The rope returned to the enemy ship. Hamlet dropped to the deck and in an instant four powerful arms grabbed him then a knife went to his throat.

This was all unreal. He barely noticed. All he could think of was the man who'd called out his name with such terrible sadness. It was Guildenstern. The fat little fool sent to Wittenberg by Polonius to pose as a friend when in truth he was nothing more than a spy.

Not a bad man. Just a weak one. A friend almost. One who, only hours before, Hamlet had despatched to a grim and certain death.

Two hundred miles south on the rolling waters of the Øresund there was an uneasy standoff between the king's vessel and the ship bound for Lübeck.

Four soldiers came on board with Voltemand, hands on weapons, ready to draw. Reynaldo the bookkeeper with one, pointing out the man he wanted. All eyes were on the ship's captain as the Lord Chamberlain of Denmark ordered him into the small cabin.

"We are, I think, correctly ordered when it comes to duties and documents, sir," the skipper said in a friendly tone. "If a mistake's been made it's an oversight, nothing more. We're all good Danes and wish to do what we can for our country. If..."

He looked at Reynaldo.

"You were supposed to be on board with us, lad. It's not our fault we left without you. A ship don't wait on passengers. No use calling in fine lords to pull us back when you're too bloody tardy to..."

"Quiet," Voltemand ordered. "This is nothing to do with your passengers. A woman gave you a letter to carry to Lübeck."

The captain laughed.

"We carry all manner of cargo, sir. Salt herring and cod. Fabrics. Hard spirits. They love that over there..."

Voltemand was on him, fingers at his throat. The two men behind drew their swords.

"If you toy with me I'll have you hanged, drawn and quartered before the morning's out. We'll stick your head on a pike for your wife to laugh at..."

"A letter?"

"A young woman named Ophelia paid you to carry it. Reynaldo here saw everything."

The ship's master smiled at the young spy.

"Well isn't he the clever one? The lady said it was a private message of an emotional nature. Nothing to do with matters of state. Simply a note to her brother in Lübeck. I..." He glanced towards the worried crew beyond the door. "No one on this ship would help or harbour any enemy of the king."

"Give," Voltemand ordered.

The captain reached inside his jacket and handed over the envelope.

"And the money she paid. You won't be earning that now, will you?"

The Danish marks were still in the little leather purse she'd used. He hadn't even counted them.

"May we resume our journey now, my lord?"

"Do that. Make no contact with Laertes in Lübeck. After that find yourself another route to ply. I've no wish to see you back in Elsinore before spring's out."

The captain shook his head.

"We've family, sir. Mouths to feed. Children to keep."

Voltemand ripped open the envelope and started to read. Then looked at him.

"And what if they're orphans? Offspring of traitors whose estates have been seized for their sedition? Who'll feed them then?"

He called his men to get ready to return to the cutter.

"Keep silent," Voltemand ordered. "Keep distant. Then, if you're lucky and I'm willing, you may live."

ONE HOUR later the new Lord Chamberlain was in the study of the king, brandishing the letter.

"This is treason. Treachery plain and simple."

Claudius looked at the careful, intelligent writing. Read the affection and concern between the lines.

"It's the truth," he said softly. "Isn't it?"

The man in front of him laughed.

"Treason usually is. If it wasn't why would it worry us?"

"The girl's lost her father." Claudius pushed the letter away. "She's distressed. Alone without her brother." He stared at Voltemand. "Forced to stay in a familiar apartment with a stranger she may find... hostile."

"The wench is trying to inflame your nephew. I suspected something was amiss with her from the start."

Claudius shook his head.

"There's another letter damning Hamlet. One that carries my seal and the words your predecessor put in my mouth. What does it matter if she thinks Hamlet's coming back for his vengeance? Within a week he'll be dead in London and I'll be damned twice over, for killing a father and his son."

Voltemand seemed taken aback by this news.

"Polonius ordered his death? Or you?"

"It was the old man's notion. I merely... acquiesced. As I usually do. Does it matter?"

"It's not just Hamlet the girl wants to toy with. Her brother..."

Claudius shook his head.

"I've enough blood on my hands already. Her brother's a decent man. He thinks she's mad in any case. Sent that way by Hamlet ..."

"Laertes won't be in Lübeck forever. He'll come back here. She'll tell him to his face what she tried to say in this letter."

Claudius gazed at the window. This cold season seemed endless. As if his brother's death had condemned the kingdom to perpetual winter.

"What would you have me do, Voltemand? My conscience labours under the weight of my brother's murder. And though I did not shed it the blood of Polonius is on my hands too. Hamlet, a child I adored and who once loved me, is now on a ship to a foreign land, there to die. My queen is slipping away from me and there's nothing else, no love in all the world, I seek but hers. What would you have me do, sir? Add a young girl's corpse to the list too?"

The man from Copenhagen scowled.

"A king rules. A king demands. We still have Fortinbras on manoeuvres not a few leagues from my home. This isn't a time for faint hearts. Besides..." He cast a cold and bitter glance at Claudius. "Once you're a little way into blood there's no turning back. Not unless you want to be wading through your own before long. I came here to serve you, Claudius. To build and maintain your grip upon the throne." He stabbed a finger at his chest. "But I have cares and ambitions, too. A wise monarch looks to keep those around him happy. Or pays the price."

Claudius didn't know whether to laugh or not.

"Is that a threat? Is this the position to which I'm reduced? Listening to the menaces of a man who not long ago was collecting tithes from herring fishermen in Copenhagen?"

"That money helped you seize the throne. Polonius told me. Much else besides..."

"I murdered my own brother with poison you were paid to procure!" the king yelled, slamming his fist on Ophelia's letter. "What else is there to know?"

"Nothing. I am your loyal servant. It's in my interests as much as yours that none of this... idle gossip becomes public."

"I could have you hanged."

Voltemand laughed.

"Not practical, my lord. I'd still have chance to speak before they put the noose around my neck. And those few words would damn you too..."

The king snatched a dagger from his belt and brandished it.

The man before him shook his head.

"You're not a murderer, Claudius. That's the problem. You've too much conscience about you. Too fond an association with the past to worry about what matters. The future. Although..." A wry smile. "You could order me to murder myself I suppose."

"What do you want?"

A shrug.

"The usual things. Money. Power. Security." He fixed Claudius in the eye. "Perhaps when you're gone they'll choose someone lowborn for a king."

"What? A tax collector from Denmark?"

"Taxes make the realm go round. Much more than weak and indecisive monarchs." He picked up the letter. "Hamlet may be headed for the grave but Laertes isn't. He could be here in days. What are your orders, my king?"

Silence.

"Do nothing?" Voltemand taunted him. "Or should I go to the chapel and pray for the Almighty to shine his eternal love upon Denmark, that we may live in peace and just prosperity till the end of our days?"

"Do not push me too far, sir. Even a weak king has his limits. If I didn't we wouldn't be here."

Voltemand placed the letter in his jacket, stared at Claudius impudently, kept silent.

"Do whatever you see fit, man. I don't want to know."

"Your highness..."

An exaggerated bow, a flourish of the hands, then he was gone from the room. Claudius sat miserable and distraught for a while. After a while he called for wine, strong red Frankish. Plenty of it.

Pinned to the mast, arms gripped hard by two hulking pirates, Hamlet had to stifle an urge to laugh. A third, a weasel of a man, had a pistol to his head and a powerful urge to pull the trigger.

He'd cost them their prize, a good number of men and left them adrift on the open sea. More a scholar than a man of action, was he? It would take hours to undo what a few strokes of his axe had achieved and they weren't happy about it.

"You'll pay for what you did," said the weasel, cocking his pistol and stepping back so he could have the satisfaction of watching the lead ball work its violence.

Hamlet looked at him, a resigned smile on his face.

"That's the trouble with pleasure. It always comes at a price."

"Pleasure? You thought it was fun, did you? Crippling our ship? All that bloody mayhem."

"Course it was! You're a buccaneer. A brave upon the ocean. In my place you'd have done the same. Stopping a pirate ship single-handed? If a chap of your blood doesn't recognise a spot of spirit when he sees it..."

"He has a point there," one of the big men holding him noted. "Mostly them merchant men wet their pants and chuck themselves over the side when they see us coming. This young fellow's got spunk, I'll say that for him."

Hamlet nodded in agreement.

"Thank you for that, sir. Kindly and aptly put if I may so. I'm offended your friend here seeks to play the aggrieved high party. After all you were about to butcher everyone on that ship. I don't think you have a lot of moral high ground in this matter."

"High or low, you're going in it," the weasel grumbled, looking down the sights of his gun.

"Strictly speaking you'll have to take me to shore first," Hamlet pointed out brightly. "To put me in the ground, I mean. Out here, you'll have to put me in the water, which doesn't sound quite as menacing somehow."

The little one with the gun was getting angrier by the second.

"Are you trying to be funny?"

"It's a gift, actually. Comes naturally of breeding. My father never loved me, you see. Comedy's a kind of defence..."

"My old dad was like that," the big man said and relaxed his grip a little. "A proper bastard."

"We share a sad burden, my friend," Hamlet agreed with a friendly nod. "Those lucky men who come from loving families will never understand it.

Happily I don't care whether I live or die. So shoot if you like, but don't expect me to dignify the moment with politeness. Speaking of which, you people all smell terrible. Did you know that? Are there no baths...?"

The weasel slapped him with the butt of his pistol then levelled it at his heart.

"You'll learn a little respect before you die, chum."

Hamlet could taste blood on his tongue.

"Not for the likes of you. My uncle's the king of Denmark and he can't get a civil word out of me. So what chance has a scrawny water-rat got?"

With a vile curse the one with the gun reached back to hit him again. Then a hand from behind stopped him, pushed the pirate to one side. Hamlet found himself facing a giant of a man with a tangled mass of straw coloured hair, a bloody scar down his cheek and very bright blue eyes.

"Ah," the Prince said. "Finally I'm talking to someone in authority."

The others gave ground.

"The captain, may I presume? Some insignia or sign of office might help, sir. If..."

He was brandishing a club of what looked like hard, dense wood with a knotty and irregular end, shiny from use.

Hamlet winced at the thing and said, "I suppose that'll do."

Then closed his eyes. This, he thought, was it. Hopefully it would be quick.

"Your uncle's that stuck-up bugger Claudius, King of Denmark?" the pirate asked.

One eye opened warily.

"So they tell me, sir."

"Then you're Hamlet, son of the old king?"

"If my mother can be believed, that's right."

The big man holding his arms spoke up.

"That's what that bloke on the ship called him, right as the ships separated. I heard the name. Thought it was a funny one. Fights good for a dandy, I must say."

Guildenstern, Hamlet thought, and his smile stalled.

"Don't suppose you've got some proof?" the captain asked. "I mean you wouldn't believe the lying toe rags we meet out here, all pretending they're of royal blood, hoping for a ransom." He tugged on his hair. "Don't work out well for them when we find out otherwise."

"Funnily enough. I have. If you reach into the pouch on my belt you'll find my father's seal. I don't usually carry it. Maybe God was watching over me after all. Seems unlikely, but still...."

They rifled through his things, produced the seal and studied it with comic caution before pronouncing it genuine. The weasel, who had obviously been looking forward to shooting him, looked most disappointed.

Hamlet shrugged and tried to look sympathetic.

"Life, eh? If it's any consolation the item that's worth a fortune to you lacks any value whatsoever to its owner."

"What?"

"My life, poltroon."

"I'll poltroon you..." he began, and lifted the pistol once more.

"Cut that out. The pair of you," the captain remarked just as Hamlet was about to point out that poltroon wasn't a verb. "We'll make our money yet. A royal ransom's got to be worth as much as a ragged merchant ship any day."

"Absurd, isn't it?" Hamlet agreed.

"Hoist sail! Set course for the Danish coast. And stick this one downstairs. Somewhere I can't hear him."

The bells from the chapel tower had tolled nine of the evening. Outside the weather was squally. Icy rain fell constantly. The castle felt freezing. She never went to the living room any more. That was Voltemand's, not that he used it much. The man seemed to drift around Elsinore like a ghost, sending out spies and emissaries, flitting in and out of the king's quarters then returning to write furiously at her father's old desk.

Ophelia had no idea when he went to bed. Or with whom. He had a carnal look to him she recognised. But since her first rejection he hadn't pestered her. And that seemed odd, though perhaps the man had better things to do.

In her head she could see Laertes receiving her letter. Imagine his immediate fury. Hope for some rational consideration once his temper had eased. She wasn't seeking forgiveness for Hamlet. Only understanding. When he returned from England the three of them could meet, speak frankly...

There was a settlement to be reached there surely. A recognition of past misdeeds: their father's, Hamlet's uncle's, the prince's own. Once that conversation had taken place they could, perhaps, discuss how to proceed. Their individual safety was at stake. But more than that the realm of Denmark mattered, too. There was open gossip among the servants about the threat to Elsinore from across the water, the return of Young Fortinbras to avenge his father and seize the crown for himself.

Growing up she'd found Elsinore tedious. The most exciting moments were the illicit ones spent in Hamlet's arms. Now the home she'd known forever seemed more a prison than a castle. A perilous one at that.

This night was like all the recent ones, all those to come until he returned. Spent alone in her bedroom with a plate of food from the kitchen. Reading. Thinking. Planning.

Then, finally, she would ask one of the maids to bring in hot water, fill the copper bath. And Ophelia would lie in the fragrant water, remembering his presence from the scent of his gift, staying there under the wan candlelight until the water turned cold and there was nothing to do but go to bed. Then wake to another cold day, hiding from sight, staying by the window to watch the grey Øresund, praying that a mast would appear from England or Lübeck, and with it good news.

She finished the stew and the bread. Knew she should be in bed before the next bell tolled the hour. Called the maid, got rid of the plates, watched as the young woman returned with buckets of hot water for the bath. Closed the bedroom door and locked it.

Two bottles of bath oil he'd left her. Rose from Paris, bergamot from Italy. The first she preferred. It was sweet and familiar. The bergamot had a strange, exotic fragrance, like perfumed citrus. It seemed... illicit somehow. Which was doubtless why he chose it.

Ophelia picked up the flask. A thing of beauty itself. Venetian glass from Murano he said, with a twisted surface of orange, tiny coloured beads within it. Too dainty and fine an object for the monochrome northern world of Elsinore.

But there was more to life than this. Had to be.

She went to the copper tub. The water was still too hot to touch. Another time she might have scolded the girl. But for that she would have had to wander outside her own small quarters, and might run into the man from Copenhagen with his staring, greedy eyes.

So she opened the bergamot and poured a measure into the steaming water, swirled it with the bottle, inhaled the scent. Wondered what Italy was like. Warm and full of colour, she imagined. One day...

Dreams.

That was all she had. Perhaps all there would ever be. Ophelia took off her velvet dress and then the long soft silk shirt beneath. Her undergarments. Stood naked on the cold flagstones in her bare feet then bent forward and put a finger in the water.

"Too hot," she muttered and looked up idly at the mirror by the window, not wanting to see herself because that made her think of him too. And the child they'd lost.

"You should whip the girl who fetched it," said a voice behind her.

Her head swam in the steamy perfume. For a moment she thought she might faint.

He'd slipped into the room while she was out with the maid. She knew it in an instant. And Voltemand was not a man who did anything without a firm intent.

Ophelia turned and faced him, didn't hide herself or blush.

"Leave my room now and I may forget this intrusion. Stay and I will scream until these walls fall in on themselves. I promise..."

He laughed and moved towards her. She retreated, back to the cold stone wall. His knuckles rapped the masonry beside her face. His mouth was close to hers.

"No one will hear you, Ophelia. And even if they did..."

He had very white, very even teeth. Too perfect for any man.

"They would never dare come. These are my quarters, girl. Not yours. A naked bitch inside them..." He shrugged. "Who should she belong to but me?"

Her hand flew at his crotch, caught him there, squeezed hard. He cried. Drew back his hand and whipped it across her face.

Strength in the man. She found herself flying towards the copper bath, knees grazing the floor.

Breath gone. Mind struggling for reason.

Voltemand was on her then, fingers to her throat, left hand yanking back her long blonde hair.

"I will fight you," she spat at him. "And when Gertrude hears of this..."

"Of what?"

His fingers tightened on her throat like a claw.

"Of..."

There was something in his eyes and it wasn't the lust she'd seen before.

"You flatter yourself, lady. I'm not a man for wooing. I take what I want when I desire it. And if she refuses..."

Pinned against the tub she flailed round, trying to find a weapon.

The Venetian bottle was just out of reach. There was nothing else.

"Here's my invitation," Voltemand said.

His hand came away from her hair, reached inside his jacket. Took out something that made her heart sink.

The letter to Laertes.

"Treason from a beautiful woman's still treason."

She snatched for the sheets. He threw them out of reach.

"You killed the old king. Murdered Hamlet's father."

"You shock me, girl. I did no such thing. I followed the orders of your father. And he the wishes of the man who now wears the crown. Good servants, both of us. Not criminals. Not like your lover, Hamlet..."

"Hamlet will slaughter you when he returns."

The laugh again. His sparkling eyes watched her.

"Hamlet's dead. Your father wrote out the orders himself, put the seal of Claudius on them with the king too afraid to stop him. Those fools Rosencrantz and Guildenstern carry his death warrant to the English court. As soon as your lover lands..."

He swept one finger across his throat and grinned.

"Liar!" she shrieked, and tried to catch him with her nails.

Voltemand was quick to dodge, quicker still to catch her with an elbow to the face.

It hurt. Not as much as his words.

"If your brother catches wind of these words I'll kill him, too. Perhaps I'll do it anyway. As a precaution."

"Why do you hate me, sir?" she asked, slyly reaching for the bottle.

His handsome face creased with irritation.

"Why? Because you and yours deny me what I want. So I must act for my own security. For my purse. My future. A man's what he makes of himself. Not what others give him."

He looked around the room, seemed distant for a moment. Her fingers brushed the orange glass.

"I grew up in a Copenhagen brothel. My mother was one of the bitches. I fetched beer for the stinking sailors who filled her bed – ten a day sometimes – while they screwed her. And you ask... why?"

"Just wondered," she said and got hold of the flask, brought it up, a wild blow at his head.

The glass shattered. Voltemand screamed. Blood, she saw that. And the smell of bergamot, like fragrant lemons.

Then she was on her feet, slipping on the wet tiles, heading for the door and safety. Willing to run naked all the way to the queen's quarters and throw herself on Gertrude's mercy.

It wasn't treason. It was justice. And the queen herself had the right to know.

One step from the door and she stumbled, caught by a stool hidden in the shadows. Went down hard onto the stone, a shriek rising in her throat.

But not for long. Voltemand's face was in hers then. Blood on his cheek, fury in his bright eyes.

"I'd thought we'd have a little sport first, lady. But now you've ruined my mood."

His fist balled, punched straight into her face. Broke something. Her nose maybe.

More blood. Hers. And pain. He was dragging her, arms hard against her breasts. The copper tub came up. He banged her skull hard against the shiny metal.

Then she was in.

The water was still hot. It hurt against her wounds. She gasped, got sight of him. Knew then this was lost.

"I will haunt your every night...".

"No such thing as ghosts," he said and caught her hair in his right hand, forcing her down.

The scent of bergamot filled her nose, her mouth. She gasped and when she did that the water came and raced into her lungs.

Ophelia shivered. Felt both hot and cold. Tried to breathe. Her limbs flailed against the shiny metal sides of the copper bath she'd used ever since she was small. A bright and hopeful child in the strange world of Elsinore. Following the little prince then. She'd always done that.

Her lungs screamed again and now the boiling fragrant water was everywhere. Coursing through her throat, racing greedily inside, racking her body with throes and spasms.

She thought she heard him laugh. And then, held deep below the fragrant water, she heard no more.

THE LAST DAYS of the voyage had been the worst. It wasn't the weather. Guildenstern had finally got his sea legs and the crossing to England had been calmer than those first nights in the open water off the Danish coast. Nor was it a sense of imminent danger. They had, as Rosencrantz kept reminding him, survived an encounter with the most infamous pirates in the area and – apart from prince Hamlet – escaped unscathed. It was, everyone said, something of a miracle, and they celebrated all the next day, with double rations of Canary wine.

Only Guildenstern felt the weight of what had happened. He hadn't been a friend of Hamlet's. Not really. He and Rosencrantz liked to pretend otherwise because it made them feel important. That deceit had earned them a little of the King's trust, but in his heart Guildenstern knew it was a lie and so, he imagined, did Claudius. They were nobodies with little money and no real talent for anything except the pursuit of fashion. In the grand scheme of things they weren't much more than clowns, jesters like that dead dwarf whose statue straddled the laughing tortoise in Elsinore.

Had Hamlet sensed this in them? Certainly. An intelligent, educated, sensitive man would see straight to the heart of the matter where people were concerned. And under the melancholy and reflective softness there was a practical, clinical hardness about the prince, a hint of mockery about him. Oh, yes. Guildenstern was under no delusions about what Hamlet thought of him.

So he remained at a loss to explain why the capture of the prince in the battle with the pirates had depressed him so much. There was the possibility that he and Rosencrantz would feel Claudius's wrath for losing their charge before they could deliver him to England. But no one could realistically expect two students to keep a prince safe when their ship was boarded by pirates.

Guildenstern spent much of the day after the pirate episode sitting in the prow, letting the salt water spray over his face, his fancy clothes, wondering what would happen to Hamlet next. They could have killed him on the spot without realising who he was. They might torture him to death for old political grievances and send his mangled body back to Denmark as a message. Or string him from the yard arm and throw his body to the sharks.

"It's not our fault," Rosencrantz insisted for the fiftieth time when they landed in Harwich and began the long, slow ride to London. "If Hamlet wants to play the warrior hero that's up to him. Stick to the story about what happened and lose the woe-is-me face. It doesn't suit you. And besides. It's the truth isn't it?"

He had a point there. The two of them had barely spoken since they lost the prince. For years they'd been inseparable but something about this business had driven a wedge between them, pointed up all that made them different. Guildenstern doubted they would still be friends when it was over. For the first time he could remember he'd started making plans for what he would like to do next, on his own.

Maybe he would take a break from Wittenberg. Travel south to Italy, perhaps. Visit Florence, Venice, get away from the frigid climes in which he had spent his entire life. He could walk through sun-splashed piazzas, pick an orange off a tree and eat it warm...

Then come back and maybe open a tailor's shop.

They were summoned to a grim place by the river called the Tower. It looked like a prison, not a royal palace. But maybe in England they thought a gloomy fortress like this passed for grandeur.

"The Queen will see you," said the attendant in terrible Danish and went to the door.

"The Queen?" Guildenstern shook his head. "What's happened to the King?"

"There is no king of England, idiot," Rosencrantz whispered. "It's that old bag Elizabeth. Give me the papers.,"

Guildenstern fished in the leather satchel and plucked out the wax-sealed parchment.

"Bit moot now."

Rosencrantz brandished the envelope.

"This is our ticket to the inner court. It shows we're on official business. Hamlet or no Hamlet."

A pair of halberdiers escorted them to the main chamber. Rosencrantz drew himself up and plastered a serene smile on his face. Guildenstern had seen it a thousand times, but for once he wanted to slap it off him.

More regal grandeur, just like distant Elsinore. Walls hung with tapestries displaying the political and military triumphs of Elizabethan England, the ceiling a complex puzzle of gilded timber buttresses. The queen wore a long golden gown. She looked surly and a little mad, a pale, elderly figure in an obvious ginger wig over a face plastered in white makeup, hunched on an opulent throne, busy in muttered conversation with a tall, severe-looking man by his side. For a long moment she didn't seem aware of their presence at all. Then the courtier next to her smiled expansively and delivered a speech in English. It lasted almost a minute but the attendant translated it simply as "Her majesty welcomes you to England."

A court official motioned for the letter. Rosencrantz handed it over with an elegant bow and made a fussy speech about how proud they were to serve their country and the English crown.

Guildenstern thought he saw a fractional sneer ghosting the woman's lips. It reminded him of Hamlet. Feeling oddly frightened he lowered his eyes.

The silence that followed was long and worrisome. Finally he looked up, catching Rosencrantz's expression of frozen concern, then returned to study the queen.

The letter wasn't long. The parchment was just translucent enough that Guildenstern could see the shadowing of the inky scrawl through the sheet, which meant she was either a very slow reader indeed or was taking in the contents several times over.

That deathly white face was utterly blank, the kind of set nothingness that politicians favoured when they wished to keep their thoughts to themselves. At last two bleak dead eyes came up over the parchment and found the two Danes before her. Queen Elizabeth of England stared at them and passed the letter to the tall counsellor who'd delivered her message of welcome. The man scanned the lines then paused, looked slowly up at Rosencrantz and Guildenstern, eyebrows raised.

The queen struggled to her feet, smoothed down her gilt robe, glanced at the door and gave the slightest of nods. The counsellor issued an order in English. Guildenstern just about understood.

"We're dead," the fat man whispered, to no one in particular, not even the trembling compatriot by his side.

In a brisk and practised movement the two halberdiers who'd brought them began moving, weapons off their shoulders, levelled at the Danes' backs. Behind them other guards stepped hurriedly from the walls in a clatter of steel.

"What's this?" Rosencrantz demanded, his voice high and desperate, all trace of his courtly sophistication gone. "What did we do? It's not our fault we lost the Prince! We couldn't have done anything! My lord, have mercy…!"

Guildenstern tried to hold the queen's eyes as she walked unsteadily from the hall. His sad smile never reached her and he knew it. Just as he understood he would never walk the streets of Florence, pick that sweet, warm orange off the tree… Yet the world would not miss him. It had scarcely noticed his existence at all.

Rosencrantz was shrieking, wailing, begging, slipping to his knees trying to snatch at the hem of the queen's long gown as she was marched out by her entourage.

Guildenstern stayed where he was. He would have, for once, a moment of dignity. They were waiting for her to leave. That was all. A monarch gave orders. Some she didn't need to see carried out.

Then, like a gilt ghost, she was gone. They were alone with nothing but soldiers and their weapons.

He didn't move to resist, to protest, to protect himself even. And he still wore that sad, lost smile as the long, slim point of the halberd came hard and deadly through his back.

~

THE WINDS HAD STALLED. After a maddening day becalmed in the Baltic Laertes had insisted he be put ashore at Rodbyhaven on the southern coast of Lollund. From there he had ridden hard, changing horses twice at inns, and taking a local ferry to Vordinborg where he had stopped, reluctantly for the night in a room above a traders' tavern. The next morning he rose at first light and rode all the way to Elsinore. It was the most ground he'd ever covered in a single day and he arrived stinking, sweaty and exhausted, but so driven by outrage that he barely felt any of it.

His first impulse had been to march straight into the castle and corner the king: demand what he knew of the circumstances of his father's death. Hamlet had not been punished. He had – it was hard to comprehend – been sent away, rewarded for killing the king's oldest counsellor with a holiday jaunt to England. No state funeral for Polonius for fear of drawing attention to the royal identity of his killer either. Claudius would answer for that.

How, Laertes wasn't sure. Storming into the throne room alone might get him killed. But he had friends in Elsinore, and – ever his father's son – had learned to keep them close and curry favour with the common folk. As Polonius had become more enmeshed in state affairs, the management of his own property and holdings had fallen to his son, who had been careful to be seen as a just and generous land owner.

So he avoided the castle and went to the country manor house Polonius owned outside the town. There he called together the steward, all the senior servants, and the commander of the local watch whose arms Polonius's family had supplied for generations. To these people the king was no more than an idea, an abstraction most had never seen, though they lived less than three miles from Elsinore.

Laertes told them of his father's death, his shamefully private funeral in the castle grounds and laid the charge for these indignities at Claudius's feet. He said nothing of Hamlet, for fear that would complicate their anger. The prince still had a reputation and was loved in some quarters. All he wanted, he said, was an escort into Elsinore: sufficient protection to ensure he'd be heard.

Given the family's generosity over the years it wasn't much to ask. An hour later they gathered in the twilight, fifty men and boys with boathooks, harpoons, clubs, and rusty pikes. They followed in grim silence at his back, reaching Elsinore as the black winter night fell, marching into the main entrance before the sentries knew they were there. By the time the alarm was raised they were across the bridge and inside the curtain wall.

Servants fled before them. The guards scattered, awaiting orders on where to take their stand. In moments they were at the doors of the Great Hall. They were locked, but Laertes banged on them with the pommel of his sword, watching out of the corner of his eyes as the duty sentries massed at the end of the corridor, muskets and halberds trained on him.

"I demand audience with the King of Denmark!" Laertes bellowed, undaunted by the soldiers only yards away. If they attacked, his men would run or fall in seconds, but that didn't matter. His point was already made.

His men had started drumming their weapons on the stone floor. The noise was deafening. The castle soldiers, watching from both his right and his left, looked uneasy. One false move, one unsteady trigger finger, and this would be a battle, and an ugly one.

"Open these doors!" he roared. "Or as God is my witness we will break them down!"

Finally an old woman came. One of his father's maids, part of the household since he'd been a child.

She'd been crying. Her eyes were still pink and full of tears.

"Bette." He remembered her kindness when he and Ophelia were young. "This anger belongs to me. As does the mourning for my father. Where is Claudius?"

"Oh, sir. I weep for your loss."

"As do I. But it's more than a week now. Leave the wailing to me."

She didn't speak.

"I've come to speak to the king. Nothing more."

"You won't find him here," she answered, and for some reason this simple remark seemed to intensify her grief.

"Why not"

She just shook her head.

"Where's Claudius?"

"By the river. Something was discovered there this afternoon. I fear to tell you..."

He was growing tired of her evasiveness.

"What?"

"I can't say it, my lord. You should go. See for yourself. I cannot..."

Enough of crying women, he thought. The river wound from the forest, past the castle, to the Øresund.

"Where's the king's party ?"

"Close to the weir near the woods. You'll see them. Oh, what a world this has become since the old king died. I fear for..."

Laertes didn't listen. He ran through the guards, back to his mob. They were looking at him in a curious way. Frightened. Expectant. As if they'd heard something.

"We grieve for your loss, lord," one of them said warily as he went for his horse.

"I know," he answered then rode for the gates of Elsinore and the river.

A MILE beyond the castle the king had gathered his men. The river was broad and swollen by the recent rains. The small island in the middle was barely above the surface. There, pinioned to the weak, bare trees, lay a bloated naked body caught on the trunks. Face just recognisable, even a few days after death.

He'd understood what had happened the night Ophelia was reported missing by her worried household staff. Had seen the look in Voltemand's sharp, bright eyes as the two of them took in the news.

And Claudius had asked not a single question. Events had begun to fall beyond his control, almost – it now seemed – from the moment he'd slunk up on the sleeping king and poured the Copenhagen poison into his ear. One foul deed to stave off another. A necessary murder that would ensure he and Gertrude would survive. Perhaps even prosper, find a kind of happiness once more.

There were a million reasons to justify what he had done. But however many he found they didn't change the act itself. Murder, of a brother. The oldest crime. From that moment on he was damned and should have known it.

There were soldiers trying to reach her using small dinghies. But the current was so strong every time they got close to Ophelia's corpse the current swept them away. Gertrude had joined the royal party once she heard. Voltemand was directing them, acting the part. Shocked, caring, full of grief.

No news of Fortinbras. None of Hamlet either. The world turned without the bidding of the King of Denmark. It was spinning on its own. Leading somewhere he could only guess at.

Claudius watched Gertrude with her servants, standing by the water's edge. She'd stopped crying. Now she simply stared at the fast-flowing river and the sad, pale body on the tiny island just a few short, impossible yards away.

The girl's long blonde hair was filthy with mud. Her lovely face damaged by something. The rushing water perhaps. Or a darker deed.

He walked over to the Queen and said, "My lady. This is no place for you. Let the soldiers recover her under Voltemand's direction..."

"Why not?" she snapped. "He put her there, didn't he?"

Claudius blinked, struggled for the words.

"I don't know what you mean."

She took his arm, dragged him to the edge of the group, beyond the hearing of all the others.

"This morning, when we heard of her death, I received this."

Gertrude reached into her cloak and he knew what she would withdraw from it, even before he saw the brown parchment.

"A copy of a letter she sent to Laertes. She left it with one of their faithful servants. To be given to me if she died. She knew he would come for her. Did you, Claudius?"

"I... am... not the master of every single act, vile or decent, that happens in this kingdom."

She brandished the parchment in his face.

"I've made inquiries of my own. Your creature Voltemand chased after the ship that carried it. Her brother never saw this, did he?"

The King opened his hands, stayed silent.

"But you did, Claudius."

"I'm only human, love."

"Don't use that word with me."

"What? Love? It's what brought us here, isn't it? If we'd never broken our vows..."

"I killed no one! I never would..."

He took her arm, told her to speak more quietly.

"The men here will tear us both apart if they knew. Denmark's fragile. In such times it's the crown that makes the sacrifice."

"Like Old Hamlet?"

So many things he wished to say. Late at night, in the comfort of their bed. Gertrude in his arms. He'd never wanted another, not since that day he saw young Hamlet delivered from her while the king, her husband, tricked Old Fortinbras and slaughtered him on the ice before Elsinore, using his own son's new-born cries to fox the Norwegian and take off his head.

"Your vile husband knew, my love," Claudius said softly, with some real regret. "About us. He told Polonius. If the old man hadn't seen me as a better bet we'd both be dead now. What choice...?"

She didn't answer. There was hatred in her eyes.

"What else could I have done?"

"Paid for your sins. As would I..."

"He was a monster, Gertrude. He never loved you. Nor Hamlet. Not the way I did. The way I do..."

"And now my son's in England. To return... God knows when. And Ophelia's dead. Like her father."

"It was a righteous act. To kill a brute who would have taken our lives for no good reason. Simply because we enjoyed the one thing he could never have. A mutual affection. A sense of... of family."

He closed his eyes and saw there the river again, sweeping towards him. But this time it was red and rank and overflowing its banks, lapping at the grey walls of Elsinore, staining the waters of the Øresund a vivid scarlet.

"It's easy enough to open a single vein," Claudius whispered. "But precious hard to staunch all the blood that follows."

"What are we to do?"

"Survive," he murmured.

Another dinghy was trying to reach the island and the body on it. She stared at it then looked back to Elsinore.

"For this?"

"This is all there is."

"Then I want none of it. And nothing of you."

Gertrude turned and left him. Talked to the women she'd brought. And then the party returned to their horses.

There were no more boats on the river now. Perhaps the body would have to stay there until the waters abated. If that ever happened. It seemed the world was in flood and a part of Claudius couldn't wait for its cold grey all-consuming waters to reach him.

A noise behind. An angry, anguished cry.

Laertes was riding towards them, whipping his steed. Hair wild in the drizzle and breeze. Eyes as crazed as any man he'd ever seen, fixed only on the still, sad shape on the island in the foaming, furious river.

Voltemand was watching too. He glanced at Claudius. A command in his face: this is mine. I will deal with it.

So the king watched, stayed back. Listened.

"Sir..." the man from Copenhagen said as Laertes dismounted. "Be calm, I beg you. Listen to what I say..."

"What is this?" Laertes roared. "My sister!"

For a moment he just stared, pale and exhausted. Young-looking. The shock seemed to have taken the life out of him. But only for an instant. Seconds later the stunned, empty sorrow was gone. The righteous rage was back. He barked at one of the soldiers to fetch him a boat.

Voltemand stood in front of him.

"She was distraught. Your father's death. Hamlet's treatment of her..."

"Hamlet...! Where is the blasted Prince?"

The boat was dragged towards him.

"I fear she took her own life, sir. We should have noticed how distressed she'd become. I blame myself..."

"I blame him. The boat! Oars!"

The man from Copenhagen put a hand out to stop him.

"The river rages, Laertes. We need to wait for it to calm."

"Nothing's calm from now on." Laertes leapt on the boat, took the oars. Got the soldiers to push him out into the current upstream of the little island.

There was silence on the bank. All watched. None moved.

Straight away the tiny boat was swept away by the power of the flow. But Laertes had planned for that and thrust the oars in, trying to take himself to the far side.

Judged it well, too. In a matter of seconds the prow hit the tiny island, not far from her. He climbed onto the nearest stump, found a branch, lifted himself out of the dinghy which span away and turned downstream, circling on itself, out of control.

He never noticed. In three swift steps he was with her, cradling her broken face in his arms, crying, wailing, shouting curses, screams and threats.

Voltemand watched. Claudius knew this man now. Understood what he'd hoped for. That Laertes would be borne away on the surging waters, too, disappear forever, one more problem solved, another body buried for good.

"Find a rope," Claudius ordered the captain of the guard. "Get it over to the island. Shoot the thing on an arrow if need be. Once it's there we can get a boat safely over and recover them both."

Gertrude was on her horse, watching him. A cold and hateful look in her eyes. He walked towards her. Perhaps there was an explanation. An apology to be offered. But she rode off without a word.

Then Voltemand was there.

"We can manage this," he said. "The queen seems... distracted."

Claudius stared at him. If he understood what Gertrude had learned perhaps he'd plot her death, too. This was man knew no limits.

"She's upset at a young woman's unnecessary death. As am I. Can you really not appreciate that?"

"Grief can be dangerous, my lord. I've caused enough to know. Is there anything I should be told?"

"Only that we need another funeral. You can manage that. I'm sure."

"True." He nodded. "But it'll have to be in the common cemetery, with the paupers. Not the castle graveyard."

The King waited, wondered, listening to Laertes howling as he clutched his dead sister on the little island in the middle of the muddy, swollen driver.

"A suicide," Voltemand added. "The girl can't be buried in hallowed ground." He snapped his fingers at a couple of soldiers, issued some orders. "I'll see it's done. Leave everything to me."

# Quintessence of dust

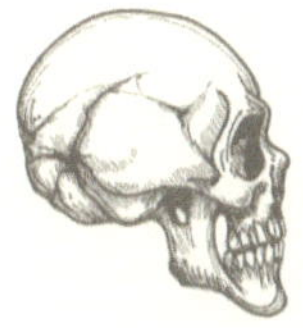

No games, Fortinbras promised the Scots. Yet that, for a difficult while, was all they got. A march south to the encampment outside Copenhagen. A tetchy standoff with the Danish locals. No word from Oslo about when the army should move on Poland.

The Norwegian prince knew what was happening. Magnus, a sick, scared old man, was keeping him away from home, organising his own succession. Buttering up the nobles who would choose the next man to wear the crown.

Blood meant nothing in the Nordic states. Unless it was spilled for glory.

And so the Scots grew restless, moaning all the time as only they could. Gregor and his men were the heart of his forces. Tough, ruthless mercenaries, ready to do anything he wished. So long as it seemed in their interest and there was treasure at the close.

In the cold, muddy fields outside Copenhagen, having to buy or barter for every bite and beer and woman, they had no such prospects. This miserable campaign appeared to be stuttering to a close without so much as a battle let alone a victory.

And in Copenhagen there stood a busy harbour. Gregor might take his men anywhere from there. Across the Baltic to Lübeck. North to

Helsinki or St Petersburg. Or out of the inner sea altogether, into the open ocean, sail for home or Europe.

They were a small but mighty force, much appreciated, expensive too. Florence, Milan, Venice... any number of troubled states would employ them without a second thought, in a land that was warm and full of plenty, rich for robbing.

Fortinbras, prince of Norway, a man who could feel the ultimate prize, the thrones of two kingdoms, slipping from him day by day, sat at the table in his campaign tent staring at a map of Europe. So many opportunities there, yet none that seemed headed his way.

Words at the door. A gruff, sarcastic voice.

"Allow Sir Gregor in," he told the guards. ". He needs no permission of you."

The Scot took the chair opposite, stared at the map.

"There," he said and planted a finger on Seville. "There." This time Florence. "There." Venice now.

"What?" Fortinbras asked.

"I have missives from all these states, my young Norwegian friend. Pleading for our presence. Offering more than a handful marks, bad beer and salt herring. We Scots bore easily. It's not good for our tempers sitting around on our arses in mud."

"Elsinore's the richest treasure in Denmark. One day's march from here. It'll take you months to reach Spain or Italy. Why not go with full purses instead of empty ones?"

Gregor laughed and scratched his grey locks.

"Because we've hung around here a week and not moved an inch towards old Claudius. Or showed any sign of it."

"Patience wins wars."

The Scot frowned.

"I told you. We're mercenaries. We fight battles. Not wars."

The Norwegian got up and went to his money chest, threw it open. The gold and silver were fast diminishing. Another week and he'd be out of funds with no easy way to replenish them.

"You want more money"?"

"We want activity, sir. I tire of saying this."

"Then..."

So few options. Fortinbras could smell Elsinore. The treasures inside it. The blood of his father leaking into the Øresund.

Another sound at the door. A messenger there, breathless, anxious.

"From Magnus?" he asked.

"Aye, sir," the man replied. "And another missive I received upon the road. From one..."

He glanced at the Scot.

"From a private source, my lord."

Gregor chuckled.

"You have spies, Fortinbras! That news cheers me up. I thought you were above such things."

The messenger deposited two letters on the table.

The first, from Magnus, was curt and to the point. The excursion to Poland was to be abandoned. Diplomacy had brought about a peaceful resolution to the dispute over taxation and borders. Fortinbras was ordered to return his forces to Norway immediately, by boat from Copenhagen. Forbidden to set foot further in Denmark. Summoned home, his troops to be disbanded, his warrant to lead armed forces withdrawn.

"How is the king?" he asked.

The messenger glanced nervously at the Scot.

"They say he fades a little more each day."

Fortinbras stabbed a finger on the parchment.

"This is not his hand."

"No, sir. I believe it was dictated by one of the nobles. They run the court since Magnus lacks the fortitude to rule."

Gregor came over, grabbed the letter, looked at Fortinbras.

"They've picked your uncle's successor already, haven't they? And once they've got your army off you..."

Fortinbras shrugged.

"Then they'll probably try and take my head. That's the way it's done in Oslo. The strongest rules."

The Scot put a hand to his arm.

"I'll have room in my boat for another. The pay's not bad so long as we find a good employer who's up for a fight. And the women in Venice..."

He cooed and made an obscene gesture with his arm.

"Don't insult me, Scot."

"I'm offering you a way out. A little gratitude wouldn't go amiss."

The second letter bore Fortinbras's name on the envelope and was unsigned. No seal. But the handwriting he knew of old.

"I'll go talk to the harbour captains," the Scot said getting to his feet. "Draw up a list of possible destinations."

"You'll stay where you are."

Gregor stopped. Fortinbras spread out the new letter across the table.

"Who sent you this?" the Scot asked.

"A well-paid turncoat in their camp."

The big man read it, nodded then shrugged.

"You reckon you can you trust him?"

"He's vain, ambitious, greedy and fearful. What do you think?"

The despatch was short, perhaps written in haste. It read, "Hamlet has gone to England and will die there. Claudius has lost his grip on the throne. Polonius, the Lord Chamberlain, is dead by Hamlet's own hand. Elsinore stands in chaos, sir. It needs a strong hand and the people themselves would welcome that. Here is an invitation, Fortinbras. Will you take it? Your friend who awaits you."

Fortinbras stared at the Scot and smiled.

"One day to prepare. One day to march. One day to win the richest prize in Denmark. After that then you can go to your whores in Venice, and afford the finest the city has to offer. Well?"

Gregor nodded.

"Well let's get started," the Scot replied.

THE JESTER TOOK a big bite of the apple in his fist, pulled an ugly face then spat out the pieces.

"Rotten to the core. Yuk. I must say I found those pirates deeply disappointing. Where was the romance? The sense of theatre? Not a single parrot or earring among them. Had I not known better I would have called them out for nothing more than common criminals."

"While we're uncommon ones?"

They were lodged in an inn in a small port somewhere south of the city. Thugs on the door under the command of a surly landlord, once a pirate himself from what he said. There was no chance of escape. Only the opportunity for ransom.

"Speak for yourself, matey," Yorick said and jumped down from the chest by the window. "I'm just an innocent bystander in this tale."

"How did you get here?" He'd been too busy during the encounter on the seas to think of Yorick and had regretted that a little later. "I thought you were still with Rosencrantz and Guildenstern."

The jester tapped his nose.

"Low cunning and sly talent. I don't wish to go into details. You've no need to know."

Hamlet shook his head.

"You get on the boat from Elsinore without my knowledge. You do the same when these cut-throats come at us on the high seas. For a clown you're more resourceful than I imagined."

The unexpected praise seemed to embarrass the little man.

"This isn't about me, is it? Haven't you noticed?"

Hamlet laughed.

"It's about your life too, Yorick. They'll hang you as readily as they'll hang me when we get back to Elsinore. Unless I can raise a rebellion. With Ophelia's help."

That seemed to discomfort him more.

"Let's get out of this hole first, shall we? One step at a time."

"Why me? Why all this attention? I don't..."

"Because my father loved you!" the jester said with obvious anger. "From the day you were born, to the day he died. He felt sorry for an intelligent and sensitive child, trapped in that grim castle with a father who didn't care for anything but conflict and blood."

"I had my mother."

"You had Claudius, too. More of a father to you than your own. Don't you recall that?"

He did. Clearly. And it made a difference, too. That was the real reason he hadn't killed his uncle at prayer. It wasn't some trumped-up religious quibble about whether the man would go to heaven or hell. It was nothing more than affection, a bond built up over the years.

"And he killed my father," Hamlet murmured.

"To save himself and Gertrude from the old king's cruel and violent wrath. You sit in judgement on so many others, Prince. Do you ever turn your searching gaze upon yourself?"

"Frequently."

"And what do you see?"

"A bigger, sadder fool than you. Why ask this? What business is it of yours?"

"I already said. I owe it my father. And there are... worse duties, my young friend."

"I'm your owner, aren't I? And you my slave. What friendship's there?"

Yorick walked to the little window and opened it. The smell of the open sea filled the room. Hamlet could just make out the shoreline and a distant horizon.

"Plenty," the jester told him. "I think. There's a world out there. If these thugs set you free why not explore it? Avoid Elsinore. Walk away from courts and kings, crowns and conspiracies. Find a life for yourself somewhere."

Hamlet looked around the little room.

"In a dump like this?"

The jester shrugged. His harlequin costume seemed scarcely dulled or dirtied by the ordeal on the sea. Nothing appeared to damage this odd little man.

"Perhaps. Life's wherever you are. Provided you're still breathing, of course."

"I promised Ophelia..."

"But you killed her father. And I doubt Laertes will be as forgiving as she."

"No." Yorick had a way of reading his thoughts. Of helping him clarify the confusion in his head. "I'm not fleeing any more. I ran from my father's ghost. From Claudius on his knees. I sought satisfaction in books and knowledge and a rational, civilised mind. But I mistook the world. It's cruel and bloody and unjust. As shifting as quicksand and it cares not a jot for the likes of us. I must face that down. Confront what's there. Hurt it as it hurts me."

Yorick came away from the window and sat on a stool in front of him.

"Don't be a silly billy. Turn round now, old chap. Back away from this mad venture. Go herd sheep somewhere. Or become a poet."

"And leave Ophelia in that hellhole? I made a vow..."

"What if she's past help? What then?"

He laughed.

"You mean promised to a minor noble. Then I'll seize the crown on my own account and take her anyway."

He bent down, touched Yorick's shoulder.

"You are my friend. No slave, little man. But I won't run away any more. Or turn back. It's Elsinore for me..."

"Even if that way lies grief and blood and pain."

The prince shrugged.

"So what's new?"

"What's new is you wish it on yourself, as much as all the others. If you could kill them all... every last man who's wronged you... Claudius even... would you do it?"

"In a heartbeat. And drag down every last damned stone of Elsinore into the bargain."

There was an expression in the jester's face he couldn't read.

"You don't believe me, do you?"

"Up to a point," the jester agreed. "But no further."

Then he clapped his hands and waddled to his feet.

"Well, I do believe it's lunch time. What'll it be? Beer and herring for a change?"

Thirty miles north in the mariners' quarter by Elsinore's harbour Horatio scanned the alley ahead, hugging his cloak about him. It was too cold to be standing around outside and the docks had become more dangerous with each passing day. Laertes had managed to rouse the town into something dangerously close to rebellion.

Elsinore felt as if it were on the edge of a dangerous precipice. Hamlet's curious absence, Polonius's bizarre death, rumours of ghosts and a Norwegian army gathering in the field in the south all made for a nervous country, and nervous people were dangerous people.

Then a page came to his room asking him to visit one of the lowlier dockside taverns after sunset to receive a private message from Hamlet. He'd pressed the boy for more but he knew nothing. And so Horatio had come reluctantly, rapier at his side, knife in his boot, and a primed pistol in his belt.

The inn was a place he would never have willingly entered, a sailor's tavern, rowdy, full of the noise and stink of the port. The harbour wasn't under lockdown yet, but the local merchants were too tense to risk much in the way of traffic with war possible every day. So the sailors, porters, shipbuilders and fitters did what they always did at times like this: they drank, argued and fought. Sometimes there were pitched battles between rival crews. Pickpockets and worse roamed everywhere. Times were hard, and so were the people enduring them.

Horatio may as well have had a sign around his neck saying, 'Rob me.' Every head turned as he took his seat at the corner of the bar. When he asked for Canary wine one of the nearest men guffawed, then took a little mincing step, arms bent at the elbows like chicken wings. Quickly he changed his order to beer but it was too late.

The man's shoulders were at least a yard across. He staggered around, dribbles of beer in his beard and the stains on his jerkin. It had been a long day's drinking.

"You from the castle?" he demanded, poking a thick finger into Horatio's chest so hard it almost knocked him off his stool.

"Just visiting," said Horatio trying to make eye contact with the landlord.

"From where?" asked the bearded man, his eyes narrowing. His two friends had turned to watch, grinning like dogs smelling a rabbit.

"Out of town," said Horatio.

"Where?" the other pressed.

"Wittenberg," said Horatio, knowing this was a mistake but unable to think of anything better. "I go to school there."

"Oooh," said one the bearded man's friends, his leer spreading. "Student. Thought as much."

"And staying in the castle as well," added the bearded man, grimly pleased with the discovery. "A friend of those stuck-up buggers keeping me and my lads from earning an honest day's pay, are you? Brought some *books* for your little holiday too, I dare say. Don't care for books myself."

"Or those who read 'em," added his mate.

"Which puts you in a bit of a pickle," the bearded man concluded. "So I think we'll go for a little walk outside, the four of us. A... tootorial. Ain't that what you call it? The subject being... what you got about you that might make the likes of us feel a bit more warmly towards your skinny little person?"

Before he could answer they dragged him off his stool and shoved him towards the door.

There was an appreciative roar from some of the bystanders. They were all stinking drunk. Horatio was wondering whether he could make a run for it. He reached under his cloak with one hand, grasped the butt of his pistol. But the bearded thug was too quick for that. He kicked his feet from under him, sent him flying down to the floor. The gun skittered under a table where someone grabbed it.

"Inside, outside... makes no difference to me," the man said, looming over him.

He pulled back a massive fist. But before he could launch the punch someone stepped in close and jammed the barrel of a long snaplock against his head. For a moment, the tavern was silent. One of the bearded man's accomplices reached for the knife in his belt but was struck hard with the pommel of a cutlass before he even saw his assailant and crumpled on the spot.

"Your name Horatio?" asked the newcomer with the pistol, not taking his eyes off the bearded man.

"I am grateful to you, sir," he answered, scrambling to his feet. "That's me."

"Message for you."

Someone thrust a letter into his hands: good parchment with a familiar wax seal.

"Read," ordered the gunman. "Then we'll talk."

Horatio staggered to the back of the room, aware of the standoff behind him, quiet, threatening words being said. Then his assailant backed off, muttering apologies to the man with the gun. And that, at least, was over.

The letter was in Hamlet's familiar handwriting and made clear that the men who'd just saved his life were none other than pirates. The one who seemed to be in charge met his gaze and grinned: one front tooth silver, the other absent entirely.

At that moment the bearded thug snatched up a stool and launched himself at him with a drunken bellow. The pirate stepped sideways, caught him with an elbow to his flank, then brought the butt of the pistol down hard on the back of his head. The man went down like an ox, unconscious before he hit the stone floor.

"Now we have a little quiet," the pirate said cheerily, turning to Horatio as if nothing had happened, "tell me, lad. Do you think we've got room for discussion here? Business to be transacted?"

The cheeky grin again.

"I do hope so. Cos if not you'll have to make your way out of here all on your own."

Horatio eyed the motionless man on the ground.

"I'll need to access to some funds, sir. But yes. We can deal."

Laertes was back, with the same company he had the previous day. The doors of the Great Hall creaked open. Seated on the throne Claudius watched as the young man strode in, rag tag band at his heels, crude weapons in their fists. They had spent the night in the castle grounds after their master had returned from the river with news of his sister's death, and their fury – which had cooled in his absence – was rekindled.

Whatever grief had dulled the edge of Laertes's outrage seemed to have already passed. He wanted answers and justice.

The guards let him through, as they had been ordered. But Claudius stopped him before the throne with a single raised hand.

"This is an outrage. Your father would never have stood for this. He'll be turning in his grave."

"The dead do not move, lord. Besides he's not here. I am and I want explanations. "

"And you're owed them," Claudius admitted.

He looked pointedly at the servants with their clubs, the farmhands and fishermen with the tools they brandished like weapons.

"But they're not."

"These are your citizens and they stand by me! They understand loyalty and the honour of my house."

Claudius turned and stared hard at them, noting how they shrank a little at that.

"It's unusual to lead a rebellion and speak of loyalty. Get rid of your... troops and we can talk."

He smiled again then, as a show of faith, turned to his own guard, and gestured with his hands, a slow downward movement, palms open. The soldiers cautiously, watchfully, lowered their weapons.

Laertes looked about him, unsure what to do. For all his defiant swagger and noble outrage he was young, out of his depth. And malleable.

Claudius waited. He felt sorry for the boy. His moment had gone. With hesitation the real danger had already passed.

"You've been wronged, Laertes. There's no denying that. Nor that I'm determined to make amends. But..." He leaned forward to emphasise the point. "This is a matter between the two of us, King and noble. Not..." He gestured at the mob. "Them."

Uneasily, knowing this was a kind of defeat, Laertes turned to his men.

"Leave now friends. With my thanks. And know – as the king does – that I may call on you again."

They went then, gratefully and without hesitation. Claudius dismissed his guards. Then took the young man into his study and poured him some wine.

"You calm down easily. When you wish it."

"I'm no fool, Claudius. I want what's mine. And I will get it."

"What's that?"

"Your nephew's head. He murdered my father. He bedded my sister and abandoned her. And now she's dead, too."

Claudius felt a stab of remorse, of guilt.

"Revenge eats everyone who seeks it. Go that way and it may devour you too. I speak as one who knows."

The young man laughed.

"You? Your brother maybe. He had enough blood on his hands. I know what you are. A quiet, civilised king. Too gentle for this present climate in my opinion and that of others." He gestured to the door. "I entered your private quarters with rough, armed men from the street. And here you are. Offering me your wine."

"Perhaps I have my reasons."

"Are they better than mine?"

"Possibly the same. You think you have good reason to kill my nephew?"

The laugh again.

"Would anyone argue with that?"

Claudius refilled his goblet, thinking about the rumours Voltemand had relayed that morning. Some sailors who'd met the vessel on the North Sea claimed it had been attacked by pirates. That Hamlet had been seized and later put ashore for ransom, perhaps intent on returning home.

"I sent Hamlet to England. He's supposed to be there for... quite a while."

"I'll wait. However long it takes."

The throne had come to Claudius through boldness, but also planning. It was in his diplomatic nature to weigh options, create several plans for possible futures to be sought. As king he'd barely need that. But perhaps it was a skill to be revived.

"It's possible he's dead already," the king said. "His ship was attacked. We don't know what happened to him."

"Then I've been denied my right to justice."

Claudius shrugged.

"Possibly. It's all rumour and gossip transmitted to me..." This thought had just occurred to him, and he knew he ought to take heed of it. "...through channels on which I may or may not rely."

"What do you want of me, sir?"

"Say Hamlet does return. He's still Prince of Denmark. You can't stab him in the night like a Roman assassin. There's..." A sudden pain afflicted the king. A headache. Nothing more than that. "There's an etiquette for royals. We must perish with more spectacle. On a deathbed surrounded by courtiers. In battle, raging against our foes."

"Hamlet and I are foes."

"But not at war. An honourable man may not murder a prince after the normal fashion. It requires forethought. Cunning. A certain theatrical skill."

Laertes nodded.

"This is beyond me. But not, it seems, you."

"I'm the king, aren't I? If Hamlet comes back will you fight him? In the open? A fair duel? By court rules?"

He snorted.

"Court rules? You mean for play? For sport? Fencing with a tipped rapier that won't so much as pierce his skin?"

"That would be the idea," Claudius agreed.

"And I surrender a loving father and my sister's lives for a game in the Great Hall?"

"Games go wrong. What seems innocuous may turn fatal. Death's a sly and cunning creature. He lies in wait in all the shadows of our lives." Claudius tried to smile, to stem the sadness. "Especially if a man puts him there."

"Tell me," Laertes said.

"I will. But first..." He nodded at the doors and the mob beyond. "After this show of force against my person I require proof of loyalty renewed."

The young man eyed him suspiciously.

"Such as?"

"Your anger's up. You want blood and don't care how you find it."

"I am the most wronged man in Elsinore! What else do you expect?"

"There may be a viper in our midst already. If so would you stamp on it with all your might? And ask me no questions?"

"Why?"

"Are you listening, boy? That's not for you to know. Will you do it?"

A moment's hesitation.

"And you will give me Hamlet when he comes?"

"The chance to take him. No head on a plate."

The young man put down the goblet and extended his hand.

"A chance is all I need. I dare damnation itself. What do you want?"

They shook. Claudius raised his goblet in a toast.

"Come to me when I demand it. And then I'll give you further instruction. As for Hamlet should he return..."

The plan had come unbidden. He had no Polonius to lean on, no man from Copenhagen to provide poison. Though there was some of that venom left, and with it possibilities.

"When you've earned my confidence we will speak more."

~

Horatio was back at Elsinore dockside, well clear of the taverns, watching a slender row boat emerge out of the dusk. Three men. One at the oars, another cloaked and muffled, the third in the stern probably covering them with a pistol under his oilskin.

When the craft reached the wall he walked from the shadows, clutching the money pouch tied to his belt.

Two men he had neither seen nor heard stepped around the corner behind him and gave him a curt nod. One was the pirate who'd saved his life in the inn. He carried the same long-barrelled pistol with which he'd laid out the bearded man, one casual finger hooked through the trigger guard.

"It's time, young lord," the pirate said. "I'm pleased to see you're a man of your word."

The boat docked. The three men in it came up the steps from the water and joined them in silence, their breath fogging the chill air, waiting. Then the cloaked figure slowly, deliberately unwound a heavy scarf and pushed back the hood of his cloak.

It was Hamlet.

Horatio's relief was so great he stepped forward and clasped the prince in a tight embrace.

In an instant the pirates' hands were on their weapons. He let go quickly.

"This is my dearest friend, sirs," Hamlet declared. "Don't be offended."

Then the prince gave him a knowing, slanted grin, and plucked the money pouch from Horatio's belt, shaking it so the coins inside shifted and clinked.

"More than I'm worth to myself, friend. But if you find value in it..."

He tossed it to the man with the gun who handed the pouch to his friend without looking at it, as if counting money was beneath him.

The pirate gave a crooked smile not unlike Hamlet's, then touched two fingers to his temple in mock salute and backed toward the ladder, the others trailing after him.

They didn't wait to watch the pirates row away.

"What now?" Hamlet asked. "Do I walk back into Elsinore and give my uncle and mother the shock of their lives?"

Horatio frowned.

"It occurred to me you might want to think things through, sir. I've been out of Elsinore these past few days organising your ransom. I'm no more familiar with recent events than you."

Hamlet took his arm.

"Well then let's ask..."

"I've secured two rooms at a coach house along the road. We can spend the night there..."

"Not you, Horatio. I want eyes and ears in the castle. Perhaps you're right and I should stay out of sight for now. But I still need to hear what's going on."

"They may know you're on your way already. Denmark's rife with all manner of gossip. There have been rumours you're hiding here, fearful to return."

"You can tell my mother then. So long as she keeps it to herself."

"How much?"

"Everything," he said, making the decision on the spot. "It's time. And let me know how she takes it. I'll stay in your tavern for now. Thinking..."

Horatio nodded.

"Like we did in Wittenberg?"

"Wittenberg was a lifetime ago. Those days are gone."

Horatio tipped his head and looked at him.

"I see that, lord. You seem.... different."

"How?"

"Calmer. More determined, maybe?"

Hamlet shrugged.

"Older. Wearier. More resigned, perhaps. It was..." He hunted for the words and opted for understatement. "A difficult though instructive voyage."

"I'll report back to you in the tavern tomorrow. If..."

"No," the prince cut in. "Not the tavern. I'll need fresh air."

"Then where?"

Hamlet thought for a moment.

"Somewhere more appropriate, Horatio. Let's say... the graveyard.

The old one. Where they bury ordinary folk. Yes." He nodded. "Make it there."

~

The next day, twenty miles north of Copenhagen, Fortinbras brought his ragtag army to a halt. The weather was vile, rain turning to snow, a bitter wind in their faces. The Norwegian men were growing ever more timid as the prospect of battle neared. Most were conscripts, forced to fight by their local lords, with little or no experience of war. They viewed the battle-hardened mercenaries with suspicion. With good reason since they knew Gregor's men would turn on them without a second thought if someone offered enough gold.

Such a short distance and still Fortinbras lacked a plan in his head. Elsinore was a formidable castle. He'd eyed that grey bastion many times as he sailed the narrow strait between Elsinore and Helsingborg. Rumour had it the place had never been taken by siege or attack. The walls were too high. The castle interior so well supplied with animals and grain it could withstand a siege for months without starvation.

He didn't have that kind of time. If they weren't inside Elsinore within a week the Scots would grow bored one last time and either depart or, more likely, cut a deal with Claudius to turn on him instead.

As he sat on his steed at the head of the column, looking at the long, bedraggled line of foot soldiers tramping in his wake, a small party came back from the advance guard. A stranger in their midst.

Fortinbras watched them bring the man. There was something familiar about him.

"Elias. I remember you from Oslo. You were an ambassador for Old Hamlet."

One of the advance guard had his sword out, aiming it towards the elderly Dane.

"Put that away," Fortinbras ordered. "We don't threaten diplomats."

The Dane laughed.

"Magnus told you to venture no further, sir. I see you are in truth embarked upon an adventure that goes against his wishes."

"My uncle's feeble and dying. Any wishes you may have heard come from the crows who peck at his corpse, not from him. I have a mind to bring some... stability to this region. A lord such as you would welcome that, surely."

The Dane nodded.

"Oh, indeed. I'm here on behalf of the new chamberlain. I think you know him, sir. You have his correspondence I believe."

"Voltemand sent you?"

The Dane drew his horse close to him. Looked serious in an instant. The guards tried to intervene, grasping his arms but not stopping his approach.

"Do you think he'd come himself? These are dangerous times, Fortinbras. Claudius trembles on the throne. His nephew's rumoured to be back in the kingdom, perhaps plotting to seize the realm for himself. The populace in Elsinore are restless and close to rebellion. No games. I lay my life on the line by being here. Get your minions' hands off me. I require words in private."

The Norwegian told them to stand down then took Elias to the edge of the line where no one else might hear.

"I must ask you again," Elias demanded. "You received the correspondence?"

"Why do you think we're here? Without it I'd be on a barque to Italy..."

"Good. Then know this. The position inside the castle grows more feverish with each passing day. Polonius's son, Laertes, has returned seeking vengeance for his father. And his sister now. Hamlet was supposed to be in England. But if it's true he's returned... The people..."

"What of them?"

"They're sheep. One moment Laertes can rouse them to near-rebellion. The next they plead for Hamlet's return, as if their incorruptible prince can set Denmark back on an honest and noble course."

"And me?"

A moment's hesitation then Elias said, "They fear you. But that's what we're taught these days, isn't it? A lord is better feared than loved. So long as they don't hate you too." He glanced around the fields. "Give them no reason for that. Leave the local populace alone. Their animals and their women."

"In that order?"

The Dane glared at him.

"I'll pretend I didn't hear that. We're not a race for grim humour."

"So I gathered. And when we get to Elsinore? How do we take it?"

"You don't. We let you in. Camp outside the east gate. Make no threats. Pillage no houses or taverns. Camp as if you were a monastery on the move."

"These men are soldiers! Ask for something I can deliver."

"If they're soldiers they'll do your bidding. Or pay the price. Wait outside the east gate until it opens. When it does treat those inside with consideration and mercy. Unless they offer resistance."

One question remained.

"And Claudius? His queen?"

"They're old and weak and tired. Gertrude still carries some popular love. To kill them would be viewed as rash and mean-spirited. If you will allow me at this stage... I will negotiate an abdication. Exile. Perhaps to one of the lesser islands."

He stared at Fortinbras.

"Is that agreed?"

"It is. And you?"

Elias took up the reins of his mount.

"Whatever reward you think fit. I must return to Elsinore now and pray no one sees me. Make your way slowly, arrive tonight and wait as I advise. Portray yourself as liberators not oppressors." He scowled. "To start with anyway. Are we clear on this?"

Fortinbras laughed.

"Elsinore must overflow with traitors. Such a quantity of messages I receive."

"The state of Denmark's changing, lord. I do what any sane man does in the circumstances. Change with it."

He gathered the reins, brought up his steed's head.

"Tomorrow. I'll see you on the throne."

And then, with a brusque word to the horse, he was gone.

Horatio lurked around the royal quarters the next morning, trying to catch the eye of a lady in waiting. It took a while but finally a woman he half-knew appeared and he told her he needed to speak to her mistress in private about her son.

An hour later, finally, he was admitted.

Gertrude closed the door herself, stood with her back to him for a silent moment, then turned briskly and motioned him into a chair.

"You've word of my son?"

No polite pleasantries about his kindness in coming, no inquiries about his schooling. Straight to it, and that was a relief.

"He's here."

"In Denmark?"

"Just outside the city."

She stood up, hands clasped to her breast, her face awash with feeling: surprise, pleasure, apprehension, but also relief.

"I thought this gossip we heard was wishful thinking. What happened in England?"

"He never reached those shores, my lady. Fortunately."

He told her about the pirate assault, Hamlet's capture, the ransom and his subsequent return to Denmark.

"Is he well?"

"Unharmed. His old self." He hesitated. "Somewhat older in his outlook I'd say."

"And this ransom...?"

"Raised within my family, madam. It's an honour..."

"An honour that will be repaid fourfold from my own coffers. But why isn't my son here to break this good news himself?"

Horatio took a deep breath. This was the part he'd been dreading. The moment where the conversation might turn on its head and see him banished from the Queen's company, or worse. If Hamlet was right, and she confided in her husband, things could go very badly indeed.

"Hamlet believes he's not safe in the castle."

"What? That's absurd. Why would he think that?"

The words of a dutiful wife, he supposed. But they came too easily and there was something beneath them, a shadow of doubt and anxiety. Even dread.

"Rosencrantz and Guildenstern carried a document which bore the king's seal. Forgive me, madam, but there's no easy way to say this. The letter demanded Hamlet's immediate execution by the English king."

She laughed, a single gasp, cut off by a hand to her mouth. Then she rose. For a moment Horatio thought she would command him to leave, and not long after he'd be dead himself. Instead she began to pace and when she spoke it was as much to herself as to him.

"That's not possible. Why would the king do such a thing? Because of Polonius? It makes no sense. Why...?" She stopped and directed the question directly at Horatio. "What reason would my husband have for wanting his nephew – my son – dead?"

"Because," said Horatio, gripping the arms of the chair, " Hamlet believes – swears – the king poisoned his father."

No laugh this time. She stared, eyes wide. This was not outrage or horror. It wasn't even doubt. She knew.

Horatio sat very still, his eyes fixed on the rush-strewn floor.

"My son shouldn't believe cruel gossip. Does he think he has... evidence? Proof?"

It wasn't a refutation or a challenge. Just a question.

"In his own mind he has no need of it."

The change which came over her was profound and instantaneous. On the bench seat she slid down into a crouch, hugging her knees to her chest like a child, tears running down her cheeks. For a long while, she stayed there, saying nothing.

"I should go," said Horatio.

"You should. Tell him something from me. Say this." Her tears had stopped, her voice was steady and low. "I knew nothing of my husband's death. Though I imagine he believes I was in some way partly responsible through my love for his uncle."

He nodded.

"Will he believe me?"

"Why shouldn't he, madam?"

"Ophelia..." Her hand to her mouth. The tears started again. "Oh my God... Ophelia..."

"I'm sorry. I've been away from Elsinore for three days arranging Hamlet's ransom. What of the lady? How...?"

"Leave me now. Leave me I beg you."

"What should I tell Hamlet about Elsinore? He aches to come here..."

"Then bring him," she cried furiously. "What's done is done. What follows no man can halt."

"And do I tell him it's safe?"

Tears streaming down her cheeks she laughed at him.

"Safe, child? *Safe?* We're human, boy. Frail and fallible. This word means... what, precisely?"

He had no answer.

"I can promise him nothing," she said. "What help I can give, he will have. For whatever that is worth. Now go." She looked at her regal dress of purple velvet. "I've a funeral to attend. And black to wear again."

Gertrude screwed her eyes tights shut.

"Black. My son's colour. He wore it before all of us. He saw the need." She glared at him, eyes ablaze. "Black, black, black... Go, Horatio! You bring news both foul and welcome. Be gone from my presence. Before I lose my reason."

THE CEMETERY WAS DESERTED except for a pair of workmen digging a grave on the western side. A thick ground mist clung to the grass. Hamlet moved slowly through the fog, black cloak billowing behind him, trying to avoid headstones rising through mist.

The sextons were always here, constantly unearthing the old bones for the charnel house or the fire, making space for the new.

"All very symbolic," Yorick declared, loping in an ungainly waddle at his heels.

"Have a little respect," said Hamlet.

"For what? Dust and clay? That's what man comes to in the end, isn't it? *Returns* to, if you believe your Bible. The stuff you might mould into a pot, or the putty for a crack in the window sill. All the great men of the past, Caesar and Alexander the Great – your sainted father too – all no more than dirt for growing plants and filling holes. Gives you a little perspective, doesn't it?"

Hamlet drifted closer to where the grave diggers were at work. One had a barrow and was dragging buckets of earth out of the pit on a rope. Another was shovelling dirt, singing nonsense songs as he laboured.

"Going to tell them to show some respect too?" asked Yorick, plucking an apple from his pocket and taking a bite.

Hamlet drew closer, kept quiet, watched. Then something like a dirty, misshapen melon was tossed up out of the grave. It bounced on the turf and rolled crazily, stopping at Hamlet's feet.

It was a skull. Could be nothing else.

Hamlet stooped and picked it up. Stained and filthy, the lower jaw had fallen away entirely and there was clay in the eye sockets.

"Quite a thing, isn't it?" Yorick said brightly. "Gazing at your own destiny. I hope you don't find it depressing. I mean... the inevitable. What's the point of going all gloomy about it?"

Hamlet's frown deepened, but he nodded.

"You think I'll look like this one day?"

"Is that a serious question?"

Hamlet sniffed the skull cautiously then thrust it away, his nose wrinkling. Yorick laughed.

"You'll need some of that fancy perfume you bought in Paris. And a lady's make up. She might need to spread it on thicker than usual..."

"Whose grave is this?" Hamlet called.

The man in the hole stopped shovelling and straightened up, flexing his back.

"Mine," he announced as if the question was idiotic.

"I meant... who is it for?"

The gravedigger still wore a bemused look.

"Dead person. At least I hope they're dead. Bit of a cock-up otherwise."

Hamlet gave him a filthy look. It didn't seem to have much effect.

"I guessed as much. What's his name?"

"It's not for a man."

"What's *her* name then?"

"Not for a woman neither," the gravedigger added, a twinkle in his eye.

"It must be one or the other."

"It's for someone who *was* a woman but is now dead."

"I knew we'd get there eventually." He retrieved the skull and held it aloft. "And whose grave was it before?"

The sexton's smile widened.

"A mad bugger, he was. Tickled me with a peacock feather once. Take a guess. Bit of a clue. He came to a sticky end."

"I've really no idea. Or time for these games."

"No? He was the king's jester. His name was..."

"Yorick," Hamlet whispered. "I remember him. Of course I do."

He gave the dwarf beside him a look which was close to anguish.

"Your father."

"My father?" the gravedigger asked. "Are you soft in the head or something? My dad was a digger of holes like me. He's safe over the other side. No sod's moving him while I'm alive. And when I'm gone..."

"No," Hamlet said wearily. "I meant... Never mind."

He turned the skull to face him and gazed into the ravaged, brown face, trying to see some vestige of the man he'd once loved. The court fool who'd carried him on his back, played with him when his father wouldn't, told jokes and shown him magic tricks. But there was nothing of Old Yorick there and no memory, however fond, could make the object any less repulsive. He offered it to the little man by his side but the dwarf just shook his head and for once was silent.

"You'd better get a move on," said the other sexton. "The funeral party's here and they got posh folk with them."

He nodded towards the cemetery gates where a group in black were escorting a coffin borne by six young men in the livery of the royal court, guards with pikes by their side.

Hamlet stood up, bewildered, scanning the faces, the women veiled in black. Horatio was there. Laertes too and, at the back, weeping, Hamlet's own mother, the king holding her arm as they picked their way across the grass.

"What's this?" Hamlet hissed. "*Who* is it?"

"I suggest you make yourself scarce, dear boy," urged the jester. "I doubt you're welcome here."

The prince dropped back behind a heavy yew tree, trusting the fog to cover his withdrawal.

The party assembled at the grave side and the priest finally spoke a name.

Ophelia.

He doubled up. It felt like a kick to the gut.

For one numb minute he crouched where he was, unable to think or feel anything. He'd no idea how she had died but his heart told him: this was fault, his responsibility. The bleak graveyard her future now, the dank, wormy earth of eternity in a pit that once held the mangled bones of an old jester.

He almost laughed at that, bitter and hollow though it was. Yorick dead at his father's hand for doing his duty, telling the truth. Perhaps that moment was the moment when this farcical tragedy began. And now it returned to its source, new bones for old, an assassin's secrets buried with them.

He fought to push down the sorrow, replace it with simple rage. It wasn't far to cross the cemetery yard. Once there he could draw his sword and plunge it into Claudius where he stood. Was that justice for her? Or brute murder? He didn't know, couldn't guess. And it was pointless to in any case. The King was surrounded by his honour guard and they'd slaughter him before he landed a single blow.

Not that he cared. About anything much any more.

He watched, hearing the dull familiar murmur of the funeral service. The coffin was lowered into the ground where old Yorick had mouldered away to fragments.

The Queen stepped forward and started scattering flowers after the casket.

Even then he might have been able to hold his peace, to keep the acid grief inside. But her brother Laertes was up and shouting, finally leaping into the grave itself.

And Hamlet could stand no more.

Out of the shadows he came, marching on, pushing through the mourners.

His mother's eyes flashed at him, an expression he couldn't read. Then Claudius, a look on the king's face of surprise and horror mingled.

The coffin had no lid as was the custom.

Laertes had his sister's body half out of the casket, a shape as stiff as a board in a white shroud. Blonde hair too clean, face so pale. A mark on her nose. Blood and bruising.

"Hamlet," Gertrude cried.

"Surprised mother?" he asked then reached the coffin, Laertes weeping over the corpse, lost to everything.

The wind was starting to howl. The mist blowing away. A new man wore the Lord Chamberlain's chain of office and stared at him, curious and aghast.

"Prince," he said. "You are welcome home."

"For a funeral, sir? Another? Elsinore seems to treat them like parties."

Laertes leapt from the grave flew at him. Two of the guards intervened, kept him back, arms held tightly.

He looked taller, stronger, older than Hamlet remembered. And his face was full of fury.

"It's true we have matters to resolve, Laertes. But not now. How did she come to this end?"

"You murdered her!" the brother cried. "As you murdered our father."

"The one but not the other. I loved Ophelia..."

"And sent her mad," this new Lord Chamberlain interrupted. "She lost her senses, sir, and threw herself in the river. It's a tragedy. But this is a sad and personal occasion. It shouldn't be damaged by discord and violence. If there's anything here to be resolved..."

"Voltemand," Hamlet said, looking at him. "I remember you now. A collector of tithes." He glanced at the chain of office. "Newly elevated I see."

He strode to the coffin. She'd fallen back onto the plain wood. Dead eyes half open. The blue he remembered had faded. There was a smell, of incense perhaps, or something more familiar.

"I'll embrace you lady one last time," he whispered and bent down, took her in his arms.

A commotion behind. Laertes was struggling to get free.

Cold clammy skin greeted Hamlet's cheek. His grip grew tighter. As he squeezed something bubbled up from her dead mouth. Liquid, water mixed with another substance. The smell again and with it a memory that seared through him like a blade.

"Bergamot?" Hamlet roared rising, letting the husk of her fall back into the casket. "Since when did the river smell of bergamot? What mischief is this...?"

A rush of bodies. Laertes came flying at him, fists pummelling, reaching for his sword.

Men intervened. Soldiers cursed and held them back with strong and certain arms.

Hamlet stared into the face raging at him. Ophelia was there somewhere. But so was Polonius.

"There's a debt to be rendered, Prince," Laertes yelled at him.

"Many," Hamlet agreed. "And for those that stand to my account I'll be responsible." He glanced at the coffin. At the silent Claudius and the weeping Gertrude. "But not your sister, sir. I never drowned her in bergamot. Any more than she did so herself."

IT WAS dark by the time the funeral party returned to the castle. Claudius and Gertrude retired to the royal quarters, Hamlet to his own. Laertes back to his sister's rooms.

When the king got to his study Elias, the old ambassador, was waiting for him. Claudius closed the door, told him to sit down and said, "Your safe return is a happy sight on this grim day, dear friend. I'm grateful for your courage and assistance. Well?"

"His army will be outside the eastern gate tonight. Tomorrow he expects entry."

"Should I allow it?"

"He says he'll let you and Gertrude enter exile. On one of the islands."

"And you believe him?"

The old man thought for a moment.

"I do. He's a decent enough man for a Norwegian. All he wants is Elsinore and the crown."

"All?"

Elias scowled.

"I'm sorry, my lord. I spend my working life trying to bring together two conflicting sides. To marry black to white. Right to wrong. To find a middle way..."

"And Gertrude will live?"

"You both will," the man said, a little puzzled. "I was adamant on that. The queen in particular carries much affection among the people. Fortinbras has no reason to enrage them. It would only make his task more difficult. Alternatively..."

He shrugged.

"The castle is well provisioned. If we hold out for a little while perhaps his Scottish mercenaries will abandon him. Should that happen our men are more than a match for the peasants he's brought from Norway. We could fight..."

"Like Old Hamlet did?"

"That was single combat, sir," Elias said carefully. "I would not advise it in these circumstances. Fortinbras is young and a warrior. You..." A wan smile. "You're older, a man more attuned to negotiation than warfare."

Claudius scowled.

"Isn't that what kings are for? To sacrifice themselves for their people?"

"Sometimes. But if we can achieve the same result without bloodshed..."

"I hear your advice, Elias. I'm grateful for it. I could have made you Lord Chamberlain. Perhaps should have." He shook his head. "Yet Polonius didn't recommend it and I always listened to him."

The old man got up.

"I bear no grudges. I serve the realm. After this I'll retire to my country estate to raise ducks and chickens. Both of which seem grateful for my attention. Until I eat them, that is. Such is life."

"And did you ask him?"

Claudius left the most important question till last.

"About intelligence?"

"Has he been receiving reports from Elsinore?" the king asked tetchily. "I made it clear..."

"Yes. Correspondence. I said I was from the new chamberlain. He volunteered the man's name himself."

Claudius sighed.

"Is there anyone in this castle I can trust save you?"

"Diplomacy takes place in no man's land, lord. It's a way of making peace with men who hate you. One must always talk to the enemy. How else may we find the middle ground?"

"Fortinbras turned round in Copenhagen and came here for a reason. He was invited. That's not diplomacy. It's treason."

Elias nodded.

"This is a delicate time. There should be room for safe passage out of

Elsinore should you wish to take it. If not we stay and fight. Either way... we've enough discord in this place already. I would advise you not to add to it."

Silence then.

"Sir?" the old man added.

"I've heard you, Elias. And thank you for your counsel. Go home now. You've served Elsinore well."

"MOTHER," Hamlet said. "You are pleased to see me, aren't you?"

She'd come to his old room, sat with him at the table. Yorick had vanished into the shadows cast by the candles near the window as he always did with visitors.

"You're my son. I feared you dead. Of course I'm pleased."

Still she didn't reach out for his hands.

"What happened to Ophelia?" he asked.

"She feared for you. She tried to send Laertes a letter telling him what the two of you believed had happened. About Claudius and your father. This new man... Voltemand... I think he got hold of it. So Laertes still hates you. And probably blames you for Ophelia..."

"This man Voltemand murdered her?"

She closed her eyes, looked ready to weep, but didn't.

"How would I know? The king and I are estranged. I don't know what his intentions are. Even if he does himself. Claudius is a gentle man by nature, trapped by circumstances. They think Elsinore could fall to Fortinbras soon. Tomorrow even. If that happens our private battles will seem irrelevant. Won't they?"

"You knew..."

"I knew none of this! What must I say to make you believe me? My sin was one of love. For a man who was kind to me. To you, too. When your father ignored us. Or bellowed in my direction." Her eyes darkened. "Or worse."

She folded her arms, hugged herself through the heavy velvet dress.

"I never realised Old Hamlet had discovered. Or that he intended to deal with us. Or that Claudius, egged on by that ambitious old fool Polonius, intended to act first."

Her voice drifted off.

"And if you had?"

She didn't answer.

"I must act," he whispered.

"Ah," said Yorick from the shadows. "More acting. Great. That's what we need."

"Quiet, fool," said Hamlet.

"Don't speak to me that way," she told him.

"Not you, mother."

"Then...?" Gertrude looked puzzled and uneasy. "You're still not well, Hamlet. It would be best if you left Elsinore."

He laughed.

"With a foreign army outside the gates? My love in a coffin?" He stared at her. "My mother torn between her conscience and her duty?"

"That burden is mine to bear, not yours." She did touch his hands briefly then. "Try and sleep. Stay in your quarters. I'll make inquiries of the harbour. Perhaps there's a ship sailing south tomorrow. A warmer land, a sunnier climate would suit you. And when matters here are clearer..."

"Mother..."

She got up and kissed him, once on the cheek, once on the lips. Then Gertrude said goodnight and left.

Yorick emerged from the corner.

"A fine and decent woman, your mother. You should listen to her."

"What? Go to Italy and learn to play the lute?"

"I could come," he said hopefully. "That statue of my father in the Great Hall? The one where he's naked on the tortoise? I told you. A Florentine made it. The original's there in the Boboli gardens of the Medici. They're a bunch of horrors but you're royal. I'm sure they'd let us take a look."

"I'm sure they would," the prince agreed, then walked to his bed and lay on the sheets.

"Shall I start packing?" the jester asked hopefully. Then he started to scamper manically round the room. "We'll need clothes for a warmer climate. And hats. New hats. Oh, summer. Remember summer? It's glorious. Down there even more so I hear. And..."

"Not now," Hamlet interrupted, worried by his sudden speed and energy. "Yorick?"

The little man stopped and looked at him. There was something lost and heart-rending in his expression. He had some clothes in his hand. The prince's. Not his own. All he ever wore was that blue and yellow harlequin suit.

"I'd have to buy you more suitable dress," the prince said. "That clown outfit's an insult. You're one of the wisest, most decent men I know."

There was an awkward moment then. It seemed the little man was crying.

"I don't need new clothes, sir. Honestly. But you... in sunnier climes. With those pretty Italian gals. Oh..." He clutched a billowing white brocade shirt to his chest. "I can see you there now. Cutting the finest figure..."

"Me, too..."

The jester went quiet. This was the first lie that had passed between them and both knew it. A bridge had been crossed. No going back.

"What now, lord?" the jester asked softly.

The prince laughed.

"Lord? Not... Your Royal Slothfulness? Prince Do-Nothing? Procrastinator General? Your Travesty? Or any of the other insults you've thrown my..."

"No," Yorick interrupted and placed a gentle hand on his forehead. "That time's past, Hamlet. You are the man you always wanted to be. Your father's son. But the better, truer part of him which the darker half managed to suppress."

His fingers came away. The prince heard his familiar footsteps patter back towards his corner.

"That's what you want to hear?" the little man asked from the shadows.

"I suppose."

"In that case my work's done."

~

The weather was worsening. A gale. Sporadic hail and rain. Claudius stood by the window in his study, watching the storm gather over the Øresund. Lightning flashes and distant rolls of thunder. Beyond the walls he could see the camp fires of the Norwegian army. Not so large. Not so brave he imagined, apart from the inevitable mercenaries. Elsinore had never been stormed. Never would be. But if the crown fell it would do so with as little blood as possible. As Elias indicated, a concordat would be reached, with Fortinbras or others. One that saved the queen, his own hide, and his citizens from the violent depredations of ravaging soldiers.

Yet such agreements had to be based on strength as much as possible. A last show of force and violence. A recognition of their mutual positions.

He'd summoned Voltemand almost an hour before. That the man was late did not surprise him. The new Lord Chamberlain scarcely sought to hide his ambition any more. He was positioning himself for the fall of the Danish crown, and the opportunities that might follow.

Halfway through the second goblet of Frankish red wine the door opened. No knocks any more. No pause before entry.

"King," Voltemand said and sat down at the desk. "You asked for me. These are hectic times..."

Claudius joined him.

"Busy indeed. News?"

A shrug.

"Laertes is furious. Hamlet's mad. The queen... I've no idea. Do you? And we have an enemy army on the doorstep."

In the distance there was the low bellow of thunder, then a flash of lightning at the window.

"These walls are thick," Claudius said. "We ride out our storms. Elsinore lasts forever. One simply has to wait."

"Elsinore is brick and stone. Kings are made of flesh and blood. There are threats here..."

Claudius stifled a yawn.

"The armoury's full. The provisions plenty. Fortinbras must feed his troops from a meagre winter countryside. And his masters in Norway don't want him here at all. I've sent couriers to Oslo asking for their assistance. They help me and I give them Jutland in return. Three days and there'll be a friendly fleet in the harbour. And this rebellious prince will hang. I'm content to wait."

Voltemand drew himself up and eyed the king.

"I was aware of no messengers. As your Lord Chamberlain..."

"You're a servant of the crown."

"All diplomatic correspondence must go through me!"

Claudius smiled.

"You were absent from your offices. No one knew where. Does a king wait on his retainers? Am I supposed to sit around like a lonely wife praying for her husband's return?"

"This post has many responsibilities. Some that a monarch never sees or appreciates."

Claudius laughed.

"You forget. I was a diplomat before I wore the crown. I know how the world works." A pause, a deliberate one. "I know that one must talk to... all sides... if a full picture of proceedings is to be had."

Voltemand's sly face fell.

"Meaning what?"

"Meaning... I understand you're an industrious man. I'm sure there are tasks yet to be done even at this hour." The king beckoned to the door. "I shouldn't keep you. The situation's simple anyway. Laertes and Hamlet will make up their differences tomorrow with a harmless fencing match before us. Court rules. No blood. Only a resolution of their difficulties. After which... we wait."

Another roll of thunder. The burst of lightning that followed seemed much closer.

"Storms pass," Claudius added. "If the ships from Norway are a day late it matters not a whit. We hold our fire. We watch the Øresund. Two days. Three. Four at the most. Then the ships from the court of Magnus are here and his nephew's head is in a noose."

He raised his glass.

"I'd offer you a drink by way of celebration. But I'm sure you've better things to do."

"True," the man grunted then got up and without another word was gone.

Claudius finished his wine. There would be more before he could sleep. A sound behind him. He didn't stir or turn. The old man, Polonius, was fond of hiding, listening, spying. It seemed a gift passed down through blood.

Laertes emerged from the vast tapestry next to the fire: Mars, the god of war, in bed with a naked Venus. In the background the shadow of her sad and cuckolded husband Vulcan, impotent in the face of lust and violence. Old Hamlet had commissioned the work from Italy and never understood the irony. Until, perhaps, the last.

"Now I know what treason sounds like," the young man said coming to the desk. "He belongs to Fortinbras, surely."

Claudius scowled at him.

"Don't be stupid! The man's a go-between. He serves no one save himself until someone wins the game." He looked Laertes up and down. Brave, strong. But he hadn't inherited Polonius's talent for espionage or cunning. "As did your father. If it were otherwise I wouldn't be here."

Laertes shifted from foot to foot, uncomfortable, gripping his dagger.

"What do you want of me?"

The King had thought this through.

"Offer Fortinbras a gift. Sure and bloody knowledge that we've recognised his strength. And met it. Make sure that should it come to negotiation he deals with me directly, not through self-serving intermediaries I cannot trust."

"And for that you'll give me Hamlet?"

The words stuck in the king's craw.

"That piece of theatre's in train already. Do you doubt my word?"

A nod and then, "I'll do it. But if the men from Norway are here in a few days we won't have to dicker with Fortinbras anyway. Will we?"

"A cautious officer of the crown plans for all eventualities." Claudius nodded at the door. "On with it. Make sure our friend out there knows he deals with men willing to be as cruel and ruthless as any he's ever met."

"Aye..."

Then he was gone.

More drink. More thunder and stark, searing flashes at the window.

For all the practice over the years Claudius had never liked lying. It seemed unworthy. Too often a way of storing up grief and trouble for the future. But sometimes...

He went through the papers on the desk. The message he'd written for the couriers to Oslo was still there. Well written. Carefully put. In it a bargain that would bring Magnus's court to his doorstep and settle Fortinbras for good. He knew that. And yet he'd never sent it.

The crown had proved too heavy. He'd only won it for Gertrude's sake. And now that murderous act had torn her from him.

If Fortinbras proved amenable under pressure...

If the two of them could escape with what remained of their lives...

The Norwegian prince was a minor obstacle along the way. One a diplomat could handle through cunning, tact and mediation.

The bigger challenge was Hamlet, his own wronged, damaged nephew.

Claudius took too greedy a swig of the wine, spilled the strong red liquid down his shirt like a tavern drunk.

Lightning lit up the window and the troubled world beyond.

"I killed your father for good reason," he murmured, still seeing the young boy only he and the jester, of all the men in the castle, had loved. "I never wanted your life too."

Yet foul deeds begat others, unseen, unimagined at the outset of the game.

He removed the slender, golden, jewel-studded crown and placed it on the desk.

A small thing: of no moment next to Gertrude.

Drink, the king thought, and yelled for his servants.

Perhaps an ocean of wine, as deep as the Øresund, might drown his sins.

Hamlet was roused by the polite cough of a young courtier standing in the doorway, an outlandish, feathered hat in his hand as he executed an elaborate bow.

With him was an embarrassed Horatio.

"Is the circus in town?" the Prince asked.

"This is Oswald," Horatio said, visibly unimpressed. "An aide in the entourage of Polonius. Laertes, now, I suppose."

"You woke me for this?"

"I bear a message from His Majesty the king," Oswald declared with another flourish of his stupid hat.

Hamlet rolled his eyes.

"Keep that bloody thing on your head. If Claudius wants to talk he knows where to find me."

The young lad looked embarrassed.

"But sir... it would be the greatest discourtesy to be behatted in the presence of the prince. A good knight's etiquette..."

The ostrich feathers twitched again.

"One more time," said Hamlet, "and I'll pluck your feathers I swear. What message?"

"The King has made an arrangement with my master, Laertes. There's to be a fencing match between you two. To clear the air. Court rules. No blood. He's bet some... swords and horses,"

"What weapon?" asked Horatio.

"Rapier and dagger. My master Laertes is rather good I must say. My money's on him."

Hamlet stood up. Oswald clutched his hat in both hands and trembled.

"Have you seen me fight then?"

"No... no..."

The Prince fished in his purse and produced a coin.

"Not much of a gambler, are you? Tell my uncle I accept the challenge. And appreciate the courtesy with which it was delivered. Horatio. Get some odds on me and put this on it."

Horatio took the money off him and said, "Done."

Oswald gave one last hurried bow and fled.

"Keep an eye on that one," Hamlet ordered.

"Of course," Horatio agreed. "Is this wise? I mean..."

"Very! I need some exercise. It clears the mind. Now..." He pointed at the door. "You too. Early night. Big day tomorrow."

When he'd gone Yorick rolled off the bed.

"Let me say from the outset I'm not enamoured of this idea, Hamlet. What kind of king goes around organising sword fights on the premises? Between nobles? One of them..." He jabbed an accusing finger. "Bearing a distinct grudge."

"Not without cause," Hamlet pointed out.

"Precisely. Kindly wipe that smartarse grin off your face. You're juggling with serpents, sonny. And you should leave juggling to the likes of me."

Hamlet took a fencing stance, waved an imaginary rapier in the air.

Yorick folded his fat arms and asked, "Florence or Rome? Milan or Venice? Which is it to be?"

"All of them, I think."

The jester's face fell. He could look quite malevolent when he wanted to.

"And when?"

The make-believe rapier slashed through the air.

"When I'm done here," Hamlet declared and dashed the invisible blade through the little man's heart.

Yorick yawned.

"Aargh. I'm dead."

Hamlet swept the imaginary rapier across his own throat.

"Not to worry," he said. "Me too."

THE CAMP WAS MUDDY, the food scarce. Fortinbras could keep his men at the foot of Elsinore's walls for a week, no more. The Scottish mercenaries he'd count in days.

And there was no word from within. No more letters. No approach from the old diplomat Elias, a man he had perhaps trusted too easily.

Gregor came in munching a bony piece of meat.

"Danish sheep are greasy and taste of muck," the big soldier grumbled.

"For a well-paid servant you whine a lot."

The man laughed.

"A Scottish habit. It's very hard to lose. Any news?"

"The eastern gate will open tomorrow."

"Your man told you that?"

The Norwegian nodded.

"Did he say when? What we're likely to meet on the other side? Fair ladies baring their breasts? Or ugly Danes brandishing their swords?"

"All in good time," Fortinbras told him.

"No such thing as good time. Just time. It's what we make of it."

"I never knew Scotland bred philosophers."

"We're a talented race. Much under-appreciated."

Fortinbras looked at him and laughed.

"I think my treasury would argue otherwise."

"We need to know some facts before we enter. The disposition of their men. The face of their politics. Whether Claudius will capitulate easily. What we may take and what we must leave. When the blood's up it's too late and I won't have you hanging my folk just because they raped some old bird when they shouldn't. We need to know the lie of this land now."

Fortinbras got up and said very slowly, "When... my... man... comes."

Gregor walked to the door of the tent. The Norwegian joined him. The storm was abating. Though still constant the thunder and lightning had moved south along the Øresund towards Copenhagen. The hailstones that followed in its wake were petering into drizzle. Soon it would be fine.

"Perhaps he doesn't like getting wet. Perhaps..."

Then he stopped. Somewhere high on the castle walls there came a cry. A shriek every soldier knew.

THE MAN from Copenhagen checked the battlements first. He wanted to see what lay between the castle and the Norwegian camp. Little but swampy earth, churned by the hooves of horses. A few guards. It wouldn't be easy. And he wouldn't be able to get back either. Perhaps Claudius had been right. He wasn't cut out for diplomacy. Voltemand wanted to find advantage, enjoy the sweet scent of victory.

Thought he had, too. He hadn't realised the king might go behind his back to Oslo. That was an oversight, one that was now impossible to retrieve.

It was time to do what any sane diplomat never countenanced. Take sides.

Kill the guards on the gate. One short walk across the quagmire separating the castle from the Norwegian camp. Then he was there. With nothing to offer but his sword. This was a bitter outcome. What power he'd possessed depended on his place in the middle, between the two opposing parties. Forced into one or the other he was just one more soldier. A lieutenant at best, dependent on the mercy and gratitude of Fortinbras.

Voltemand checked the distance between wall and tents again. The Danish guards he could manage. Any foreigners who got in his way he'd deal with as they came. If Fortinbras didn't know the men in Oslo were chasing him there might still be opportunity for some bargaining...

"No choice," he muttered, and turned for the tower stairs down to the guard room, hand on his belt, thinking of how he'd silence the men at the gate.

Three steps and then something moved behind him. Voltemand tried to turn. Tried to speak. But there was something both cold and hot at his neck. His hands found their way there automatically.

Recoiled at what they met.

In the thin light of a winter moon breaking cloud the man from Copenhagen stared at his gloved fingers. Blood dripped from them. The words he wanted failed him. His throat gagged. His eyes dimmed. Whirling round he saw a black shape moving out of his vision.

A picture then. A man had waited, come out of the shadows, slashed at him with a sword.

Found his neck, his throat. His very being.

"Why...?" he thought and couldn't say.

A face caught in the silver light then. Young, familiar. Angry and determined.

Laertes, son of Polonius, drew back his sword once more, swept it out in a fast horizontal arc that decapitated the man before him in one clean, powerful movement.

The body fell in a heap. Laertes walked over and picked up the bloody head.

Mouth agape, eyes open, trim moustache now covered in gore.

"You're a pretty sight, traitor," Laertes whispered. "And tomorrow you'll give me a better one."

Then he strode to the battlements, found a gap, leapt up onto the step.

Out into the night he bellowed, "Fortinbras, prince of Norway. I have your friend Voltemand. He wants a word."

His fingers took a tight grip of the dead man's hair. Laertes whirled the grisly head beneath his arm and propelled it out into the black night.

A thud somewhere. The sound of men coming. Curious at first. Then horrified.

~

MINUTES later in the Norwegian campaign tent Gregor looked at the thing and laughed.

"Is this your spy then, Fortinbras? Our free passage into the castle?"

The Scotsman picked up the severed head, put his ear close to the gaping, dripping mouth.

"What's that you say, pal? Everything's just wonderful, is it?"

He threw the thing into a corner.

"Don't talk much these Danes, do they? Anything else you've heard, my lord?"

"One way or another we enter Elsinore tomorrow."

"How?" Gregor demanded. "Can't scale those walls. Can't starve them out. Either you find another friend inside that place, one who's still got a mouth he can use, or we're buggered here."

"Tomorrow we go in."

The Scot picked up his gloves and looked at the dark night beyond the tent flap.

"From this point on our camp's our own, Prince. Do not enter. You or your men. If you want to speak with me you send in a minion to request it. If we're still sitting in this shit tomorrow, eating greasy lamb and polishing our blades..." He stabbed a finger across the table. "Then we'll settle this matter. Once and for all."

# Now Cracks A Noble Heart

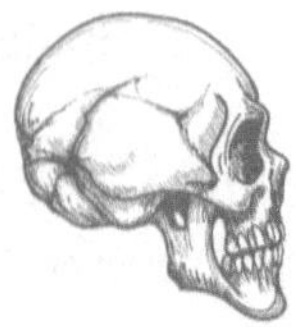

The next morning a bright sun rose over Elsinore. Gulls hung in a blue and cloudless sky above the still waters of the Øresund. Sheep grazed the fields beside the port. But no boats moved. No farmers brought their wagons into the town. A foreign army was encamped at the gate. There were rumours of defections. Of a vanished Lord Chamberlain with treacherous intentions. The court was close to chaos.

Inside the castle the atmosphere was feverish, unreal. Gossips whispered about an abdication, a pact with the Norwegian forces, discord at the summit of the royal family. And there was excitement, too, since another show was on the way, perhaps one as strange and shocking as the visit by the English players which seemed to prompt the kingdom's present crisis. Two men, a prince and a high-born noble, would settle their differences with a duel. A harmless counterfeit battle, unlike the bloody encounter on the ice between Old Hamlet and the father of Fortinbras, now threatening the very crown of Denmark.

It seemed an odd piece of theatre to offer with an enemy army at the walls. Yet these were strange times, and had seemed that way since Old Hamlet died. In the face of conflict Claudius was adamant. The duel would take place. After that distraction the business of court, of diplomacy and defence, could resume.

The Queen stayed in her quarters, solitary with her ladies-in-waiting, praying that the meeting between Hamlet and Laertes would bring to an end the bad blood that had seemed to infect the throne of late. In his room Hamlet practised with his rapier, taking guidance from Horatio, a man who seemed to know more about fencing than his mild and scholarly appearance would suggest.

Yorick was nowhere to be seen. Every inquiry of Horatio and the servants drew a blank look. The jester had vanished yet again.

So Hamlet focused on his rapier, the cut, the thrust, the thrill of action. And in that world was lost, seeing no one but himself.

Across the royal quarters, in the King's study, Claudius briefed Elias, one of the few men he'd come to trust within the court. Whatever happened this day the die were, to some extent, cast. Fortinbras would enter Elsinore, one way or another. It was important that happen on the best, least violent terms possible. With the treacherous Voltemand out of the way Elias was the only man for the job.

"You understand me fully? There's no room for doubt," Claudius asked when he'd finished as sound and detailed a diplomatic briefing as he'd given in his life.

"I believe so, sir," the old Dane answered.

"You look at me askance, Elias. Do you think I have other options?"

"If you had them, you'd take them, wouldn't you? Few men would give up the most precious thing they own so lightly."

"Nothing here's done lightly," the King snapped. Then he took his circlet of gold and silver and placed it on the desk. "And you read me wrong. I've something far more precious than this worthless bauble. Were I to lose my lady, my love..."

Elias nodded and kept quiet.

"You're a brave man," Claudius added, and patted him the shoulder. "I apologise if I seem harsh with you."

"You're the King," the old courtier said with chuckle. "You do what you like. It's not my place to question it."

"Perhaps it should be. How many battles have you fought? How many wars?"

Elias had to screw up his eyes and think about that.

"Enough. Too many. Your brother was overly fond of fighting, if I may be so bold. I did my best to seek peace where it was available. And keep the bloody side brief and confined to the military." He scowled. "Not that I was as successful as I'd like."

"You fought for your country. All I ever did was talk. And..."

"The state needs men who can negotiate and bargain," the old Dane interrupted, as if he wanted to hear no more. "Perhaps they serve the people better than warriors on occasion."

"You didn't hear me out," Claudius complained.

Elias picked up his gloves and the white flag of truce he'd brought with him.

"Best I be on my way, lord. This signal of yours...?"

"Look for it on the walls. Leave when you see it. Once this piece of theatre with my nephew and Laertes is over you'll see it again. Then you know what to do. If there's an agreement we proceed."

The old courtier didn't blink.

"And if not ... then I owe you my gratitude. And my admiration for your courage. They will honour a well-meant truce, surely?"

"Only one way of finding out," Elias answered with a grim smile.

Claudius stood up, shook his hand, wished him well then watched him leave, taking the piece of cloth with him.

After that he sat alone with his bleak thoughts and two gifts from Voltemand he still possessed, supplied by the dead man's wife, supposedly from the Medici court. A place that had the best poisoners in Europe.

The first was a vial of purple liquid, venom for a dagger. Not so different to the potion Claudius had poured into his sleeping brother's ear. The second he hesitated over. Perhaps his nephew would best his stronger, more skilled opponent. What then? His story had to end. There was no reconciliation between them and both knew it. The murder of a father – however foul – was not a matter to be forgiven.

If Polonius's son missed his mark then Claudius alone must act.

He looked at this exotic instrument of murder. A pearl, large and beautiful. A tiny hole drilled in the base, arsenic, sudden and deadly, filling most of the space inside.

The King placed the thing back in the velvet pouch it came in, at such a high and painful price.

Then he called a servant.

"Fetch me, Laertes," he ordered. "I wish to speak to him before this... entertainment."

Outside he could hear the drumbeat of foreign soldiers, shouts from their marching drills, their voices harsh and violent on the bitter breeze.

The Great Hall had been cleared, benches and chairs pushed to the walls, tables removed entirely to make room between the doors and the low, sad statue of Old Yorick. The same space had been given over to the play that had so inflamed the King. Now it was set for more dark theatre.

An hour before the combat was due to start Horatio had delivered Hamlet's rapier and dagger to the castle smith and watched as that burly craftsman rounded the sharp end of each and tipped them with cork plugs. Then he'd returned to the hall and waited as they were measured for length and thickness against the blades Laertes had proposed. His were all fine Saxon weapons with swept hilts and inlaid handles. Horatio had tested one and found it light and finely balanced. The choice of a man who knew something of swordsmanship.

Hamlet's by contrast, was the blade he always carried, a workmanlike weapon, sturdy and effective, but nothing like so refined. It had been a gift from a visiting French dignitary when Hamlet had turned eighteen and he'd worn it ever since. The parrying dagger, unlike Laertes' carefully matched pairs, came from somewhere else entirely.

Horatio's unease about the fencing match wouldn't go away. The Prince was different since his bloody adventure at sea, more focused in some ways but also more resigned, as if he could see an end coming and no longer cared to prevent it. He was a skilled fencer though Laertes – if he kept his head –was faster and more practised. Not that it was the ignominy of losing a fencing match that worried Horatio.

Twice before the duel he checked the swords carefully to make sure there was no trickery. None was apparent, though he didn't like the fact that Oswald, Laertes' aide, was to be in charge of judging the contest.

"My master issued the challenge," Oswald said tetchily when Horatio raised the matter. "Court rules. The king himself will serve as final judge in case of dispute."

That was no better, but it was too late to object.

The crowd started to arrive a half hour later. Normally such an event would have been pleasant diversion made more notorious by the royal standing of one of the participants. Today there was an enemy army at the gates and here were the noble lords, quarrelling among one another when every man in Elsinore might be fighting for his life, and that of his loved ones, before the day was out.

The spectators quietly found their places around the room. The King and Queen sat at opposite ends of the area set aside for the duel. Horatio doubted that was merely a matter of symmetry. Perhaps it was to indicate that each backed a different party in the fray.

When everyone was in place one of the guards at the king's elbow banged the butt of his halberd on the floor and the hall fell silent. Oswald rose, bowed to the king and queen in turn, then took his place in the centre of the field of play and addressed the room.

"This fencing match is the result of a challenge issue by my Lord Laertes to Prince Hamlet. Court rules apply. The winner is the first to ten hits. There will be a break after each five points scored, and fencers or their seconds can request one other pause each. My Lord Horatio will be Prince Hamlet's second. Reynaldo will serve the same office for Lord Laertes. I will keep score. Appeals will be settled by his majesty the King." He turned to the two men dressed in cloaks, white shirts and long black pants, before the throne. "Fencers, choose your weapons."

A rack had been set against the chamber wall. Hamlet snatched his rapier and dagger, barely looking at them, though Laertes, who had submitted several from which he might choose, lingered before selecting his. Horatio followed this closely, trying to get a better look at the blue steel sword he'd picked. He didn't recall seeing the weapon earlier. But it was hard to see properly and when each fencer presented their weapons to the king, Claudius merely tapped their corked tips and nodded, smiling.

"Take your places, my lords," said Oswald.

Claudius rose, an ornate chalice of wine in his hand.

"I drink to you both," he said, raising the cup and taking a sip. "And will award this precious prize to the victor."

He showed the pearl to the crowd then dropped it into the chalice, and set the cup on a stand, retaking his seat as the crowd clapped politely.

"Before we begin..."

Hamlet turned to address the assembled court, shrugging out of his cloak and handing it to Horatio. "I wish to say something."

There was a murmur in the crowd. The King and Queen watched avidly. Laertes became very still, something close to a sneer on his face.

"Laertes. I've hurt you grievously. The manner, the circumstances are more complex than anyone realises. But I make no excuses. What I did, I did. Believe me when I say I'm sorry for that. Sorrier, perhaps, than you'll ever know or imagine. It was, I suppose, a kind of madness, though some lunacies are shared, caught from others, like diseases. What drove me to these acts I do not wish to say. But..." He bowed to the man across from him. "I never meant you harm or sorrow, sir. I hope for your forgiveness. Perhaps there will never be another day for it to be granted. Nevertheless..."

He sighed. The crowd watched, rapt by the performance. There was an uncertain patter of applause from the gathered courtiers, and several faces turned to Laertes to see if he would respond.

The son of Polonius took a breath and nodded. Still with a scowl on his face, he said, "Your words as usual are most compelling. You have my forgiveness if you wish it, Prince." At that he flexed his blade. "But for the sake of my family's honour you will satisfy me with this contest."

Hamlet's eyes met Horatio's and a wan smile appeared on his face.

"I wouldn't ask for it to be otherwise."

Oswald stepped between them.

"Then if both parties are ready let combat begin."

" Laertes took position, face set, body taut with anticipation.

"Ready!"

"I've been ready all my life," Hamlet answered languidly, swishing at the air with his sword. "Come on, sir. I think it's time."

Horatio folded Hamlet's cloak and set it on the chair reserved for him where a servant with a pitcher of water hovered at the ready. When he turned back, the two fencers were in position, dagger hands raised, sword blades just touching so that in the silence they seemed to chime softly like distant bells.

Laertes moved first, a plunging, eager attack. Hamlet took a step back, caught the rapier blade on his dagger, swinging his own sword in an easy, precise swipe that made his opponent leap backwards. Even so the blade missed his chest by no more than an inch. Hamlet grinned. Laertes came on again, swinging high this time, cutting with his sword and stabbing with the smaller blade so that Hamlet had to parry both deftly.

Horatio shifted to get a better view as Laertes returned, cutting at Hamlet's shoulder. The prince twisted away, deflecting the attack with a touch of his dagger and lunging low. His rapier point found Laertes' doublet and Hamlet gave a wordless shout of triumph.

One point to the prince.

Laertes backed off slowly, conceding the matter. Oswald nodded to the applauding audience to show he'd registered it.

"Well played, Hamlet," said the Queen.

"It's not a play this time, mother," he said pleasantly. Then he nodded to her with a smile that was the most heartfelt Horatio had seen from him in weeks.

The Prince won the next point, too, and the one after that, in both cases keeping his head as Laertes's frustration drove him to wilder swings.

"Three hits to nothing, Hamlet leads," said Oswald, his smile a little strained.

Hamlet winked to Horatio, over his shoulder.

"Not just a schoolboy, eh?"

Laertes heard and his face darkened. He sprang forward, a long, unsteady lunge which Hamlet cut to the side and rolled from his body moving in close that Laertes could not turn his dagger in time, while Hamlet's came up and touched him lightly on the throat.

"Four to the Prince," Oswald announced.

For all Hamlet had said, this was theatre of a kind. The crowd were fully engaged now, the enemy outside the walls forgotten in the drama of the moment. Men began to take sides and call out encouragement to one or the other. Horatio hooted and clapped every sortie. All might yet be well.

The fifth pass was the longest, a steady back and forth tussle that took the pair of them careering around the room. The crowd shrank back at the force and violence of the encounter, gasping, cheering.

Laertes cut from the elbow and the shoulder, broad strokes, slow but full of power which drove Hamlet back. The Prince countered with sudden, speedy lunges at which Laertes flailed wildly, only just managing to sweep them aside. He was sweating heavily now, while Hamlet still seemed calm and unflustered, almost clinical in his precision.

One more charge, Laertes with his sword high over his head, crying out with fury. A lesser man, thought Horatio, would have fled such an attack. But Hamlet held his ground, dropped to one knee and angled the corked tip of his sword into Laertes' belly.

Oswald signalled the point, but for a fraction of a second Horatio thought Laertes would complete his attack anyway. He held his rapier over Hamlet's head, frozen, his eyes full of fury, face flushed and dripping sweat. Horatio took a hurried step forward.

"That's five. Time for a break."

"Indeed," agreed the king, standing and indicating the chalice to his nephew. "Take some wine, Hamlet."

"Wine, uncle? This is a contest of arms. Not a drinking match."

Claudius came closer and extended the goblet to him.

"You need refreshment, nephew."

"Are you deaf, sir?" Hamlet kept his eyes still on Laertes who had yet to lower his sword. Something here was wrong. "I'm not thirsty. And even if I was I doubt I'd like the taste of pearl."

A sudden movement. The Queen came between the two of them and snatched the cup.

"I'll drink to my son. I never knew he could fight like this. Pearl or no pearl. In honour of your play so far!"

The cup came up. Claudius fought to stop her. But she stepped back.

"I may raise a glass to my son if I wish it," Gertrude insisted, staring him down.

Then she brought the chalice to her lips, gulped greedily at the wine. Red liquid on her lips. And in the King's eyes a sudden dismay.

Laertes retreated.

"Hamlet," Horatio whispered.

The Prince looked elated.

"What is it?" he asked.

"Keep your shoulder turned. You're showing him too much of your chest."

"If he keeps driving like a berserker it won't matter how much of my chest I show him. Where's that jester when you want him? He should be watching this!"

Horatio shook his head.

"Jester?"

"Old Yorick's son, for God's sake! He almost lives in my quarters..."

"The old jester never had a..."

"Oh enough of this," Hamlet declared, casting wildly around the room, seeing nothing. "Never mind. Come on." He cut a circle in the air with the rapier. "We begin again."

THE SIGN WAS SIMPLE: Elias waited by the eastern gate and kept his eyes on the keep tower. Eventually a standard emerged. The Dannebrog, the national flag, a white cross on a red background, thrown down from Heaven by God to the Danish forces struggling through a famous battle in Estonia centuries before.

Perhaps Claudius had a sense of irony rare in one of his kind. For after this day it was unlikely the Dannebrog would be flying over a free nation.

He turned to the surly pair guarding the gate and told them to open it. The biggest, oldest, ugliest stared at him in astonishment.

"There's a thousand or so stinking Norwegians out there, sir. No offence but are you off your head?"

"Not yet," Elias answered with a laugh. "Just do it, man. There's matters afoot here you needn't worry about."

A crack opened big enough for an old Dane to squeeze through. Elias picked up his square of white fabric attached to a small pole and walked out into the bright day waving it.

The Norwegians were encamped just a hundred yards away, surly, hungry men, staring at him as he approached. To the right were the tents of the mercenaries under the Scot Gregor, a cunning, experienced man whose history Elias had studied at length the previous night as he went through the intelligence reports gathered over the weeks since Fortinbras first moved to Helsingborg, opposite on the straits.

There was division here. A physical one between the two camps. A point worth noting.

He walked forward beneath the white flag. A man in armour on a grey stallion rode out to meet him. The Norwegian prince himself, face wreathed in fury.

Elias smiled.

"This is a fine morning, Fortinbras," the Dane said. "Too beautiful to stain with blood. I'm sure you'll agree..."

Armed men round him, halberds in their arms, swords raised. He had no weapon. Only the white flag which he raised again, still looking up at the figure on the horse.

"Would your compatriot, Voltemand, agree?" Fortinbras demanded.

The old man nodded.

"Oh yes, him. A gift from Claudius, I believe. A greeting designed to tell you that whatever we may be... however fragile the kingdom..." The smile vanished and the white cloth came down. "We're Danes, my friend. Offer us suitable terms and you'll find no more faithful friends on earth. Push us too far and we will fight. Any way we can." He glanced towards the sea. "As your father discovered all those years ago."

"Perhaps I'll send Claudius a gift of my own then," the Norwegian prince roared. "Seize him! Search him! Take him to my tent for interrogation."

Then he snatched the meagre banner Elias held and his massive charger stamped the white standard into the mud with its hooves.

Laertes had started the duel in a foul mood and now it was even blacker. He saw how Claudius glared at him after the last lost point, storming back only to be bested again. Even the Queen was toasting her son and all knew how estranged they'd been of late.

Claudius had been clear in his instruction. Play the contest properly. Fight fairly to begin with. And reach for the deadly weapon only at the end, when Hamlet's collapse might be attributed to excitement or exhaustion, not the skills of an Italian poisoner.

Even so he wanted to win those early bouts, and was furious to have been bested so clearly.

"This sword's no good," he snapped, throwing it at Reynaldo. "The balance is off. Get me the one with the gold hilt."

The second came close to him and whispered, "I'm not sure that one was checked by the weapons arbiter. If you like I can ask..."

"Just get it. We're ready to start."

Reynaldo nodded, walked quickly to the rack and drew the gold hilted rapier. The tip, he saw, was uncorked. He returned to Laertes, holding the weapon carefully in his arms.

"My lord," he faltered, "I'm not sure that one's... eligible. The point..."

"Whose side are you on, minion?"

"Yours, sir. Naturally."

"Then give me the sword I asked for."

At that Laertes snatched the hilt.

"And a towel now."

Reynaldo nodded and fetched the cloth he'd brought to mop his master's brow.

Something had happened in the meantime. Laertes grabbed the towel, wiped the tip of his sword, then slipped something into the pocket of his doublet. A vial or flask it looked like. There was a stain on the end of the blade. Purple, thick. Wrong.

He opened his mouth to ask what it was but Laertes's eyes met his and stared him down.

"This is for my sister," he hissed. "And my father. Say a word and you'll regret it."

After a long moment Reynaldo lowered his gaze, took a step backwards towards his chair. Then Laertes re-joined the duel.

THERE'D BEEN WORSE treatment over the years, Elias thought to himself. All the Norwegians had offered was a little rough handling. A couple of men spitting in his face. A kick or two. Now he was seated in a chair in the command tent, wiping his face clean, watched by Fortinbras and the Scot.

A foot soldier came in at the Norwegian's command and brandished something bloody and grim. A severed head.

"Why show me this?" Elias asked. "Do traitors in Norway receive the nation's thanks and a pair of kid gloves?"

The Scot laughed at that and shook his head.

"I like this one. He's got guts. Making a fool of you out on the field like that. Then walking in here bold as brass."

He picked up what remained of Voltemand and kicked it out of the tent flap.

"You should listen to our friend here. He's got more brains than that dead fool..."

The Dane bowed politely.

"Which means," the mercenary added, "we can't let you back in that castle alive. Not till this is over. Now you know we have our..." He winked at the Norwegian. "Differences."

"What do you have to offer?" Fortinbras asked with a surly stare.

"What do you want?" the Dane asked getting another guffaw from the Scot.

"I want Elsinore. I want the crown."

Elias sighed and smiled at him.

"We've been here before. Give me the guarantees – safe passage, no plunder, fair treatment of our people – and we have something to discuss. Or test the mettle of your men against our walls."

Fortinbras snorted with disgust.

"Why should I bargain with a coward like Claudius? A king who sends an old man beneath a white flag to haggle for him? Open those gates for me now and I'll spare who I choose. Force me to sit here in your filth one day longer and we'll slaughter every last one of you. Man, woman and child. Take that message back to your king. "

A shrug from Elias. No answer. Not a move.

"Perhaps I'll put that in a letter and stuff it in your mouth," the prince from Oslo said. "Then throw your head back behind those walls as you threw my man's to me."

The warrior from Scotland groaned.

"Etiquette's not your strong point, is it?" Gregor leaned forward and placed his elbows on the table. "This chap has something on his mind.

Out with it, Dane.' He nodded at Fortinbras. "His problem's imagination. Mine's patience. Best you don't tempt both."

~

Gertrude returned Hamlet's pleasant smile as he adopted his fencing stance to begin the duel again. He was doing well. Better than she'd ever expected. Laertes was supposed to be the better swordsman. But Polonius's boy seemed clumsy, flustered. Strangely nervous and, if she was any judge, over compensating with anger.

The wine she couldn't finish. It tasted odd. A few of the more senior courtiers had left the room. Claudius had promised negotiations with the Norwegians. A peaceful end to the half-hearted standoff outside the walls. Territory or submission would save them. Elias, a good man, better than the vanished Voltemand, would see to that.

Then Hamlet would be restored to health. With her and Claudius. Or without his uncle. One way or another.

She applauded as he led the next bout though her hands felt strange. Weak and unmanageable.

A further hit for Hamlet. Laertes broke away shouting his frustration with foul curses. She glanced at her husband and got no response in return. This duel was his idea, a way of brokering peace between two families. Yet he looked downcast. Lost even. As if he'd wanted Laertes to win to spite her. Or perhaps...

She closed her eyes and tried to think. Her mouth felt odd, tingly and numb. Her throat, too. When she moved her tongue around it felt sluggish and thick. The sensation reminded her of an opiate from the east the old king had made her take once, to sate his desire. Not unpleasant in itself though the memory of what followed was bleak and vile.

Thirsty she reached for the chalice to drink.

Another point lost and this time Laertes's fury got the better of him. After the hit had been called he closed on her son and leaned in to say something. Hamlet hesitated, straining to hear over the applause, and in that moment Laertes made a sudden movement with his sword. Hamlet stepped quickly back, clutching his forearm, and Gertrude could see a slim cut close to his wrist, dropping blood.

Silence in the room. Though not in her head. Something there, like a distant ocean, was starting to roar.

"Hamlet..." she whispered.

But already he was bellowing his fury, sword forgotten, grabbing Laertes and punching him in the face. Laertes dropped his blade and the two men wrestled briefly, till Oswald and their seconds leapt in to pull them apart.

"Hamlet, my son..."

The words were so faint she wasn't sure she'd even uttered them. Gertrude felt feverish and sickly sweaty. Her breathing became laboured and shallow. Sick. She was sure of it.

Her right hand began to twitch wildly so she had to drag it away from the chalice for fear of knocking it over.

The wine...

Her eyes slid from the struggling fencers – back on guard, their swords somehow switched in the melee so that Hamlet had the rapier with the golden hilt –to the cup beside her.

Confused, head aching, she watched as the two men rejoined the fight with different swords. Hamlet clutching the blade of Laertes now, fighting back violently. Polonius's boy wild-eyed and anxious with his opponent's slender rapier.

It seemed to her there was blood and that seemed wrong.

Her thirst was raging. She reached unsteadily for the cup again, remembering at the last moment not to down every last drop all because her husband had dropped a pearl there. A trophy for the victor.

Gertrude glanced at him then. Claudius caught her eyes and immediately looked away.

She stared into the goblet. Yellow wine, cloudy, with a dusty substance swirling at the surface not quite dissolved...

Down she fell, legs starting to spasm, and her gaze went past the fencers to where the king sat, face ashen, eyes on nothing in the hall but her.

A BIGGER PRIZE, Elias said and then they listened. That was the reward on offer.

"How big?" Fortinbras demanded.

The Dane relaxed and told them.

"Two thrones instead of one." Gregor nudged the Norwegian's arm. "Now there's an offer to turn any prince's head. And those of the men behind him."

Fortinbras hesitated, looked at Elias and then the Scot.

"You included?" he asked.

"If we can trust this one," Gregor replied looking closely at the man opposite. "Well, Dane? Can we?"

Elias met his gaze.

"Your name's Gregor Macbeth. Lord of Moray."

"You like to know your enemies," the Scot agreed.

"More than five hundred years ago an ancestor of mine, Sueno, then the King of Norway, met an ancestor of yours on the battlefield. Your territory, not ours then." The Dane shrugged. "Scotland. Down the Great Glen, at Inverlochy."

Gregor grinned.

"This is a long way to come for a history lesson, mate."

"This isn't history," Elias insisted. "It's about who we are. Sueno was old and stupid. He lost."

"Your point, man? What..."

"My point's your ancestor Macbeth treated the King of Norway honourably. Let him sail home for a suitable ransom. Then went about his own business." He opened his hands in a generous gesture. "We're modern men, not savages. If our forebears could behave with such expedient decency, is it really beyond the likes of us?"

"When the hurlyburly's done and the battle's lost and won," Gregor murmured, smiling. "Two thrones not one. I can do business with a man like you." He nudged his neighbour's elbow. "So can he. Can't you, Prince of Norway?"

"We need guarantees..." Fortinbras began.

"We need a sign," the Scot cut in. "What is it?"

Elias got to his feet and walked to opening of the tent.

"The Dannebrog," he said. "The flag of Denmark. When it appears on the keep tower we move. If I walk before you, sirs, none will do you harm or offer anything but a wary welcome. That I guarantee."

The King watched her fall and felt his world tumble with her. One death he'd wanted in all his life. A deserved one. That of her murderous husband. No one else.

Yet blood beckoned blood. Ophelia, Polonius, the vile man Voltemand followed in Old Hamlet's wake. And now Gertrude's son. Laertes' had reached for the venom-tipped blade. Even so, ever the diplomat, a man for planning, Claudius had erred on caution. So he'd dropped the pearl drilled with arsenic into the chalice, determined to keep hold of it in case Polonius's boy failed.

Too late. Claudius watched helpless as the poison from Voltemand's Italian wife took hold, powerless to intervene.

Falling to the hard stone Gertrude convulsed in front of his eyes, staring at him and he thought... she knows.

The courtiers and servants had noticed, too. Only the duellists fought on, oblivious to the tragedy in their midst, Hamlet stabbing Laertes deep in the gut with the venomous tip of his sword.

Claudius got unsteadily to his feet, walking out into the stalled contest, all eyes on him now as he made for the woman he loved.

The woman he'd killed. Was this justice? Or the wrath of God for all his many crimes? Vengeance taking vengeance itself, stealing the life of the one thing he truly loved, trampling her in the dirt?

He pulled aside a servant. Told them to make the sign from the walls they'd used earlier. Then walked as if in a trance, blind to the chaos around him, not hearing the shouted accusations of the fighters. Paying no heed to anyone as he made his slow, tortured way to his dying queen.

Outside the walls the three of them, Dane, Scot, Norwegian, stood by the command tent, watching the keep. A glittering, armoured arm appeared. And then a red-and-white standard.

"Follow me," Elias ordered. "Leave your main forces where they are. Bring an honour guard of your most trusted warriors. Tell them to keep their weapons sheathed."

"We said nothing about leaving our army outside the walls," Fortinbras objected. "You could cut us down the moment we're behind your doors."

The Dane shook his head.

"Why would we do that, sir? You're our new king. And with you we'll conquer Norway. Two realms. Two thrones. If you doubt my word perhaps we have no bargain to strike."

"I want my army in there..."

"No!" It was the Scot who intervened, with force. "Put a thousand men inside that castle and they'll be drunk and pillaging before nightfall. However much you threaten to hang them. I've seen your so-called soldiers, Fortinbras. If they were any good you wouldn't need the likes of me."

He barked some orders to his own men and a group of them started to come over.

"We'll be your honour guard. I like this Dane. There'll be no trouble."

Before Fortinbras could answer Elias grunted his thanks then set off for the walls. The eastern gate was opening ahead of them already.

THE DUELLISTS HAD STOPPED, breathless, unsteady on their feet. Blades down. Both watching Claudius bent over his stricken Queen.

"You're dead, Hamlet," Laertes said, clutching his stomach. "Minutes at most. Me, too." He pointed at the tip of the sword Hamlet had snatched from him. "When you stole this blade you stole a little present from Italy too."

"There's justice," the Prince whispered staring at the smear of blood, the traces of a thick, purple fluid on the weapon's tip. Close by, with his dimming vision, he could just make out two figures on the stone floor close to the statue of Old Yorick.

"Forgive me, as I do you," Laertes begged, sinking to his knees. The wound Hamlet had inflicted on him went deep. The venom was acting swiftly. "I know my sister loved you."

Hamlet nodded and reached for his hand. Laertes clasped it then his body was racked with a convulsion that doubled him up grimacing with pain.

"The King," he mumbled. "Claudius gave me the poison. He's to blame."

The hall began to spin. The light to darken.

"I know, Laertes. And so does he."

Unsteadily Hamlet lurched towards the scarlet-cloaked figure bent over the fallen Gertrude, and pricked him in the back with the tip of the poisoned sword.

Claudius uttered the softest cry. Two guards with halberds ran towards them, but Horatio was there, rapier out, protecting the Prince.

The King looked up at him.

"Don't worry, uncle. It was just a scratch. My heart races. Not yours. Most of the poison's gone already. But you... and I... we will die this day." His eyes wouldn't leave the sad, still shape before him. "Mother..."

He let the last word hang there. Next to his wife, pale and terrible in death, Claudius sighed, a great breath released as if he'd been holding it for years. His whole body seemed to sag and shrink. Tears ran down his face.

"My beloved queen is dead. And I have murdered her son, whom I loved as a child and as a man."

"With love comes agony," Hamlet murmured.

"And we know it." Claudius struggled to his feet. "I won't offend you by asking your forgiveness or understanding, nephew. I deserve neither."

The two men faced each other, Hamlet looking at him along the length of the blade.

Then Claudius reached casually behind him for the poisoned chalice, closed his eyes and smiled.

"Remember when you were a boy? You had a horse called Zeus. Your father gave it to you."

"No lies now, uncle. The stallion was your gift, not his."

"Ah." Claudius looked at him, lifted the cup in a toast and took a deep draft. "You knew that too. Yes. He came from me. You remember how we rode together along the shore when the tide was low, for hours sometimes? And your mother would greet us on our return...?" He smiled bleakly, lost in the memories, drinking more of the poison. "I thought that if your father was gone then those days would be our future, our life. I am so sorry..."

He drained the cup and threw it away, grimacing as he felt the first of its effects.

Hamlet lowered the sword. The blade clattered to the floor.

"I remember..."

Claudius doubled over and stumbled to the flagstones. With the last of his strength he crawled to Gertrude's side and reached for her.

"Love," Hamlet said to Horatio. "Perhaps it's easier in death."

"Everything's easier in death," said a low, familiar voice in his ear. "But you'll know that soon enough."

"Yorick...?"

The hall was like a dream now, hazy and uncertain. Hamlet could feel the poison starting to clench his limbs. His heart was thumping hard and fast as a beaten drum. There was so little time before him.

"Your Majesty?" the jester asked.

And yet the voice...

Hamlet strained his neck and saw. The little man was by the statue speaking, almost a part of it. The same coarse, brute face, not quite human, flesh and stone looking to meld together.

He pointed at this spectre and asked, "You see him, Horatio? You hear him?"

The young man peered at him in grief and puzzlement.

"I hear nothing but commotion, sir. And soldiers. Our own. Foreign. Lord Elias..."

"You tricked me, clown," Hamlet said, laughing, choking, he wasn't sure which.

The dwarf on his plinth shrugged, not that anyone else noticed. The colour in him was almost gone now, all the blood and the bright and energetic life.

"No, Prince. You tricked yourself. Court jesters do not beget sons. There was but a single Yorick. A lost soul trapped in Purgatory alongside your father, though full of grief and guilt."

Unseen to all the world, he leaned down naked from the grinning tortoise.

"You summoned me. Your fears, your suspicion, your knowledge of this castle's secrets put flesh upon my bones."

The march of soldiers' boots. Voices of many accents and different tongues.

"You were real," Hamlet whispered.

The last, familiar chuckle.

"As real as you. The antic actor in your head."

There was the metallic rattle of armour around him and the sound of harsh, military voices.

"I must leave now, Hamlet. Just as you..."

His wraithlike hand came out and matched the pose of the statue's arm, outstretched in a mock greeting to the tumult in the hall, freezing into stone.

"This play is run."

Another voice, fierce and foreign.

"What bloody theatre is this?" Fortinbras demanded. "Where's my crown? Where...?"

Elias took Gregor by the elbow and led him to the Norwegian.

"Your new Lord Chamberlain can tell you, sir," the Dane said then patted the Scot on the back. "He'll tell you what to do."

Fortinbras stared at the two of them.

"Lord Chamberlain...? I recall no words of mine to that effect."

But Gregor Macbeth was issuing orders already. For peace in the castle. A decent respectful attendance to a dread scene that shocked even his hard troops.

All this was nothing but a dying murmur in Hamlet's failing mind. He felt himself tumbling through memories, moments in time, days, weeks, months, Ophelia's arms around his neck in a meadow by the water, then further back, drifting through the swirling tangle of recollection to a day he could not possibly remember, had only heard of from the ghostly jester, the loud and bloody moment of his birth, his father victorious on the ice outside, an infant's cries echoing through bright cold air from a high window...

One last time the jester's voice came, warm, fond, caring, grimly amused at a finale they both knew must come.

"And now, Prince?"

Hamlet closed his eyes and heard his own final, fragile words.

"And now the rest is silence," he said, then slipped into the endless dark.

~

# Afterword

## *Hamlet*, The Play

You'd think that after more than 400 years people would have run out of things to say about Hamlet. Not so. Like most of Shakespeare's plays Hamlet is a constant source of new ideas and arguments, the play seeming to shift as our culture evolves and finds that it somehow keeps pace, holding as t'were the mirror up to us.

Some of those debates concern the text of the play itself, there being several early versions of different lengths and emphases, and we know for sure – or as sure as we ever can be about such things – that even the earliest of these texts was not the play as it was first written and performed. While Shakespeare's play in the forms we have it seems to date from about 1601, there was at least one other version floating around a decade or so before that, though whether it was written by Shakespeare or someone else, we can't say.

What we do know is that the version most people read in school today was never performed in Shakespeare's own lifetime and represents a cobbling together of parts from those early versions. The earliest of these, the first quarto – sometimes called the "bad" quarto – is half the length of the later texts and reads like a very different play. It lacks much of the digressive rumination which became so central to the eighteenth and nineteenth century's romantic notion of what the play was – and who its title character was – feeling much more like the blood and thunder revenge tragedies of Shakespeare's early contemporaries.

In our novel we have used few of the specifics from that first quarto choosing, for instance, to stick with the familiar name "Polonius" instead of Corambis. But one thing David and I wanted to capture from that version of Hamlet is its story-driven thrust, its emphasis on action over rumination. Hamlet, in the popular consciousness, isn't generally thought of as a thriller; but there is evidence to suggest that when it was first staged, it was rather closer to that than to the existential or Freudian musing which it subsequently became. Hamlet is a tragedy of blood, and we wanted to find something of that original fire in our retelling of the familiar story.

That meant, among other things, giving time to show those elements of the story which go by quickly in the play because Shakespeare knew the limitations of his own theatre. As we did with Macbeth, a Novel, we have given more scope to battle scenes, to landscape, to the background intrigues which surround the core story, and to potentially thrilling moments which get fairly cursory treatment in the play such as Hamlet's boarding of the pirate ship.

But our boldest decision, perhaps, was to rethink the great soliloquies for which the play is famous as dialogue between the title character and someone who never actually appears in the play. Yorick may well be the most famous non-character in literature, enshrined forever in quotes and half-memories and jokes because of a casual utterance made by Hamlet in the graveyard. "Alas, poor Yorick. I knew him, Horatio."

It's an oddly inconsequential thing to confer such literary immortality, but the play was made to be performed and the key to the line is actually a visual motif which the quotation doesn't actually articulate. When the line is delivered, Hamlet is gazing on Yorick's skull, casually unearthed by the gravedigger. Yorick's fame grew out of being the line which accompanied what is, perhaps, the single most recognizable, iconic image in literature: a man in black considering a human skull. Show some form of that picture to most moderately educated people – and plenty who aren't – and they'll know the man is Hamlet. Such things don't find their way into the popular consciousness by accident, and trivial though the line may sound, it speaks to the heart of the play: a man compelled by circumstances outside his control to confront his own mortality.

In order to extend this idea, to make Hamlet's reflections on life and death more dynamic, we brought Yorick – or a version of him – back to life. Whether this works as a device or not, I'll leave to you to decide, but I'll say why I like it, and I can do so without boasting because I'm pretty sure it was originally David's idea. We wanted this to be a story of passion, of hard or bad decisions, and of love, all driven by the pace of a modern thriller.

Hamlet is not a mystery in the contemporary sense because we quickly learn who the bad guys are and we are pretty sure we know how things will end up. It's a thriller because thrillers focus on the "how" of a story, on its pace and its pressure on the protagonist. But we didn't want to lose that crucial image of the man with the skull, staring down death, trying to make sense of it. Inserting Yorick into the story as a foil for Hamlet, to goad him into action, to inject a little bleak and bawdy humor that would undercut his posturing, but also to show unflinchingly the enormity of what he did was, I thought, a neat way of extrapolating elements which are present in Shakespeare's play and indeed in the title character himself but which might otherwise get ponderous in our version of the story.

It isn't the original, but then in all likelihood, neither was Shakespeare's, and our purpose was never to replicate or replace that original, but to create something new which grew out of it, a journey – if you like – through a familiar story which sees it from a different perspective.

*A.J. Hartley*

## *Hamlet*, The Background

Shakespeare produced plenty of work based around his own, sometimes biased, interpretation of history. This is not one of them.

There is no indication in the text to suggest in which century *Hamlet* takes place. We've set it around the time the play was written, at the start of the seventeenth century, in part to reflect Hamlet's conflict between present and past as a child of the Renaissance. But this is an interpretation of the original, just like the common depiction of Hamlet as a medieval student in tights. Whatever period one chooses for the play you will find no historical prince of Denmark named Hamlet, no King Claudius, no conflict resembling that between the state and its Norwegian neighbour. Even the names Shakespeare uses for his principal characters – Polonius, Claudius, Laertes, Gertrude, Ophelia – rarely suggest any Nordic origins.

While stories of wronged sons seeking revenge on their father's murderer are common from the earliest of times, a single source suggests itself for the tale of Hamlet. The story was recorded around the end of the twelfth century by the historian Saxo Grammaticus, a clerk to Absalon, the fearsome warrior-bishop who expanded the Danish empire in the Baltic, converted to Christianity some of the last Pagan Viking communities in the region, and founded Copenhagen.

Grammaticus recounts the tale of Amleth, a Danish prince, whose fate mirrors much of Shakespeare's Hamlet. Amleth's father is killed by his own jealous brother who then marries his widow 'capping unnatural murder with incest' as Grammaticus writes, in an echo of the play. The suspicious Amleth is then sent to England with a letter that is his own death warrant. He alters the missive to ensure his own escape and the death of his retainers, then returns to Denmark and murders his uncle. Later, after further adventures, he dies in battle.

It is a folk story, probably one that Grammaticus recorded after hearing it on his travels with Absalon. There are none of the psychological nuances of the play – Hamlet's hesitation over his revenge, and his multifaceted relationship with his uncle, for example. As usual Shakespeare applied his genius to a simple, raw original and reinvented it as a complex and textured tragedy that goes far beyond mere revenge.

If the history behind *Hamlet* is fictitious at least the geography does bear some resemblance to the real world. Elsinore is an Anglicisation of Helsingør, a town in eastern Denmark, set on the narrow straits of the Øresund which separate the country from Sweden. The place was never the permanent seat of the Danish monarchy but there is a large and impressive castle, Kronborg, widely touted by the local tourist trade as 'Hamlet's'. There have been occasional performances of the play within its walls, with stars ranging from Laurence Olivier to John Gielgud, Christopher Plummer and more recently Jude Law.

In truth though today's edifice is picturesque and largely Renaissance in style, with none of the dark, enclosed atmosphere one associates with Hamlet. Its predecessor, known as Krogen, was probably very different, a forbidding military fortress built to enforce the duties payable by shipping using the straits to reach the wealthy Baltic nations.

A little of that forbidding bastion remains, and with it a reminder of the violent, Viking past that would have been part of the fictional Hamlet's heritage, one that, in our version, he longs to shrug off. Deep within the bowels of the beautiful Renaissance chateau of today lies the hulking statue of a Viking warrior, with a long beard, a metal helmet, burly arms crossed, broadsword on his lap, shield by his side. This is the slumbering hero Holger Danske, the Danish King Arthur, ready to awaken and fight for Denmark in her hour of need.

*David Hewson*

# About the Authors

**A.J. Hartley** is the *New York Times* best-selling author of the Will Hawthorne fantasy series and several thrillers, as well as the Darwen Arkwright books for younger readers. He is the Russell Robinson Distinguished Professor of Shakespeare at the University of North Carolina at Charlotte.

Twitter: @authorajhartley

Web: ajhartley.net

**David Hewson** is the author of more than 30 novels including the Nic Costa series in Italy, the Sarah Lund adaptations of The Killing and the Pieter Vos books in Amsterdam. *The Garden of Angels*, set mostly in wartime Venice, appeared in mass market paperback in August and *The Medici Murders*, a mystery set in Venice in hardback in October. His audio adaptation of Romeo & Juliet, performed by Richard Armitage, won the Audie, the audiobook Oscar, for best original work in 2018. A former journalist with the Sunday Times and Times, He lives in Kent.

www.davidhewson.com

Twitter: @david_hewson

# Also by David Hewson

The Medici Murders

The Garden of Angels

The Savage Shore

Romeo & Juliet (Audible adaptation w/Richard Armitage)

# Also by A.J. Hartley

(Also with David Hewson) *Macbeth, a Novel*

(With Tom Delonge) *Sekret Machines: Chasing Shadows*

*Sekret Machines: A Fire Within*

*Cathedrals of Glass: Planet of Blood and Ice*

*Cathedrals of Glass: Valkrys Wakes*

*Steeplejack*

*Firebrand*

*Guardian*

*Act of Will*

*Will Power*

*Impervious*

*Burning Shakespeare*

*Cold Bath Street*

*Written Stone Lane*

*The Mask of Atreus*

*On The Fifth Day*

*What Time Devours*

*Tears of the Jaguar*

As Andrew Hart:

*Lies that Bind Us*

*The Woman in our House*

# Friends of Falstaff

Thank You to All our Falstaff Books Patrons, who get extra digital content each month! To be featured here and see what other great rewards we offer, go to www.patreon.com/falstaffbooks.

**PATRONS**

Dino Hicks
John Hooks
John Kilgallon
Larissa Lichty
Travis & Casey Schilling
Staci-Leigh Santore
Sheryl R. Hayes
Scott Norris
Samuel Montgomery-Blinn
Junkle

www.ingramcontent.com/pod-product-compliance
Lightning Source LLC
Chambersburg PA
CBHW020621110726
47899CB00002B/596

* 9 7 8 1 6 4 5 5 4 1 8 2 0 *